PRAISE FOR CAROLYN RAE'S
Romancing the Gold

Romancing the Gold received a Top Pick and a 4 1/2 star review from Night Owl Reviews.

Night Owl Reviews gave *Romancing the Gold* a Top Pick and 4 1/2 stars. Here is what the reviewer said, "I absolutely loved the characters, and found myself cheering repeatedly for both Megan and Josh as they bravely fight through the South American jungle for their lives. This novel is a wonderful book that readers of most ages will absolutely adore. One word of caution: the love scenes are HOT! Which, in my humble opinion, made it even better."

OTHER BOOKS BY CAROLYN RAE

Hiding from Love
Witness Protection Series, Book One

Protected by Love
Witness Protection Series, Book Two

Tempted by Love
Witness Protection Series, Book Three

HIDING

from

Love

Witness Protection Series, Book One

Carolyn Rae

Williamson Press
Hurst, Texas, USA

HIDING FROM LOVE
Copyright © 2015 by Carolyn Rae

Williamson Press
Hurst, Texas, USA

ISBN: 978-0-9965873-0-3

Cover Art © by Charlene Raddon, Cover-Ops Cover Art
Interior Formatting by Author E.M.S.

Published in the United States of America.

Acknowledgments

With thanks to former U.S. Marshal Dub Bransom for information.

This book is dedicated to my critique partners, Pepper, Jan, Dorothy, and the DFW Writer's Workshop, and to NTRWA, DARA and Yellow Rose RWA for their help and encouragement as well as writing teachers, the late Dwight Swain, the late Jack Bickham, and the late Rita Gallagher.

Chapter 1

"Who's she?" Alex Brandon swiveled on the scarlet bar stool. Silhouetted against the red door, the woman appeared to be scanning the casually dressed patrons of the only place alive tonight in Grandville, Texas. Her form-fitting green dress revealed nice curves. Lightly tanned with a determined looking chin, her face looked interesting beneath a cloud of dark hair.

The short Asian bartender held up a forefinger, then resumed jiggling his shaker. He poured a frothy yellow liquid and slid the glass across the black counter inlaid with images of golden pagodas.

He tilted his head toward the lady at the door. "Don't know her. I bet she's a patient of Doc Gittleman. He's a plastic surgeon, treated lots of these folks. They come to the Oriental Energies Spa next door for therapy."

Dr. Gittleman—the name stirred a memory. Wasn't he the surgeon they'd mentioned at headquarters when agents needed to become less recognizable?

Behind the bar a sign proclaimed, "Today is the First Day of the Rest of Your Life." Especially true for his friend, Sam, who had to disappear when his cover was blown.

At least Alex hadn't needed to do that. However, he wished he'd been able to settle down like his family had always encouraged him to—except it was too late now.

Alex sipped his drink. Laced with pineapple, it was refreshing after the hot muggy air outside. For now he wanted to forget the past and let the measured rhythm of oriental music sooth his troubled spirits. Inhaling the scent of cloves and fennel from a ceramic incense burner, he wished it could somehow renew his enthusiasm for life.

Bathed in the glow from red lanterns, the attractive dark-haired woman threaded her way between crowded tables. As she walked past a carved wooden screen toward him, he could see a flesh-colored bandage on her nose.

The man behind the bar leaned closer. "Probably some society snob from Austin who doesn't want anyone to see her before the swelling from her facelift goes down. Lots of them hide out in Grandville."

As Alex watched the graceful sway of her hips, snatches of nearby talk revived memories of London and Paris. Someone mentioned Moscow's chilling cold. He'd definitely agree.

Sipping his drink, he watched the woman in the green dress approach. She barely glanced at the carved screen depicting cherry blossom trees with Mount Fuji in the background.

With her dark hair brushing her shoulders, she reminded him of Amy. About twenty-five, the age Amy would have been now if....

He blinked, then wondered why this woman had come here. She didn't seem the type to venture into a place like this alone. Maybe like him, she was tired of her own company.

Hesitating, she looked around and headed toward the only empty stool, the one next to him. The bartender, barely a head taller than his seated customers, stepped in front of her. "Name's Charlie, when you're ready," he said.

"I'd like a frozen pina colada."

"Lady, I can fix a virgin one, but not one with rum. This is a juice bar and cafe, not a tavern."

"Okay," she said in a low husky whisper. She stared at the mirror as if trying to locate someone.

Alex took a sip and set his glass down. "Somebody joining you?"

She looked startled, then shook her head. Dark waves rippled over her shoulders. Her auburn strands shone in the light from the glass-enclosed candle on the counter.

He smiled. "I'm Alex Brandon."

"My name's Lee." She hesitated. "Lee Marshall."

She smelled like gardenias. Now that she was closer, her heavy makeup didn't quite hide the dark swollen areas under her eyes. Touching her cheek, she winced, then dropped her hand to her lap. A tentative smile brightened her face as she smoothed back her hair. "I'm new in town. Have you lived here long?"

Alex grinned. "You stole my line. I just moved here." He looked into her soft brown eyes. "Came to start a new business. How about you?"

"Well," she paused, "I plan to look for a job in the next few days. What kind of business are you setting up?"

Her ruby lips, delicately parted, made him wonder how soft they'd feel against his skin. What was he thinking? A woman was the last thing he needed or wanted. "I'm opening a travel agency."

"That sounds interesting."

Leaning back, he sipped his drink and wondered about the bandage on her nose. Maybe she hated the shape of the nose God gave her and was hiding out until bruises from surgery healed. On the other hand, she could be covering up injuries from an abusive husband. He hoped it wasn't that.

Even so, she looked pretty and smelled good. He breathed in the heady scent and grinned. "The way that perfume smells on you — ought to be illegal."

She smiled, and then looked up as Charlie brought her drink. She pulled it close, her fingers gripping the glass. "It's called Island Gardenia. I can tell you where to get it if you want to buy some for your wife."

"I'm divorced," he said, regretting the mistakes he'd made. "Signed the papers almost a year ago."

"Oh." She leaned closer, making him even more aware of her sweet smell and her feminine curves. "Why do you want to open a travel agency here?"

"I've always wanted a business of my own. Done a lot of traveling in Europe. I wrote several chambers of commerce and picked this area. I'd hoped my wife would give living here a try — but that was before — "

"She didn't like the idea?"

He shook his head. Instead of being happy he'd resigned from the CIA, his wife had thrown a fit when he proposed starting his own business in another town. "She said she wasn't about to leave our prestigious Westlake Hills house in Austin for a cheap house in some podunk town. The next day I got served with divorce papers."

"That's too bad. I worked in a travel agency at one time. Maybe I could give you some tips."

Through the hubbub of conversation, Alex heard a gravelly voice ask for a shot of Jack Daniels. Charlie, the bartender, shook his head. "Don't serve whiskey here. How about a ginger carrot zinger?"

"Yeah, whatever," the voice intoned. Charlie poured an orange mixture, and then pushed the glass forward.

Seconds later, the man's beefy arm, straining the seams of a loud yellow plaid blazer, shoved it back. "Who drinks this stuff?"

Charlie pointed to the glass. "Folks around here like it."

"Tastes like shit. They must be health nuts."

The bartender held up a hand. "Sorry you don't like. I won't charge you."

Alex turned his attention back to Lee. "It's too noisy here. I'd like to hear some of your tips for running a travel agency. Walk with me to the cafeteria down the street. I'll buy us both dinner."

She met his gaze, but seemed to be listening for something. Finally, she said, "I haven't eaten, but — " She glanced in the mirror and gasped. The man in the yellow plaid sports jacket was elbowing his way toward them. "Bubba," she murmured. She scribbled something on a red cocktail napkin and shoved it toward Alex. "Excuse me, please."

The swish of her dress as she slipped off the stool was almost drowned out by the buzz of chatter. He glanced at the numbers, slid the napkin into his pocket, and then looked up as she hurried past the carved wooden screen.

"Hey, you can't go in there," the bartender barked. The clang of cookware almost drowned out Charlie's warning. Alex caught a glimpse of green disappearing through the kitchen door as the aromas of soy sauce and frying fish wafted past.

The man called Bubba headed after Lee and shook off a waiter's restraining arm as he marched toward the kitchen. The scowl on the belligerent Bubba's face said he'd make trouble for Lee.

Alex slid off the barstool and strode toward the beefy man. He tapped the guy's shoulder. Catching a whiff of B.O., Alex wished the guy had bathed more recently. "Sit down. I'll buy you a drink."

"Not now," Bubba barked. "Gotta talk to someone." He pushed his way past Alex.

Sticking out his foot, Alex tripped the big guy. He fell onto a table. Glasses crashed onto the floor. His loud curses made heads turn. "Who tripped me?" he bellowed.

Alex grabbed his arm to help him up. "Who knows? Place is packed."

Bubba's scowl fixed on Alex. "You're closest. You tripped me."

"Why would I do that? Hell, I don't even know you." Alex hoped the delay gave Lee time to get away.

Bubba pushed his way to the kitchen door. A muscle-bound cook stood in the doorway, meat cleaver in hand and a determined look on his face. Bubba halted, and then turned and elbowed his way through the crowd toward the front door.

Alex followed, hoping Lee had disappeared by now. Bubba

stood in the open doorway and rubbed his knee. "Damn it all to hell, she's gone."

A tall, thin waitress tapped Alex on the arm. "You forgot to pay your tab."

Alex pulled out his money clip, and the red napkin slithered to the floor. He snatched it up.

Bubba turned and leaned forward as if trying to read it. "Whatcha you got there? Her phone number?" His knowing grin grated on Alex's nerves.

Resisting the urge to swing at the guy, Alex pocketed the napkin. "Just some doodling." He slapped some bills in the serving girl's hand. With a smile, she took them and walked away.

Bubba growled, "Tell me where I can find Laura Lee Leventhal."

"I don't know any Laura whatever you called her."

"Oh, yeah. I saw you talking with her, you know."

Ignoring him, Alex strode out, heading for his car. In the parking lot he was reaching in his pocket for his keys, when he felt someone grasp his shoulder.

Fists clenched, he whirled to face a belligerent looking Bubba. "Look, buddy, I don't know what your problem is, but I was just leaving." He assumed a fighting stance. "You want to fight? I'll take you on, but you could get your face messed up."

Alex waited, feet planted, muscles tensed.

Bubba scowled. "Stay the hell away from Laura Lee." He stomped off.

A few minutes later, seated in his beloved Jag convertible with the top down, Alex pulled out the napkin and tried in vain to read it in the waning light. Giving up, he tucked the napkin back in his pocket.

She hadn't given him her real name. Tomorrow he'd find out if she'd given him her real phone number.

Exiting the parking lot, he spotted a flash of green down the side street and turned. He'd better find her before Bubba did.

Chapter 2

The back door of the kitchen banged behind her. Lee cringed but kept running. She hoped clatter in the kitchen masked the sound of her footsteps. She ran along the alley, crossed the street, and shot down another alley, running between the yards of modest homes. Reaching the corner of a solid wood fence, she ducked behind it and gasped for breath. With each breath of clean air, her heartbeat slowed to a more normal pace. Little by little the insects and other night creatures resumed their chorus.

Finally, she peeked around the corner. Live oak and mesquite branches waved in the wind, but no one followed. She ran down the alley until she came to the street. Dark alleys were no place for lone women, but she'd rather be here than face that guy with a belly and an attitude.

Knowing Bart Sheldon was in custody helped her feel safer, but she wasn't taking any chances. She'd wanted to call the D.A.'s office to ask if a high bond had been posted, but Joe, her contact from the Witness Security Program, had advised against it. He'd said he'd find out, but so far he hadn't told her anything.

She crossed the street and headed down another dark alley. Her side hurt from running. She ducked behind a tree to catch her breath. Peering past the thick trunk, she looked back. The way she'd come was empty.

She hoped she wouldn't see Bubba again. Thank goodness, she'd only have to see Sheldon once more. One day in a Dallas court. She shivered. She was scared to testify, but she would. There was no other way to stop Bart Sheldon from building his miniature mafia into a bigger one.

On that day she'd wear a strawberry blonde wig, styled the way she used to wear her hair.

She'd put on her glasses and use makeup putty to give her nose the aquiline shape it had before the operation. Her new brown-tinted contact lenses she'd leave at home—well, wherever she was staying. And for one day only she'd be Laura Lee Leventhal, the name she'd been born with.

After catching her breath, she took off again, walking briskly this time. It seemed strange answering to Lee when she'd always been Laura. She'd felt like a fraud telling that guy Alex her name was Lee Marshall. He seemed so lonely. Somehow she felt comfortable with him, even though he must be at least six feet, two. His smile alone was enough to bowl her over. She wondered what had gone wrong in his marriage.

After glancing over her shoulder, she turned south on the next street. She missed her family and friends. She hadn't expected giving up her name would make her feel so cut off from everything she knew. Now if only she could remember to answer to Lee until she got used to the new name.

If this Alex was on the up and up, she hoped he'd let her work for him for a few months at least. It wasn't as if she had a lot of choices. The two places she'd considered didn't appeal to her. The cafeteria would insist she stay in the kitchen, standing on hard concrete floors all day, and working in the blind factory would bore her stiff.

She'd talked her way into a job in another town, but it wouldn't start until fall. That was months away. The allowance they'd given her until then was barely enough to pay the next month's rent on her apartment and stock the refrigerator and the cupboard with a few necessities.

Katydids and crickets almost drowned out the faint sounds of someone's television. She thought she heard her name. Was someone calling her or was she imagining it?

A metal storage building stood behind the cyclone fence beside her. If she could get over the fence, she could duck around the storage shed or maybe hide inside. Grabbing the top of the fence, she wedged the toe of her shoe in a diamond shaped opening. She hoped her skirt wouldn't catch on the sharp barbs on top.

Lee was halfway up when racing footfalls drew her attention. A big black dog ran around the edge of the house, barking furiously. She tried to jump back down, but the toe of her shoe caught in the fence. The dog grabbed the toe of her shoe in his teeth. Growling and slobbering, he tugged at her foot.

"Let go," she ordered. He kept on pulling her shoe. Finally she wrenched loose and heaved a sigh of relief. Hoping no one would come to investigate, she took off running again.

"Lee, Lee Marshall." The voice was definitely masculine.

It wasn't her imagination. Someone was calling her. Was it Sheldon's pudgy messenger whom she'd seen in the bar, Joe from the witness protection program, or Alex Brandon, the man she hoped would hire her?

Her pounding footsteps echoed through the alley. So did her pursuer's. She looked for somewhere to hide. She ran faster until her side ached. Her heart beat a tattoo against her ribs. She dashed through a yard and behind the shadowed trunk of a large oak tree.

"Lee." The man sounded closer now. She strained to see his face, but it was too dark. His athletic figure told her it wasn't Bubba.

That left only her witness protection contact and Alex Brandon. But why would Alex chase her — unless Sheldon had sent Alex? She stepped up her pace.

The wind picked up, chilling her. Mist from a sprinkler

blew over her. No, it was rain. Good, maybe whoever was following her would give up. Spray dampened her skin as she rushed on. She ran across another street, conscious now of a steady drizzle and the smell of damp earth.

The next yard had a gate. She tried the latch. It gave. Relieved, she shoved it open.

Heading down a narrow yard between two houses, she hoped there was no dog. She darted between rose bushes and a hedge of fragrant gardenias. The crunch of her footsteps echoed on the pathway of large stones. Loud footsteps behind spurred her to run faster.

Emerging from between the houses, she looked both ways, trying to decide which way to go.

A hand gripped her shoulder, sending her heart into a tailspin.

She whirled to face her pursuer.

❦

Alex struggled to catch his breath. He saw the look of fear on her face. She must have thought that jerk of a husband was chasing her. "It's me, Alex. Don't panic. Why the hell didn't you stop when I called? I just want to give you a ride home. It's raining, and that guy in the bar you don't want to see is looking for you."

She looked wary. "What if he followed you?"

"No one followed me. When you ran into this alley, I parked my car and called your name. You didn't answer, so I ran after you."

"Oh." Her lip trembled.

"Will you let me take you home, or don't you trust me enough to tell me where you're staying?"

She swallowed. "Guess if I want to work for you, you'll want to know where I live. You don't look like-like—"

"Like what?"

Lee hesitated. The look in her eyes said she was still afraid of him. "Well, you don't exactly look like a big, bad wolf."

Relieved, he laughed, his chuckle bouncing off the nearby house. "I should hope not." The rain picked up its pace, spattering off wet leaves of the tree above and intensifying the smell of wet dirt. Fat drops polka dotted her dress. More landed on his shirt, chilling his skin.

"Come with me to my car before we drown."

She crossed her arms protectively beneath her breasts. Shivering, she still hesitated.

A porch light came on, flooding the front yard. A woman called, "Who's out there?"

She ducked into the shadows. "Shhh. She'll hear us and call the cops."

He extended his hand. "Come on."

"Okay." She let him grasp her hand. It felt soft, but trembled in his bigger one. He led her back between the houses. Glad for darkened windows, he hoped no one saw them. He didn't want to waste time explaining why they were trespassing.

The skies opened up, chilling them with liquid bullets as they raced down the alley.

When they reached his open Jaguar convertible, he yanked the door open. "Get in. If you stay out here in the rain, that guy you're running from will find you."

❧

Lee frowned, but slid inside. Good gosh, she'd trusted her fate to some idiot who drove around in the rain with the top down. She faced him. His cerulean blue eyes seemed to search her soul. "Thought we were going to get out of the rain."

"We will be soon."

"How come you didn't put the top up already?"

He pushed a button, then struggled with the heavy canvas

top. "It wasn't raining then, and I didn't want to take the chance of missing you or worse, give that bully time to find you."

"I was doing pretty well eluding him all by myself."

"But I found you." He scowled. "This damn top doesn't work right. Gotta get it to a mechanic." He pulled the top over the car and jumped into the driver's seat. Clamping the fastening shut on his side, he grumbled, "I expected at least a 'thank you,' but all I get is an argument."

"I'm sorry. I do appreciate the ride." Her damp skirt clung to her thighs. She shook it loose. Glancing down, she was chagrined to notice how her damp dress clung, outlining her breasts.

His arm snaked out, leaning against her left breast. Tingling from his touch, she leaned back to slap him. Then she realized he was only trying to fasten the roof on her side of the sports car. She tried to shrink against the seat, but there wasn't any more room.

Something clicked. He glanced at her with a sheepish look. "Sorry about that, but it doesn't always catch, and I don't want the rain blowing into the car."

⁂

Alex started the car, enjoying the faint smell of her perfume. Having a woman around at work would be nice. With the CIA, he didn't need a secretary. You couldn't very well tote a woman around from country to country. And his cover as a small time American businessman didn't require a secretary to travel with him.

As he pulled away from the curb, he scanned the area from force of habit. In some places it might have been nice to have someone along to help, but the one time he did, he had to worry about her safety as well as his own, and things ended badly.

He'd never let Kathy and little Tanya come with him, even when he went to Paris. He'd always been glad to return to the warmth of the home Kathy provided—when they weren't fighting, that was.

He'd resigned after she'd complained about his being gone so much. He'd been about to set up an office in Grandville for his new business when she said, "Don't bother to come back. I'm filing for divorce. You can stay at a motel or with a friend. I don't care where as long as it's not here. And I'm keeping the house until I can find something better."

Too shocked to think clearly, he'd said, "You're not selling the only home she's known out from under Tanya. And you can't stop me from seeing her. She's my daughter, too."

With tight lips Kathy had taunted, "You didn't see her more than once or send her letters for six months. That makes a good case for me to get sole custody."

Amazed she had the gall to suggest that when he'd taken dangerous assignments to provide for her and Tanya, he'd tried to ignore the gut-wrenching pain slamming into him. "You'll hear from my lawyer," he shouted.

Now he didn't care where he lived any more, nor would he let himself care too deeply for any woman. His main joy in life was his monthly visits with Tanya.

He'd regretted telling Kathy he planned to move to Grandville. His wife's damn lawyer had changed the twice a month visitation to a once a month visitation schedule for a parent living over a hundred miles. Alex had kicked himself for not catching that before he signed it, and the decree was sent to the judge. Still smarting from her ugly accusations, he hadn't wanted to face her in court again so he'd skipped the final hearing.

Lee's teeth chattered, bringing his thoughts back to the present. Arms crossed beneath her breasts, she was shivering. He had to take her some place warm or get the heater working fast.

"How about some hot peach cobbler at the cafeteria?"

She shook her head. "They're probably closed. Besides, that guy may be there."

He drove slowly down the street, keeping an eye out for any vehicle that might follow them. "So, is he really your husband, and why is he chasing you?"

She rummaged in her purse and retrieved a comb. She tried to work it through her shoulder length auburn hair. She was silent for so long he wondered if she were trying to come up with a plausible story. "He's pestering me to do something I don't want to. I can't tell you any more right now."

So, that subject was closed for the time being. Maybe she'd reveal more later. He pulled to a stop at the intersection of the street and the highway leading west. "I know a place in the next town that serves great chicken fried steak with fried okra and a hot fudge brownie sundae that's out of this world. I promise I'll take you home immediately afterwards. Okay?"

"I look a mess."

He liked the way her dress clung, revealing the soft shape of her breasts. "You look great. Besides, as long as you have on a shirt and shoes they'll let you in."

She smiled. "Then I'm game."

"Good." Surprised how pleased that made him, he pulled onto the highway and stepped on the gas. He turned on the radio, found a light jazz station.

She leaned back and closed her eyes. "Ummm. That's perfect."

They'd gone almost two miles out of town before he noticed a black Camaro tailing them.

Chapter 3

Alex slowed. Maybe the black Camaro would pass. Instead, the car kept a steady distance behind. He stepped on the gas. The other car sped up. He swallowed. He wasn't afraid for himself, but how had he managed to be responsible for someone else's safety again? Scanning the road ahead, he stepped on the gas and hoped the police in the next town had at least one cruising patrol car.

Lee grasped his arm. "What are you doing, trying to get a speeding ticket?"

He shook his head. "Trying to shake our tail."

"Oh." Her voice sounded shaky. Her eyes widened, and she spun around to look. Her fingers bit into his arm.

"Better let go of my arm. I might have to turn suddenly."

"Sorry." Lee jerked her hand away.

He blinked, trying to shut out the memory—another time, another place, another woman—one who'd expected his protection—and died in his arms. Even now he could still feel the pain—and the guilt. God help him if it happened again.

Lee's worried voice jerked him back to the present. "They're getting closer. Are they trying to run us off the road?"

"Not if I can help it." Gritting his teeth, he jammed his foot down on the accelerator. He wished he'd had his old Jag tuned up.

"What if they ram us? They could turn your Jaguar into junkyard bait."

"Be still and let me concentrate." He tried to remember how far it was to the next town.

Lee craned her neck to watch behind. The thin, tight line of her lips betrayed her fear.

Hell, she couldn't be more scared than he. They were sitting ducks. At least the top was up, but if someone started shooting, it would hardly stop a bullet.

The Camaro inched closer, until its bumper and mud-smeared license plate nearly touched them.

"They're going to hit us," Lee screamed.

He shoved his foot harder against the pedal, but couldn't get more speed.

The bump jolted him. A scraping sound made him wince. That driver meant business. Alex's mouth went dry. He gripped the wheel so tightly his knuckles turned white. Trees flew by. His Jaguar widened the gap by inches. The Camaro bumped them again, harder this time, jerking his neck. Alex glanced in the side mirror. The driver held a gun out the window, pointed at him. Alex caught his breath and scrunched his head down into his neck. He doubted the headrest would deflect a bullet. His heart pounded furiously. Lee gasped as if trying to get her breath. He shoved her down. "Stay low. He's got a gun." The shot blasted his ear drums. His stomach lurched. Lee screamed and ducked.

The next bullet nicked the left side mirror. Sparks flew. He gripped the wheel, fighting to keep control. He managed to widen the gap between them and the Camaro. More shots rang out.

"Can't believe they didn't hit us. Maybe they were aiming for the tires." He hated to think of facing the thugs on foot. He had a gun, but if there were two of them, they'd have the advantage. They'd shoot him and then Lee.

Or perhaps they'd shoot her and make him watch. He

flinched, then swerved the car to make it more difficult to hit.

She clapped a hand on his shoulder. "Look out. There's a steer on the road." Long horns shone pale in the headlight's glare.

He slammed on the brakes and jerked the wheel to the left. Then he stomped on the gas pedal and zoomed ahead of the animal. Lee gasped as they barely missed the animal. The steer paused, then trotted down the middle of the road, holding its longhorns high as if to say, this is my territory, don't mess with me.

Behind them brakes squealed. Alex caught a whiff of burnt rubber. With the head start the longhorn gave them, they should outrun the Camaro. He glanced in the rear view mirror.

Seventy-five yards back, the Camaro slowly pulled out of the ditch.

He shoved his foot harder on the gas, hardly daring to breathe. He topped a hill, flew down the other side. Not until they hit a long straight stretch without seeing their pursuer did he breathe easier.

Lee looked back, then touched his arm. Her brown eyes glowed. "You did it. We're home free."

"Maybe, maybe not. Now I hope I can find a police station in the next town before they try something else."

"It's not they, just one guy."

"Bubba from the juice bar, right?"

She sighed, her entire body seemed to sag. "Yeah, it's him all right."

"What's he want with you?" Surely she wouldn't consider going back to that guy. If she did, she didn't have the brains he'd given her credit for.

"It's a long story. Let's find the police station. We'll be safe there, won't we?"

He wanted to tell her 'yes,' that he'd protect her from that piece of garbage, but he wasn't sure he could deliver. If she were one of those battered wives—hell, he didn't know enough psychology to convince her that guy was bad news. And he didn't need to get involved with another woman. Hell, he'd signed the papers a year ago, but the bad taste from his ugly divorce lingered.

He almost didn't see the city limits sign. A big magnolia tree hung over it. The sign said "Middletown, population 15,080." At least it was big enough for a police station.

Lee pointed to the right. "There, turn down that street."

He frowned. "What?"

"The police station's down there."

He slammed on the brakes and careened around the corner. "Why didn't you say so?"

"I thought it was obvious."

He scowled. "Hell, I didn't know what you were pointing at." After pulling to a stop in front of the station, he ran around the car, and grabbed her hand. "Hurry."

"I'm coming. Just let me get my purse."

"Forget it. You'll be a sitting duck if that guy pulls up," he barked.

Frowning, she shoved the car door open. "Do you always have to be right?"

He took her hand, but turned away to hide his grin. The way she said it reminded him of Amy. His sister had always complained when forced to admit he was right. Now he'd give anything to hear her complain again.

He held the station door open for Lee and placed his hand on her back, trying to hurry her.

She stepped through and turned to face him as he slammed the door. "Sorry, I didn't thank you for rescuing me. No telling what Bubba would have done if he caught me back in that alley." She shivered.

He hustled her to a small cluttered oak desk. Where was the officer on duty? Bubba was a wild card. Might even march in here and shoot them. He scanned the wanted posters, looking for Bubba's face.

"Hello, anyone here?" he called.

"That's Gin," cried a man in a back room. Chairs scraped and footsteps echoed. Someone walked down the hall.

A man turned the corner. Dressed in black, his shirt straining against a rounded belly, an officer with thinning gray hair shuffled to a chair behind the desk. His name badge said 'Lieutenant Harmon.' He smiled. "What can I do for you, sir?"

"Some guy's been chasing us."

The officer leaned back in the chair and put his feet on the desk. "You didn't by any chance get his license number, didya?"

"Hell, no. It was too dirty to read. Besides, I was too busy trying to get away. He bumped my car, and I almost ran into a longhorn steer on the road."

The officer scratched his head. "Can't do much without a license number. What kind of car was it?"

"A Camaro," Lee said.

"What color?" Lieutenant Harmon asked.

"Black," Alex said.

"You even sure it was a Camaro? Was it new or old?"

Alex frowned. "An older model, and I'm sure it was a Camaro."

"Shoot, lots of folks here have black cars, or ones that could pass for black at dusk."

Alex leaned over the desk. This cop was useless. "You're wasting time. He's getting away. Can't you radio someone to watch for him?"

"Don't rightly know as we could nab the right person— can't just stop anyone that looks suspicious."

Alex gripped the edge of the desk. "You mean you're not going to do anything?"

Officer Harmon brought the chair back on all four legs with a thunk. "If it'll make you folks feel any better, I'll send my second in command out to look around."

Lee stepped closer. "Don't you have any officers out there patrolling the town?"

The cop shook his head. "Me an' Oscar are the only ones on duty, and he's in the back room smokin' one of his Havanas." Alex caught a whiff of cigar smoke in the air.

Lee turned to Alex, fear lurking in her brown eyes. "Don't think visiting that cafe you mentioned would be wise."

Officer Harmon leaned forward. "Tell you what. Let me send Oscar on a quick run-by, then he can go with you to the cafe. He'd probably welcome a coffee break."

Lee smiled. "That would be nice. Thanks."

Twenty minutes later, Oscar, tall, lanky, and rather quiet, followed them into the Middletown Cafe. He sat in the next booth, his back to the wall, scanning everyone who entered.

Alex whispered. "I feel as if I'm on a date with a chaperone."

"We could sip soda through a straw like that old song says."

Alex chuckled and laid his hand over hers. "My grandmother used to sing that. I seem to remember something about lips slipping into a kiss."

Seeing her struggle for a reply, he watched her lips. Red and full, they would definitely be worth kissing. But she wouldn't welcome it now. He could feel her trembling hand beneath his. Obviously she was still shaken. Hell, he'd had to concentrate on relaxing his fingers to let go of the wheel.

When a waitress approached with menus, Lee reached for one, but he waved them away.

She frowned. "But I want to see what they have."

"Do you like chicken-fried steak and fried okra?" They had the best for miles around, but he supposed he should check to be sure she liked them.

"Yes."

"And hot fudge sundaes?"

"Sure, but that's—"

20

He turned to the waitress. "Bring us two chicken-fried steaks with some of your breaded, fried okra and then two hot fudge brownie sundaes."

As the waitress left, he glanced at Lee, and then did a double take. Scowling, her face radiated fury. What had he done to tick her off?

"You didn't even let me look at the menu."

"But you said you liked all that stuff."

"That's not the point. I like to decide things for myself."

He scratched his head. She sure was independent. Women—he'd never understand them.

Oscar leaned over the booth. "Lady, he shore made the right choice. Place is known for miles around for their fried okra and brownie sundaes. An' the chicken fried steak here ain't bad neither."

Alex took her hand. "Now, suppose you tell me why that guy was chasing us."

❧

Lee swallowed. She didn't want to tell outright lies, but could she trust him with the whole story? What if he let it slip that she was in the Witness Security Program? Not sure if he'd bought her allusion to an abusive husband, she racked her brain, trying to think of a plausible story.

"Isn't that our food?" She pointed to the waitress carrying two plates piled high with crispy golden nuggets. Huge chicken-fried steaks hung over the edge of the plates. Her mouth watered.

She grabbed a hot breaded piece of okra and popped it into her mouth. Tucking into the food with gusto, she hoped he'd drop the subject of Bubba. Later, she pushed the empty plate away.

Alex leaned forward. "Now, tell me, why do you think that guy was chasing us?"

"He wants me to do something. I just want him to leave me alone."

"Can't you get a protective order against him?"

"He'd ignore it. I just have to stay away from him."

He stared at her, perhaps wondering why she put up with such treatment. If Bubba didn't leave her alone, she'd have to move again—but she didn't want to miss out on getting to know this fascinating man facing her. He might be a bit heavy-handed, but the look in his eyes when he wasn't ordering her around said he was definitely interested in her.

The waitress cleared the table and brought two hot fudge brownie sundaes. Lee slid a delicious spoonful into her mouth and savored its chocolatety goodness. "Mmmmm."

Alex leaned back against the booth and smiled. "Watching you enjoy that dessert is almost as good as eating it myself." He took another bite.

She savored the last bite of brownie and pushed away a plate with nothing but crumbs. "I'll have to admit you're right. The steak and okra were tasty, and the sundae was out of this world."

Alex grinned. "Told you so."

She slapped his arm playfully.

"You hit me."

"It's bad enough that you were right. You don't have to rub it in. By the way, you wouldn't need a secretary, would you?"

Alex scratched his head. "Not sure I can afford one right now."

She leaned closer, her chestnut eyes earnest, her skin a rosy glow. "Wouldn't you rather have a human answer the phone than an impersonal machine?"

He scribbled some figures on a notepad.

"So, what do you think—can you afford a secretary?"

"Can't afford to pay much. What experience do you have?"

"I was the administrative assistant for a Dallas import-export business owner."

"Can I phone him for a reference?"

She shook her head. "His business closed down. I'm not sure where he is now."

"What did you do for him?"

"I made travel arrangements, typed letters, answered the phone, made lunch and golf appointments. I also interpreted for him in French and Spanish for business with foreign companies."

"That could be an advantage."

She leaned forward. "So, can I help you get your new business started?"

"Be nice to have someone answer the phone, but I don't know much about you. Would you work on a trial basis for two weeks?

She nodded.

"When would you be able to start?"

She touched the bandage on her nose. "You mean because of this? I'm sure Dr. Gittleman would say it's okay to start work. I'd rather stay in the background—I mean because of how I look."

"The bandage on your nose is all that's really noticeable." That was stretching it a bit, but he didn't want to make her feel self-conscious. "Does it still hurt?"

She shook her head, but didn't meet his gaze. "I-uh ran into a door—in the dark—should have turned on the light." She rose and fished in her purse. "I need to visit the powder room."

He caught a glimpse of a gray twenty-two before she snapped the bag shut. Either she was really scared of Bubba, or she had a past with a capital P.

Had he just made a first class blunder?

He took a deep breath and nodded toward her bag. "You won't need a gun in my office. I don't deal with rough customers." At least not anymore, but she didn't need to know that.

She pushed it further down in her purse. "I carry it for protection."

"From what I've seen, the folks in this town seem fairly law-abiding. You won't bring that gun to work, will you?

She shook her head. "I'd stay in the back room if you have one. I don't think Bubba would try to drag me away with you there."

Later, Oscar followed them in his squad car to the city limits, and then turned around. Alex leaned back in his seat. "Keep an eye out for that steer. It may still think it's king of the road. I'm glad you liked the food there. What else do you like?"

"Movies where you cross your fingers for the hero because you want him to win despite impossible odds. Then you feel like standing up and cheering when he does. But I don't like ones where they're caught in a storm. That's scary."

"Storms don't bother me. Who's your favorite movie star?"

"Tom Cruise. He's not very tall, but he has the sexiest smile. And Richard Gere always treats the woman so nicely. Who do you like?"

"Helen Hunt. She's blonde and witty."

🜁

Lee looked down at the floor. Fat chance of a relationship with him. She barely remembered a joke long enough to tell it to someone, let alone come up with one of her own. On the ride home, Alex kept checking the rearview mirror. He seemed lost in thought. Was he thinking about his ex-wife? She could understand his not wanting to talk about her, but he didn't seem to want to talk about himself either. Was he hiding something, too?

At her doorstep she put her key in the lock. Alex grasped her arm and turned her toward him. Was he expecting a kiss?

"Lee, I've been thinking."

"And?"

"Do you want me to spend the night on your couch? That guy may not know where you live, but you might feel safer if I stayed."

Relief flooded her. "I appreciate your offer, but won't that take time away from setting up your office?"

He shook his head. "You can pay me back by helping me choose furnishings in Middletown tomorrow. Then Bubba can't find you here alone." He gazed at her quizzically. "Well?"

She took a deep breath. He didn't act as if he were going to take advantage of her. Visions of Bubba breaking in during the middle of the night spurred her decision. "Thanks, I'd appreciate that. Come on in. And I'll be glad to help you choose stuff for your office."

Shutting the door behind him, he met her gaze. "That Bubba may keep on looking for you. You sure you want to work in my office? Maybe you should move to another town."

She bit her lip. Perhaps after he learned the truth, he wouldn't want any part of her messed up life. "Can't. My rent's paid up for two months, and I don't have enough money to go somewhere else."

"I see."

After spreading sheets and a blanket on the couch and setting out a towel and washcloth for him, Lee took a shower and went to bed. He seemed like an okay guy, but she locked the bedroom door.

Lying in bed, she listened to him sing 'Some Enchanted Evening.' His deep voice blended nicely with the shower sounds and made the apartment seem more cozy. She wondered if there were any significance to that particular song. Then he sang, 'If Ever I Would Leave You,' from Camelot to her. He sounded like Robert Goulet. His voice sent delicious shivers through her.

The next morning Lee was sleeping like a downed tree in the forest when she heard Alex knocking on the door.

Blinking at the bright sunlight from the window, she yawned. "What time is it?"

"Time to get up."

She unlocked the door and got back in bed. Seeing his eyes on her and suddenly conscious of her clinging nightgown, she pulled the sheet back up. "Why so early?"

He sat on the edge of the bed. "I'm going to Middletown. I need to buy furniture for the office. You said you'd help me shop. Besides, you shouldn't stay here alone."

She rubbed her eyes. The sheet slipped down again. "It's too early," she said, pulling the sheet back up. She lay back down. "Please let me sleep. I have my gun. I'll be safe here. If there's no car parked outside, it will look like no one's here."

He looked at her and smiled. "It's hard to resist the pleas of a pretty woman."

"Then you'll let me sleep?" She snuggled beneath the sheets and burrowed into the pillow.

"For a little while."

It seemed like only minutes later he was shaking her shoulder. "I want to be out of here in ten minutes. You want to go in your nightgown?"

She glared at him. "Did anyone ever tell you that you're a tyrant?"

"Yeah, my sister Amy." He grasped her wrist and pulled. "Come on. Get dressed."

"But I haven't had breakfast. Promise you'll let me grab an Egg McMuffin on the way."

"I don't like anyone eating in my car."

She frowned. "You think I'll spill something. Come on, I can be careful."

"I don't even eat in it."

"If I don't take time to eat, I'll get faint."

"Just get dressed. We'll stop somewhere on the way."

Lee shrugged into her robe. "I'll be ready in just a few minutes."

He paused at the bedroom door. "I want to be at the store soon after it opens. I'll pick out furniture and have it delivered this afternoon, so I can arrange the office. Then I'll choose computers and buy office supplies. After that I can start making contacts and arrange for advertising on Monday."

"You don't stand still long enough to leave footprints do you?"

"Once I've made my mind up, there's no point in delaying what needs to be done."

"I see."

During the ride, he didn't say much, but his brows stayed knotted. Was he thinking about setting up the business or wondering what happened to his marriage?

Either way, he wouldn't be part of her future after September when she was supposed to move to a different town. And she wouldn't have to worry about putting his life in danger, too. Why should she care whether he went back to his wife or found someone else?

She tried to visualize herself working in a new town and making new friends. She'd argued with the U.S. marshal assigned to her about applying for job at a private school. He'd insisted she'd be too visible, wanted her to work in a cafeteria or hospital kitchen somewhere.

Starting a new job in the fall seemed somehow less appealing than it had before — before she met Alex. Going away and not seeing him again would leave an empty place in her life. She tried not to think about that.

She concentrated on watching the rolling Texas hill country with clumps of stubby mesquite trees and waving grasses. Here and there a sprawling one story ranch home nestled between post oaks and sweet gum trees. Signs and brick walls of subdivisions told her they were approaching Middletown. He stopped at a McDonald's and bought Egg McMuffins for them. A little while later Alex stopped in front of a large furniture store.

By the time he'd selected furniture, visited an Office Depot store, picked out two computers and a printer, and arranged for someone to set them up, her head swam from the speed with which he made decisions.

After she helped him carry office supplies to the car, he took her to a Red Lobster Restaurant where they dined on succulent fried shrimp and melt-in-your-mouth cheese biscuits. He ate quickly, and then began sketching furniture arrangements on the floor plan of a two-room office suite.

He took her hand, his touch electrifying her senses. She almost pulled back, afraid he'd notice her reaction. He was nice, but rather bossy. Why did he make her feel this way? She didn't have time for this—not while she was on the run. And what about his ex-wife? Was he really over her?

Apparently unaware of the conflicting emotions roiling through her, he pointed to the diagram of his office. "I'll put your desk behind the door of the back room where you can't be easily seen."

"But won't it look strange not to have a receptionist greet customers?"

"I'll deal with them. I can't let you sit out there. That Bubba guy might come looking for you. Did you get many people just walking into the office in that import-export business?"

"Yes, but I suspected most were fencing stolen goods." Noting his inquiring stare she added, "That's one reason why I left."

"I wouldn't think there'd be much profit in selling a few pieces overseas."

"Sometimes we'd have whole truckloads of something to ship."

"Didn't you deal with any legitimate businessmen?"

"A few, but most of those contacted us by telephone or letter." She wiped her hands on a napkin. "Well, most of the people who come into a travel agency want to plan vacation trips. Business travel I expect will be handled mostly by phone.

"What I'm concerned about is someone coming in to harm you. Besides, I expect to get most of my business from a web site." He turned the diagram around to face her. "What do you think of this arrangement?"

"Didn't you say the building faced south? If you turned the desk this way, you could still see the door, but the afternoon sun would be behind you instead of glaring in your eyes."

"You're right. I didn't think of that. I wouldn't have until I sat down with the sun staring me in the face." His smile would have melted M & Ms. It made her wish she could lean on his shoulder and tell him everything. She could sink into his strong arms and show him with a kiss how she appreciated his protectiveness. She bet he'd kiss her right back with those sensuous lips.

She shook her head. This was madness. She handed the diagram back. Even if her daydreams came to naught, this would be a pleasant change from working for Sheldon.

On the way back to Grandville, he smiled at her several times. He acted like they were old friends. He drove straight to the office and unloaded two folding chairs. He parked his firm buns in one and was soon engrossed in measuring and redoing his diagram. She stepped into the back office and arranged office supplies on the shelves in the walk-in closet.

At three-thirty two hefty men stopped a truck outside, then unloaded furniture. Sounds of shuffling feet and grunts accompanied them as they set the heavy pieces into place. After they left, Alex told her he wanted to change a few things.

She helped him move a credenza and a bookcase. "I thought all your diagrams would have prevented this," she grumbled. Hot and perspiring, she slumped into the desk chair in the back room.

He took a look at the way she'd set things out on the shelves and started to rearrange them. Seething, she swallowed a retort. It was his business after all, and she'd soon be leaving.

At five the computers arrived with a guy to set them up. Alex dogged his steps. By seven she was famished, but he was still moving things around. Was he going to be that particular about everything?

She tapped him on the shoulder. "How about letting me run out and pick up something to eat?"

"No," he barked.

She blinked. "Aren't you hungry?"

"Sure, but I'm not letting you run around this town by yourself. Why don't you order a pizza?"

She bowed. "Yes, sir, your worship. Shall I grovel now?"

He smiled. "Am I that bad?"

She nodded, but couldn't suppress a smile.

When the food arrived, she had to practically drag him away from his desk to the glass topped table in the kitchenette, but he brought pen and paper with him. He took a few bites, then pushed the pizza away and scribbled on the paper. Then he picked up the manual that came with the computers and began reading.

So much for pleasant conversation. "Are you always like this?"

He raised his eyes from the manual. "Like what?"

"So busy organizing things you forget to eat."

"I've got to get things right. I don't feel comfortable until I do."

"When you ate meals at home with your wife, did you read at the table?"

"Mostly just short articles. She was always chattering about buying something. Then I'd have to stop reading and talk her out of something really expensive, which we probably didn't need."

"No wonder.... She clamped her mouth shut. It wasn't her place to comment. Besides, she'd be leaving at the end of the summer. After September, she could forget about him, couldn't she?

He looked her in the eye. "No wonder what?"

"Never mind."

He laid down the manual. "What were you going to say?"

"Forget it."

"I want to hear it."

"No, you don't."

He touched her arm, sending an electric current through her. "I insist you tell me."

She hesitated. "You'll probably pester me until I do."

He grinned. "You're right."

"Well, I was going to say no wonder she asked you for a divorce."

He looked incredulous. "Just because I read magazines at the breakfast table?"

She shook her head, wishing she hadn't brought it up. "Because she probably felt ignored."

He looked surprised. "At least I wasn't watching TV and ignoring her completely. What do you think I should have done, just eat?"

"I don't know, but you can at least talk to me while you eat."

❧

He pushed the manual aside. That's what Kathy always said when he read magazines during dinner. Could Lee possibly be right—could a little thing like reading at the table make Kathy ask for a divorce? No. It had to be more than that. What had happened to the togetherness they'd had when they first got married?

After wiping his hands on a paper napkin, he made some notes on a piece of paper.

She touched his wrist. He was surprised at the electricity that seemed to spark at the contact. "You're doing it again," she said.

"I'm just trying to figure out the best way to set up the business here."

"Have you ever run a travel business before?"

He shook his head.

"I worked at one once. I might know more about it than you do."

He glared at her. "You're the most outspoken secretary I ever had."

"So how many have you had?"

He grinned. "Just how do you mean that?"

She reached over to swat at his hand. "I'm serious. I mean working for you in an office.?"

He stared at her for a moment. "Believe it or not, so did I."

"Well, how many?"

&

Alex looked sheepish. "Just two. One was older and one was just out of high school, but both were very respectful."

She leaned forward. "You mean they didn't have the nerve to offer suggestions?"

"That's right. After all, I was their superior."

"But that doesn't mean you have a monopoly on good ideas to run a travel business."

"In my last job, I probably did."

"You may have traveled a lot, but arranging it for others is different."

"Okay, give with some good ideas."

"I speak French and Spanish. English is a second language for a number of Texas residents. We might sell more tours if I translated one of your web pages into Spanish." Then she outlined some of the possible pitfalls in selling on credit that her agency had run into.

Instead of brushing her off, he listened intently and asked questions. Maybe he wasn't all ego after all.

When she'd finished, he rose and shoved back the wrought iron chair. Keeping his gaze on her, he stepped around the table. "Thanks for helping me set up things. And your idea about where to set my desk was right on target."

His words and his broad smile warmed her heart. Grasping her hands, he pulled her up, and hugged her. She melted into his embrace, loving the feel of his strong arms holding her against his rock hard chest. She felt safer than she had for days. It was almost as if she'd come home at last.

Need to pull away — will in a moment. But being in his arms felt so good. She nestled against him, trying to summon up the strength to do that.

His face came closer. His warm lips descended on hers. He tasted of tomato sauce and sausage and hunger. His arms tightened around her. He tasted and nibbled, sending tremors of delight throughout her body, making her toes curl. She leaned into his strength, put her arms around his neck and met his lips with fervor — until common sense set in. She shouldn't do this — shouldn't get involved with him when she might have to leave at a moment's notice. As she pulled away, she saw surprise in his eyes. He brushed his finger over her bottom lip, then backed away. A sudden coolness washed over her mouth. She studied his face wondering what he thought.

He grinned. "You sure aren't bashful."

She felt awkward, but she wouldn't let him see it. "Are you saying I'm too forward? You started this."

"I've wanted to do that all day, but I probably shouldn't have." However, his grin said he didn't regret it one bit.

She felt as if she were sinking into a soft pile of pillows, cushioning and hugging her.

He grasped her hand, his fingers locking with hers. He gave her hand a gentle squeeze, then released it. "I signed the divorce decree ages ago, but if Kathy finds out about you—" He rubbed the back of his neck. "Knowing my ex-wife, she'll probably say something nasty if she gets a chance. I don't want to put you through that."

Lee swallowed. She could ignore his ex-wife's taunts, but what if Alex stole her heart? He could without half trying. She steeled herself against it, even as she looked into his eyes. His heartwarming grin pulled at her, but she said, "Don't worry. I'm a big girl. I know the score."

"Do you?"

"You've offered me a job and protected me. I don't expect anything more." 'Liar, liar,' chanted her heart. She could get used to more of those kisses real easy.

He marched back into his office. She stayed where she was and set up the file drawer. She wouldn't let her feelings lead her to heartbreak before summer was over. She studied the manual that came with the computer, but the way she'd felt in his arms and the memory of his lips meeting hers kept getting in the way.

After picking up the manual again, she concentrated on setting up an Excel spreadsheet. An hour later, feeling as if her brain were on overload, she leaned back and closed her eyes. At the sound of Alex's footsteps, her eyes flew open.

He yawned. "I had no idea it was so late. "I'll take you home. I can finish later."

Lee's landlady met them in front of the door to her apartment, wearing a duster and curlers in her hair. Rubbing her back with a pudgy hand, the woman said, "Thank goodness you're back. I was beginning to worry about you." She glanced at Alex, then at Lee. "It's none of my business, but I thought you should know. Your husband came asking for you earlier, wanted to know when you'd be back. I told him I didn't know. He said he'd come back later."

"My-my husband?" Clutching Alex's arm, Lee pushed back a wave of panic.

Chapter 4

Lee stared at her landlady and edged closer to Alex. Bubba must have come here. "I might have known he'd find out where I lived. Did that jerk tell you he was my husband?"

Mrs. Wilson nodded, setting pink spongy rollers in her hair bobbing. "I don't think I'd want to be married to the likes of him. Demanded to know where you were and shouted at me when I told him I didn't know when you'd return."

Lee gritted her teeth. "I'm sorry he bothered you."

Mrs. Wilson's lips formed a tight line. "If you like, I can tell him you've moved. Maybe he won't come back."

"He better not," muttered Alex.

Lee pushed down a wave of fear. "You can try, but he doesn't discourage easily." He'd never stop pestering her until she agreed not to testify against Sheldon. She'd have to call the U.S. marshal and tell him. He'd probably make her move—and she'd never see Alex again, never have a chance to really get to know him.

As the landlady waddled off, Lee said, "I wish I knew how he found me. I didn't tell anyone where I was going."

"Not even your family?"

Lee shook her head. "Not even my sister." She tried to keep from trembling, but her hands shook.

Alex looked her in the eye. "You must really be scared." He took her hand, his warmth and strength calming her.

But when his gaze met hers, a different kind of warmth filled her, one that alarmed her with its intensity. She shouldn't be attracted to this man. His compelling personality threatened to sweep her along with whatever he wanted, and his take charge attitude would make it hard not to go along. And besides, he'd just been through a divorce.

He faced her. "If he's your husband, why don't you divorce him? And if he isn't, why is he threatening you?"

She swallowed. If she let Alex think she were married, he might leave her alone. She really needed to distance herself from him. She didn't want Alex to believe she and Bubba were married. That left Sheldon. She shuddered at the thought of being married to the man. He had a way of overwhelming women he favored with flattery and gifts, but she'd never feel right living a life of ease on money that had been gained by fraud.

"I'm not supposed to talk about it because Sheldon will be on trial soon." She took a deep breath. "Bubba's not my husband. Bubba and I both worked for Sheldon in his business before—before it closed down. Sheldon sent Bubba because he's afraid I'll implicate him."

"So he's afraid you'll spill something to the cops?"

She nodded.

So you're going to testify against Sheldon?"

"I can't let him get away with what he did, all the people he ruined financially."

Alex stared at her for a long moment. "It's time you leveled with me. Just what is your situation?"

Lowering her voice to a whisper, she said, "You mustn't tell anyone, but I've been put in the Witness Security Program. However, I don't really feel safe. I can't understand how Sheldon's hired goon found me so quickly."

"Maybe they put a tracking device on your car."

"I didn't bring a car. A U.S. marshal brought me here."

"Sounds like you need a friend. I know what those devices look like and where to look. They might have put one on something you have. Or maybe a bug. Let me search your apartment."

She hesitated. Although she hardly knew him, she could probably trust him enough for that. Nodding, she stuck her key in the lock.

He grasped her wrist. His voice low, he said, "Don't say anything until I check for bugs. After we go in, bring me your suitcase. They may have put something in it."

Pushing the door open, she stepped inside. She wouldn't call this place home exactly, but after she'd unpacked, set her sister's picture on the entryway table and hung a few pictures, it had felt comfortable — until she'd seen Bubba.

Alex followed her in. She was glad the place still looked neat — not that he'd say anything. He'd been polite, except when he'd ordered for her without asking her first. Why did some men always think they knew what women wanted?

He leaned close, then whispered. "Get your suitcase."

She hurried to bring it to him. After inspecting it inside and out, he went into her bedroom and checked the bathroom. He returned, shaking his head. "By the way, the latch is broken on your bedroom window. Give me your purse."

She opened it, pulled out the gun, and laid it on the end table beside the couch. He took the purse, his fingers brushing hers as he did, sending a current of awareness up her arm.

As he sorted through her things, she felt as if he were sizing her up from the contents, but if someone had slipped something in her bag, she wanted Alex to find it.

He handed the purse back and motioned to the gun. "Hand that over."

She took a deep breath and looked into his eyes. Could she trust him?

He didn't smile, just held out his hand.

Lee hesitated, and then met his gaze. Trusting the look in his eyes, she laid the twenty-two in his palm.

He unloaded, and then reloaded it. "Seems in good condition. Nothing's attached." He handed it back. His gaze fastened on the overstuffed couch. He made quick work of removing the pillows and cushions to search underneath. Then he lifted the couch and peered below. He stared at the walnut end tables and old-fashioned pole lamp as if trying to think where else to search. Then he removed the large print of a waterfall from the wall, inspected the back and rehung it. Other pictures received the same treatment.

After returning the twenty-two to her purse, she dropped the bag on the end table. Fists clenched, she paced the floor. She thought she'd escaped Sheldon's control. How dare that two-bit mafioso boss invade her privacy like this?

Alex peered under tables and above doorways. The sound of kitchen cupboards being opened and shut resounded through the small apartment.

Finally, he returned, scratching his head. "Can't understand why I haven't found anything."

He scribbled something on a piece of paper and laid it on the table beside the phone. "I'm leaving now, but if someone tries to break in, call 9-1-1, and then call me at this number. I'll get here as quick as I can."

Reluctantly, she opened the front door. She could ask him to spend the night on her couch again, but after that kiss, she wasn't sure it was a good idea.

He took her hand, his touch warm and comforting.

"Lock your door after I leave."

"I will, thanks." She started to close the door.

"Wait," he said. "I forgot something."

She swallowed and looked into his cobalt blue eyes. What else did he have in mind?

He strode in. "Let me see your sister's picture." He snatched it off the table near the door. "I'll bet you kept this on your desk at the office."

"How did you know?"

"Just a lucky guess." He pointed to a lump on the back and held a finger to his lips.

After pulling the back cardboard out of the frame, he held up a small object. "It's a tracking device, not a bug." He stuffed the round disk in his pocket. "I'll throw it in the lake on my way home."

She imagined Bubba burning in the hot sun, hunting along the shore for it. Now that was something she'd like to see.

Alex paused at the door. "They've traced you here. You better let me drive you to a motel tonight."

Lee shook her head. "It's late. I'll look for another place tomorrow."

Alex frowned. "It's your funeral. Better barricade your door and lock the windows." He strode out and unlocked his car. She followed him to his car and watched him slide behind the wheel. Smiling now, he waved. He had such a nice smile. Too bad he didn't use it much. Maybe he had demons of his own to face.

Glad the rain had cooled the air a bit, she mounted the steps and went back inside. The resounding clunk of the deadbolt sliding home made her feel more secure. A cool breeze from across the room gave her goose bumps. The bedroom window must be open.

She stepped into the bedroom and pulled the window down, shutting out the chill and the smell of wet earth from the sprinklers. She returned to the living room.

A sneeze echoed from the next apartment. It sounded awfully close. She hadn't realized how thin these walls were.

Another sneeze sounded, louder and closer this time. Her skin crawled. Was someone hiding in her apartment? She snatched the phone, dialed 9-1-1. Damn, the line was busy.

With trembling fingers, she pushed it again. Still busy. Pulse pounding, she grabbed her purse and tiptoed to the front door. As quietly as possible, she unlocked it.

The sound of the bedroom doorknob turning made her jerk around. The door flew open.

Paralyzed, she took in Bubba's evil grin, then screamed and yanked the front door open.

She rushed out and collided with Alex.

He shoved her aside and marched in to face Bubba with fists clenched. "Leave her alone."

Bubba laughed, darted around Alex to grab her arm, and yanked her against his flabby body. "She's my woman, you know. We just had a little disagreement, but she's coming with me. Now bug off."

Alex turned to Lee. "That's not true, is it?"

"No." Almost gagging from Bubba's body odor, she wrenched out of his grasp and backed away a few steps.

"You're coming with me, Laura Lee."

Lee gasped. "Why should I?"

Still holding her purse, she glanced at Alex. If he got Bubba's attention, she could whip out her gun.

As if on cue, Alex strolled over to the bedroom doorway and pointed to the window. "This how you got in? What if someone saw you and called the cops?"

Bubba shrugged. "I came around the back way. No one saw me."

"You sure no one saw you?"

Bubba turned and toward the window.

Lee yanked her gun from her purse. As if realizing his mistake Bubba faced Lee and drew a gun from his pocket, but Lee was faster. She aimed for his arm and pulled the trigger. The recoil wasn't bad — it was a small gun, but the boom had her ears ringing so that she barely heard Bubba's gun clattering to the floor.

He swore like a sailor and grabbed his arm.

Alex snatched up Bubba's gun, pointed it at him. "Stay right where you are. I'm calling the cops."

Bubba stared at his arm as if he couldn't believe what he saw. "You shot me, bitch. I'm bleeding."

Alex grabbed Bubba's wrist. "You're not going to bleed to death. You can see a doctor later."

"They can't hold me, you know. They should haul her in for questioning, not me."

Alex waved the gun toward the phone. "Lee, call 9-1-1."

As Lee reached for the phone, Bubba scowled. "I'll get you for this Laura Lee. Sheldon ain't gonna let you ruin a good thing." He struggled in Alex's grip, then jerked his arm loose and sprinted toward the door.

Alex aimed the gun.

"Don't kill him," Lee shouted and stepped between them.

"Move, Lee." Alex raced to the door. "He's gone. Damn it, you distracted me just long enough for him to get away. It's too dark outside to see. Shouldn't take the police long to catch up with him though. Now call them."

A uniformed officer came in five minutes. Lee and Alex described Bubba. The cop took notes and asked questions. The officer pocketed his note pad. Pausing at the door, he said, "We'll keep this place under surveillance. I doubt he'll dare return tonight. And, miss, I need you to come down to the station Thursday when our police artist will be available, so we can put a drawing on the wall in the post office and show it on TV."

When the patrol car drove away, Lee let out the breath she'd been holding. "That's just great. The rent's paid for two months, but I'm afraid to stay here. Sheldon will send someone more dangerous than bumbling Bubba next time."

"Pack some clothes. You're coming home with me."

Chapter 5

Lee stared into Alex's earnest blue eyes. She couldn't stop trembling. "Come home with him," he'd said. She tried not to think how appealing that sounded. Strange sounds wouldn't keep her awake and worrying, but....

She took a deep breath. "I appreciate your offer, but I can't do that. This is a small town. I'm supposed to blend in, not make people talk. And if anyone finds out I spent the night with you — the gossips would have a field day."

"Would that be so bad? People don't make much of that these days. You can't stay here. Bubba could sneak in at night and slit your throat."

She shuddered. Her insides felt as if some macramé expert were tying a knot in her stomach. "Maybe I should call the guy from the witness security program and ask him."

Alex shook his head. His warm hand on her arm was reassuring. "If that man had done his job right, you wouldn't have this problem."

"It might not be his fault. Sheldon has several men to do his bidding. And most of them owe him favors."

"Your protector, the man from the U. S. marshal's office — what's his name?"

"I'm not supposed to give it out."

His hands gripped her shoulders. "Use your head. What if something happens to you, and I need to call the guy?"

She swallowed. "I keep his first name and phone number in my purse."

Alex frowned. "And I suppose you have it labeled 'witness security adviser?'"

"You think I'm stupid."

"No, but you might need help sometime. So what's his name?"

"Joe."

His hands gripped her shoulders. "Joe what?"

"Just Joe. That's all I know."

"Is that his real name or just a code one?"

"Darned if I know. That's what he answers to."

"That's just great. I can see it all now. I rescue you from some bad guy. You're unconscious and bleeding, and I need your medical records. If I just ask for Joe, you suppose anyone there will tell me anything?"

"Well, once when I was talking to him on the phone, I heard someone call him Iceberg, but I don't think that's his last name."

Alex scowled. "Iceberg." What kind of protector can he be? Look, we need to get out of here." He turned her around and gave her a gentle shove toward her bedroom. "Pack what you need. And make it quick. We can come back for more later."

Lee frowned, then headed for the bedroom. He sure was a 'take charge' kind of guy. No wonder his wife divorced him.

❦

Alex perched on the loveseat, resting his chin in his hands, and watched her slender form retreating. He couldn't believe he'd told her to come home with him. But what else could he do? She'd put on a brave front, but he couldn't leave her here.

He didn't know what he'd expected when he offered to drive her home, but he hadn't planned on taking her to his place. How could he look at her soft curves and not want her in his bed? More important, could he keep her safe? He'd damn sure better or he couldn't live with himself—not after last time. He shut his eyes. He wouldn't think about that now.

Wishing she'd hurry, he glanced at the print of a mountain waterfall cascading down wooded hills. More restful than his painful memories, it added a nice touch to the drab furnishings. He'd stayed in so many different furnished rooms that never really seemed like a home, but Lee had managed to make the apartment look livable. Like him, she couldn't go home again. From now on he'd only have women as friends or spend time in their beds. Little Tanya was all the family he'd have. Lee definitely needed a friend, but he didn't want to get involved.

❦

In the bedroom Lee threw underwear and three changes of clothes in her bag, then added toiletries and slippers. She hated cold feet. After laying a sweater over the rest of the things, she tossed in her swimsuit, hoping his apartment complex had a pool.

She rushed into the living room with her suitcase. Alex sat on the loveseat, his eyes closed. He must be worn out. She set her bag down and put a hand on his forearm, felt his muscled strength. "Alex, wake up."

Instantly alert, he glanced at his watch. "Sorry, didn't mean to fall asleep."

Rising, he yawned. "Turn out the lights, then sit down."

"I will when we leave."

"Do it now."

"Why?"

"If someone's watching your apartment, I want them to think you went to bed. I don't want anyone to see us leave."

That made sense. Why hadn't she thought of it? Would she ever get used to looking over her shoulder all the time? She flipped out the lights, then stumbled back toward the loveseat and proceeded to trip over his feet. His arms came out to steady her, but she lost her balance and fell into his lap. He smelled of English Leather, and his warm breath fanned her cheek. His arms closed around her, pulling her against his hard chest, making her feel strangely safe.

In the light from the window she could just make out an amused grin on his face. She struggled to get up. "How clumsy of me. Sorry, I should have waited until my eyes adjusted."

She scrambled off him and moved to the edge of the loveseat. Mortified, she sat there, acutely conscious of his heavy breathing across the narrow space between them.

Finally, she couldn't stand it any longer. She stood. "Can't we leave now?"

He shook his head and whispered. "We need to wait longer."

"How long?"

"Long enough for anyone watching to think you're in bed. Come sit down."

Not wanting to stumble around trying to find the couch, she sank back down, again aware of his heady aftershave. Heat from his body flowed over her. She was sitting too close. She inched away, only to be stopped by the arm of the loveseat.

After five minutes without talking, he seemed to be breathing heavier. Was he going back to sleep again? She reached out and touched his arm, felt firm muscle.

He flinched. "Where's your bag?" he whispered. She shoved it closer.

He grabbed it and took hold of her hand. "Let's go." He pulled her toward the door.

At the threshold, she yanked her hand loose. "I should leave a note for the landlady. She might think Bubba's dragged me off."

He scowled. "You want to leave a note in her mailbox where anyone could read it."

"No, I guess not."

"Come on. You can mail her a note and tell her you've gone away for a long weekend."

"But it's Tuesday."

"Well, for a short holiday." He grinned. "Or you could say you've moved in with me." He swallowed. What had made him say that? The only women he'd let stay for more than a night would be those who knew the score and didn't expect anything more than great sex. She seemed so innocent—he wanted to keep her safe, but that didn't keep him from wondering how her breasts would feel in his palms. He'd felt their softness when she fell against him. He caught her quick intake of breath. Could she guess what he was thinking? He swallowed. Wouldn't do to let her know she attracted him.

"Okay," she said, "I'll mail her a note."

He could barely see her dark form as she rose and stepped next to the wall. A zipper rasped. He gasped. "What are you doing?"

"Putting my sister's picture in my bag."

He rose and took hold of her hand. "Come on," he whispered. "We can leave now."

After she locked the door, they ran to the car. He held a finger to his lips as he opened the door, careful to make as little noise as possible. "Shut the door quickly so the light will go off."

Once behind the driver's seat, he scanned the area, and then drove away.

The rain had stopped, and the moon peeped from behind a cloud. A few stars blinked, making the sky seem friendlier.

❦

Lee reached behind to unzip her bag. She pulled out her sister's picture, barely visible in the moonlight. Would she ever be able to see her and talk to her face to face again?

The moon came out from behind the cloud. Things didn't look so scary with more light. Alex was driving around in a haphazard pattern, making lots of turns and even doubling back.

She drew in a deep breath. "You think we're being followed?"

"You can't be too careful with headstrong types like Bubba. I hope we convinced him to leave town, but if your Sheldon has something on him, Bubba won't give in that easily."

Her skin prickled. "I'm afraid you're right." The city-limits sign fell behind them. She glanced back, thankful to see no car lights. "Where are we going, to the next town?"

"Until I get my business set up, I'm staying in a little place out from town." He kept glancing at the rearview mirror, and then made a sharp left onto a road that skirted the lake. He stopped the car, opened the door, and got out. "Come stand by me. You can really see the stars from here."

Uh oh, she'd heard that line before. "You sure it's safe to stop here? What if someone is following us? Maybe somebody put a tracking device on your car."

He shook his head. "I checked."

Hoping he was right, she walked around to stand beside him. The rain had cleared the air. Stars shone brightly overhead. "All I can recognize are the big dipper and Orion."

"See those four stars that outline the shape of a kite. That constellation's called booties."

"Where? I don't see it."

Alex's face was so close to hers she could smell the fresh scent of his aftershave—he was close enough to kiss her.

Instead he pointed. "See those three stars arranged in a triangle. Now follow my finger down to the bottom star."

"I see. It's a diamond-shaped kite, but longer on one side."

He clambered up onto a large rock, then pulled a disk-shaped object from his pocket, a tracking device he'd called it. He threw it sideways as if he were trying to make it skip. It didn't—just slid into the water with a soft plop. He jumped down and walked back to where she stood. He grinned. "Should take Bubba a while to figure that one out. Let's go."

She imagined Bubba hunting along the shore for it, sweat dripping off him in the hot sun. Now that was something she'd like to see.

Minutes later, he pulled back onto the highway. About three miles farther he turned in at Riverview Mobile Home Park.

She swallowed. "You live in a trailer?" Would it even have a couch? She certainly didn't intend to share his bed.

Alex pulled to a stop in front of a modest mobile home. Fully skirted, it had a few shrubs with a scattering of flowers along the walk. "My place isn't much. I didn't expect company."

"I'm sorry. I'm putting you out, aren't I?"

He didn't comment, but merely opened her car door and hefted her bag. He mounted the few steps, unlocked the door, and swung it open. He stepped to one side with his arms outstretched. "Welcome to my humble abode." After shutting the door, he reached past her and flipped on a light, brushing her arm with his muscular one. Her skin tingled where he touched it.

Off to one side, a sink and small counter were surprisingly clean. The loveseat looked like it could be a sofa-bed. However, the coffee table and TV facing it didn't leave enough room to pull it out. She hoped the narrow hallway led to a bedroom or better yet, two bedrooms. He set her case on the coffee table.

She unzipped the side pocket, took out her sister's picture, and set it on the coffee table.

Alex glanced at it. A frown flitted across his face and then vanished. "Are you and your sister close?"

She nodded. "I'll miss our long talks on the phone. But the man in charge of keeping me safe said it would be too risky. I'll have to be content with letters. He told me to mail them to him at his office."

Alex frowned. "To Joe, you mean?"

"Yes, Joe. Anyhow, he'll mail them to Libby. Do you have brothers or sisters?"

"Just one sister. We were very close. Growing up, she always came to me for help and advice, even with boyfriends. Until the last time…."

"You're not close anymore?"

He blinked several times. "She's dead."

"Oh, I'm sorry." She glanced away from the pain in his face. "Was it an accident or would you rather not talk about it?"

"It's okay. She died in childbirth following a car accident."

"How sad. Was her husband killed too?"

"She wasn't married."

"Oh. Did the baby live?"

Alex nodded, then blinked again.

"What happened to the baby?"

"My mother takes care of him. He's just learning to walk now, calls me Lex-lex."

She imagined him swinging the child to his shoulder. Would she ever have a chance for a home and family with a guy like Alex" She sighed. "Bet you're a great uncle."

He smiled, and his eyes twinkled. "He loves it when I swing him over my head. You should see the way he crinkles up his nose and giggles."

Alex stepped into the narrow hallway, and then opened a cupboard. Seconds later, he tossed a towel, sheets and a blanket onto the loveseat. "I'm sleeping on the couch. You can have my bed in the back. I'll let you have the first shower, but don't be too long. My water heater is small."

"I won't take long, but I'm not kicking you out of your bed. I'll sleep here on the couch."

"Of all the stupid—that's the most dangerous spot in this place. Someone could bash in your head before I could get to him."

Lee opened her mouth to object, then shut it. Damn him, he was right.

He glanced out the window. "I'm going outside to be sure no one's lurking around."

After he left, she ducked into the bathroom, then slipped off her rumpled dress and half slip.

Later, after toweling her body in the tiny shower cubicle, Lee slid into her slippers.

The outside door clicked shut, and Alex called out. "I'm back."

Suddenly she realized she hadn't brought in her nightgown. Then it dawned on her. She'd left her suitcase in Alex's living room. Not wanting to put the underwear she'd worn all day back on, she wrapped the towel around her and tucked it in above her breasts.

The thin, damp terry cloth clung to her body, exposing too much thigh for comfort. She peeked into the living room. He sat on the couch reading the paper. If she made a quick dash for her nightgown, maybe he wouldn't notice much.

In the living room, holding her towel in place with one hand, she made her way to the chair. As she bent over her open suitcase and rummaged for her nightgown, she was conscious of cooling skin on her thighs where she'd missed a few drops.

Close by a newspaper crackled. Glancing toward Alex, she caught him quickly returning his gaze to the paper.

"Nice legs," was all he said, but she wondered if he'd been watching all along.

Her face and neck heating from embarrassment, she slid her nightgown from her bag, then hurried back to the bathroom. She'd packed in such a hurry she'd thrown things in. The gown she'd grabbed was clinging and almost transparent. Darn. It covered more than a bathing suit, but she still felt exposed. She glanced in the mirror, wishing it didn't reveal so much cleavage. A sweater would cover her up some.

She marched back into the living room in a no-nonsense manner and grabbed a sweater, hoping he wouldn't get any ideas. "You can have the bathroom now."

He glanced up with an interested look in his eyes. Maybe he already had ideas.

Chapter 6

Lee took in Alex's interested look. Just because she'd let him kiss her—and wow, he sure could kiss—she wasn't going to encourage him. Right now she had all she could manage trying to set up a new life. She pulled on her sweater to cover up her revealing nightgown.

"Good heavens, woman, you'll roast. The air conditioning doesn't work, and my box fan blew a fuse last night. Take that sweater off or you'll sweat."

She sank onto the couch. "My grandmother used to say, 'ladies don't sweat or perspire. They just glow.'"

"Well, you'll glow a lot." His glance roved over her as if he expected to see drops appearing on her skin.

Already the muggy air threatened to suffocate her. Must be eighty-five degrees outside.

He rose. "I'm bushed. If you'll stand up, I'll pull out the hide-a-bed." He moved the TV, and then lifted the coffee table as if it were a cardboard box, though she could see muscles ripple beneath his shirt. He set it in the kitchen area.

As soon as they finished pulling out the hide-a-bed and putting on the sheets, she turned toward the hall. "I'm going to bed now."

He touched her shoulder. "No so fast. Sit. We need to talk."

What had she gotten herself into? She slid out from under his hand, made her way around the end of the sofa-bed and perched on the opposite side facing him. "About what?"

He smoothed back his dark waves, then shot her an intent look. "It's time I learned more about you."

She gazed into his intent blue eyes, then swallowed. "What do you mean?" She buttoned her sweater.

He grinned. "Wish you hadn't done that. Liked the view better before." Reaching over to pat her shoulder, he smiled. "Relax. I don't have designs on you, but you'd better tell me who does."

She let out the breath she'd been holding. "You've been wonderful, but I don't know how you can help me escape Sheldon."

"Try me."

"You don't know what he's like." She shivered. "He stops at nothing."

He shrugged. "Tough guys I can deal with."

She stared at him. "You're an ordinary businessman. I wouldn't expect you to have experience with guys like him."

He frowned. "So maybe I've done other things."

"Sheldon was always wheeling and dealing—probably most of it illegal."

"Did you see anything to prove it?"

"One night I when was working late, a truck drove up, and two men unloaded a whole bunch of really nice furniture—couches, love seats, easy chairs, and end tables into our warehouse. I read the tags. They were all made by Broyhill, nice stuff. The next morning I asked Sheldon if I could buy a couch from him at the same discount he was offering retail stores. He glared at me, and then said they'd all been shipped out long before I got there."

"Sounds like a quick turn-around."

"It seemed too quick for me. When I looked for the invoices and shipping manifests to file them, I couldn't find any. Then I remembered other shipments that came without invoices."

His gaze met hers. "You think those were stolen goods?"

She nodded. "Not only that, but men kept coming in with cash."

"To pay back money they owed?"

She shook her head. "I don't think so. There were too many for that. Sheldon set out large envelopes for me to give them. One day I peeked inside."

"What did you find?"

"Lists with names, addresses and details of money owed. That's when I figured out that bookies and drug pushers were working for him. When the police came with the IRS investigator, they wanted invoices for the last shipment. Sheldon gave them a few and claimed the rest were misplaced. After the IRS looked at his books, they took him away."

"So he's in jail now?"

She nodded. "His lawyer probably got him out on bond, but I hope not. I'm sure he's got hit men at his disposal, even now when he's in jail. I'm afraid the authorities don't have enough proof to keep him locked up for long."

"So what you need is someone to get enough evidence to nail him?"

"Right. If he and the men working for him are in jail, maybe I can go back to living with my sister in the house our parents left us. Except I can't ask you to help with that."

He ran his fingers through his hair. "I've done a bit of sleuthing before."

"You were a private eye?"

"More like a public eye."

She raised her brows. "I don't understand."

"I used to work for the government."

"The FBI?"

He shook his head. "CIA."

"But you don't any more?"

"Took too much time from my family. Got burned out."

"Was your family relieved when you quit?"

"That's when my wife said she wanted a divorce. Since then I haven't seen as much of my daughter as I'd like."

"That's too bad. How old is she?"

"She's five and darn cute. I get one weekend with her a month. I'm learning to enjoy cartoons again. It's one thing we can still do together." His eyes looked sad.

She was beginning to like him, but he seemed tied down by his past. Besides, she had no business getting involved with a man who loved children. She'd better keep hands off. She only hoped he kept his hands off too.

"Enough about me," Alex said. "Why are you so afraid Sheldon will find you?"

"When they arrested him, he vowed to get even. He claimed I put the finger on him."

"Why'd he say that?"

"First an accountant came to audit the books for a loan, and then I showed the IRS investigator the wrong ones when he arrived. How was I to know he kept two sets?"

"Was he charged with income tax evasion?"

"Sheldon claimed the accountant had made a mistake, but they got a search warrant and found both sets of books. He threatened to wipe out the cop that came to search. That's what got him thrown in jail."

Alex whistled. "No wonder you're scared. What do the feds want from you?"

"They want me to give them the names of all his contacts and testify to that in court. They want to nail the whole ring."

"So Sheldon was just your boss, not your husband. How come you stayed with him so long?"

"I was getting ready to leave, even threatened to quit, but my sister needed an operation. I wouldn't have minded doing without to pay for it, but I couldn't scrape up enough money. Sheldon offered to lend me money for the operation. He said I could pay him back out of my salary."

He frowned. "Couldn't you have gotten a loan at a bank?"

"I hadn't established a credit record yet. He gave me a raise as an incentive. I was only going to stay until I paid back the money. When Sheldon got arrested, he looked me in the eye. In a cold voice he said, if he got a jail term because of me, he'd see me in hell before he'd let me live."

"So what did you do then?"

"I walked out with the cop. I went straight to the District Attorney. He arranged for me to be in the Witness Security Program if I promised to testify."

"Doesn't look like they did much to protect you."

"They got me a different social security number and a new driver's license with my picture and new name. They brought me here, arranged for surgery on my nose—I'd already planned to have my deviated septum fixed. My health insurance had okayed it.

"Joe, my U.S. marshal contact, paid the deposit and the first month's rent on an apartment. Then he told me I needed to find a job so I wouldn't look so obvious to townspeople. Joe promised I'd be safe in Grandville, but—"

"But Bubba found you anyhow."

"When a policeman escorted me to their office to pick up my things, I didn't realize someone had put a tracking device on Libby's picture. For all I know, they made a copy of it so they can find her, too." She rubbed her eye. "I'll never forgive myself if they harm her."

"More likely, they'll threaten you with hurting her—if they find you again that is."

She sighed. "This little town was starting to grow on me. I don't look forward to having to move again, but I guess I'd better."

He leaned closer, his spicy aftershave teasing her senses. "Not if you can make Sheldon think you've left town. I take it Bubba's one of Sheldon's hit men?"

"One of his yes-men. Sheldon's probably got something on

most of the men who work for him. Don't think anyone likes him."

"You should have found another way to pay him back."

She frowned. "Even with the money Sheldon lent me, I could hardly scrape up enough to pay the deposit for Libby's surgery. I haven't bought a new dress in ages, but my sister's health is more important than new clothes."

"Kathy looked good in what she wore, but she was always buying something new." He shrugged. "Don't know what it is with you women."

Lee frowned and leaned forward. "We're not all like that. Don't set yourself up as judge unless you've been there."

"I try not to be judgmental." The hint of a smile flashed across his face. "Actually, I try to keep that tendency a deep dark secret."

"Sure you do."

His eyebrows furrowed. "I can't understand why you didn't get another job and quit sooner. But what's done is done. Tomorrow I'll take you to tell your landlady that you're moving out. Say your mother is ill and you have to go take care of her. You don't know how long it will be so you're canceling your lease and—"

Her hand came down on his forearm, harder than she meant for it to. "Wait a minute. You want me to march up there in broad daylight and tell her some cock and bull story. You've got to be kidding."

He flinched. "I'd hate to be near when you lose your temper. Bet you pack a mean wallop."

"Sorry, didn't mean to hurt you. I don't like being told what to do as if—as if I'm incapable of thinking for myself."

"I didn't mean that. We'll wait until it's dark when Bubba or someone else Sheldon sends is less likely to see you."

"Shouldn't I call first?"

He shook his head. "Someone might come asking about

you. She could let something slip. Don't need to alert them to your plans."

She swallowed. "Tomorrow's a holiday. You want me to stay holed up here all day then?"

He nodded. "And after that, since that I've got my office arranged, you can work in the back room and answer the phone back there."

"What if someone comes in and sees me?"

"They won't—not with your desk back behind the door."

"But anyone who remembers seeing me with you will wonder where I am. Maybe they'll think you did away with me." Holding her breath she watched his face. What had possessed her to blurt that out"

He scowled. "Don't be ridiculous." He moved to the window, pulled the drape back a notch and peeked out. "I can hang around the Red Door Cafe looking like I lost my last friend." He let his head droop, and a sad look spread over his face. I've done a bit of acting in my day. I'll fool the lot of them."

"What about food? Won't someone notice if you buy anything besides beer and TV dinners?"

"You think I can't cook?"

She leaned against the back of the loveseat. "I suppose you're going to tell me you're a gourmet cook."

He grinned and took her hand in his. "Wait 'till you taste my beef stroganoff." You'll beg for seconds."

Lee's gaze met his arrogant one. "You're so sure of yourself. Do you ever admit to making a mistake?"

"I make damn few." He opened the front door. "I need some fresh air."

As he shut the door behind him, she wondered why he had referred to his wife in the past tense. If she were dead, why hadn't he mentioned it? And who was taking care of his daughter?

Chapter 7

Footsteps alerted Lee to Alex's return to the living room/kitchen of the trailer. "I've got it," he said.

She leaned forward. "What?"

"Tomorrow I'll take you to the bus station. Buy a bus ticket to somewhere—like Houston and mention in a loud voice where you're going—only you won't. Later, I'll cash in the ticket. Then after dark, I'll take you by your apartment for the rest of your things."

"And I can shove a note under the landlady's door."

"Or better yet, mail it to her."

Lee's gaze swept the living area. "Your place is cozy, but awfully small. If I have to stay cooped up here all day—well, it's not how I want to spend the 4th of July."

He frowned. "They didn't put you in the Witness Security Program to be entertained. If staying here is what it takes to keep you from being shot or your throat slit, you'd better do it."

She glared at him. "I didn't expect everything to be fun and games, but couldn't you drop me off at a museum or an art gallery and pick me up at five. I should be safe enough there."

He scowled. "No way. I'm not leaving you alone for Bubba or anyone else to grab. Besides, the museums and art galleries may be closed." He stood. "I'm going to take a shower." He strode down the hall.

He had an answer for everything, darn him.

At the bathroom door he paused. "If you don't like staying here, call your marshal guy. Tell him to find you another place."

She frowned. "At this hour? He's probably in bed or out somewhere."

"Then you're stuck with me. Maybe tomorrow we can drive to Fort Worth and watch the fireworks."

"That's better. I'd like that."

Later, in his bedroom she snuggled under the sheet and was almost asleep when she heard the phone. He must have snatched it up after one ring. His angry tones flowed down the hall. All she could make out was, "Damn it, Kathy. Why now?"

Well at least his ex-wife was still alive. Except their poor child was caught in the middle. Alex could be bossy at times, but he'd been so protective and even put his plans on hold to keep her safe. However, if his ex found out Lee were staying here, there'd probably be a different kind of fireworks.

The next morning, he insisted she call her U.S. Marshal. Alex got on the line and convinced Joe he could protect Lee for a few days until Joe could set her up somewhere else.

Alex fixed fluffy scrambled eggs, crisp bacon, and toast. After eating her fill, she was rising to leave the table when he touched her arm and grinned. "Don't know why I didn't think of it before. I'll take you on a picnic at the lake."

Lee smiled. "That's a great idea. Can we stop at Kentucky Fried Chicken? Bologna sandwiches aren't my idea of a picnic."

"Mine neither. I'll take you to the lake house of a friend I went to high school with. He invited Kathy, Tanya, and me for his annual 4th of July picnic. I declined because Kathy and I had split up. But last night she asked me to take Tanya for the day. Seems she has a hot date, said she doesn't want the guy to see the little minx."

Lee leaned back against the seat. "So it was your wife who called last night?"

"Ex-wife. I was hoping the phone wouldn't keep you awake."

"It didn't. I went right back to sleep."

"I can't believe Kathy wants to keep Tanya a secret. I'm proud of my daughter. Any woman I date is likely to meet her. Carl's 4th of July picnics are always great fun. There'll be swimming and water skiing and burgers cooked on a grill. Want to go?"

At least this time he'd asked instead of telling her, but did he really want to take her, or was he just being polite?

He took her hand and squeezed it. "Say 'yes.' I'd really enjoy your company."

She smiled. "Sure, sounds like fun." If she saw him with Tanya and his friends, she might see the real Alexander Brandon—and maybe see why Kathy divorced him—instead of thinking about how sexy he looked with that tan T-shirt outlining his well developed muscles. It wasn't smart to get too attached to him. He might be divorced, but what if he and Kathy decided to remarry for the sake of the child?

He looked at his watch. "It's later than I thought. I have to meet Kathy and Tanya at the bus station. Get your bathing suit and come on." As soon as she pulled it from her suitcase, he grabbed her hand and practically dragged her out the door.

After he pulled to a stop at the bus station, he snapped his fingers. "Damn it, I forgot Tanya's car seat. Kathy will have a fit if I don't have it."

"Isn't the bus due any minute now?"

"Yes, but Kathy's always harping about my being late to pick up Tanya. Would you wait for them inside the station? The bus might come before I get back. With all the people there, you should be safe. Tell her to wait and that I'll be right back."

"Why doesn't she drive her here?"

"She hates to drive, says the freeways make her nervous. She offered to bring Tanya because she has a hot date. Otherwise, she wouldn't even let Tanya visit today."

"I see," Lee said. Things didn't look good for his daughter. The air was warm as Lee got out of the car. A gentle refreshing breeze carried the scent of honeysuckle and freshly cut grass. Inside she bought a ticket to Oklahoma City, making sure to mention the destination loudly. Then she strolled outside to wait for Alex and watch for the bus with his wife and his daughter. People were coming and going. She should be safe enough.

Leaning against a tree, she closed her eyes for a moment. Heavy footsteps seemed to be coming closer. Her eyes flew open.

A beefy hand grabbed her arm. "Well, what have we here, but Miss Annie Oakley herself?" Bubba's exaggerated drawl sent shivers down her spine.

Trying not to shake, she jerked her arm loose. Stepping away from the tree, she inched closer to the sidewalk. Would he dare try anything with people walking by? Her gaze roved the area. Frantic, she looked for Alex. All she saw was Bubba's black Camaro parked nearby. Why couldn't a friendly cop be cruising around?

She cleared her throat and struggled to keep her voice even. "Let go of me, you pervert."

His bushy eyebrows came closer together. "Bitch, I'm straight, and you know it. I should break your arm for shooting at me last night."

"You would have shot me if you could."

"Not if you promised not to testify."

"Why'd you come here, Bubba? The cops will be hunting you. Why haven't you split?"

He laughed. "Been looking for you, baby. Figured you'd try to run." He frowned. "Don't call me Bubba. Name's Frank, you know." He stuck out his bandaged arm. "Aren't you going to ask how my arm is?"

She stepped back, wanting to run, but forcing herself to speak calmly. "Okay, Frank, how's your arm?"

He scowled. "Better—as if you cared."

"Hey, you'd have shot me if I hadn't winged you first." She edged toward the door of the bus station. "I'm going inside and call the police."

"No, wait. I won't shoot you here."

"Darn right you won't. There are plenty of witnesses to nail you." She hoped her loud voice would attract attention. One woman scurried into the bus station—to call the police, Lee hoped. On shaky legs, she backed nearer the door.

Just then a bus pulled up, and passengers filed out. A young blonde in a micro-mini skirt held tightly to the hand of a bouncing girl about five years old with red curls.

The blonde pulled the little girl back. "Be patient, Tanya. Your father may not be here yet."

So that was Alex's ex-wife, barely out of the cradle. Whatever had he seen in her? A quick look at the girl's slim hips and tight fitting T-shirt stretched over ample breasts answered her question.

She had to get rid of Bubba. Lee swallowed and faced him, hoping Alex's ex-wife and child would go inside. Bubba mustn't suspect Lee had anything to do with them. She edged toward the station door.

It took concentration to keep from trembling. Where was Alex? He said he'd be right back. She swallowed. Got to deal with Bubba myself. He wouldn't dare try anything with all those people around would he?

She held up her bus ticket. "Damn, this has the wrong time. I need to get it changed." Backing up to the entrance, she reached behind and groped for the door handle, but all she touched was air.

He had her arm in his beefy grasp. "Just a minute, Laura Lee." He pulled her away from the door. "Let me see that ticket."

She waved it in front of his face. If her pulse weren't racing so, she'd enjoy trying to fool him.

Bubba grabbed her wrist, pulled her close and stared at the ticket. She gagged at the odor of garlic and unwashed flesh.

He grinned. "Sheldon will want to know that you're going to—" He read the ticket. "Oklahoma City."

She tried to shake her arm loose. He held on like an alligator.

"Let go of me or I'll scream."

"Hey, I won't hurt you." He smiled, showing yellowed teeth. "Got a proposition for you, Laura Lee. You don't need to squeal on Sheldon. He wants you back, you know. Said you were the best secretary he ever had, an' he'll give you a raise if you come back."

She yanked her arm away from his protruding belly, tried not to inhale. Being this close made her nauseated. When he let go, she glanced at her watch. What was taking Alex so long? Sticking out her chin, she edged toward the door. "I'm not interested."

"Forget the ticket. Sheldon will make it worth your while— might even forgive that loan he made you for your sister's operation if you lay low until after the trial."

"And what else"

"Shit, ain't that enough?"

Got to keep him talking. What can I suggest? "Would he take me on a trip to the Bahamas? Heard he was thinking of setting up some business there."

"Hell, I don't know. He don't tell me everything, you know."

She glanced at her watch again. Alex's wife might get impatient and page him. Need to get rid of Bubba fast. Her mind raced. I could step inside and ask the clerk to use the phone to call the cops, but Bubba might follow me. Or I could hide in the restroom and call on my cell phone, but then Alex won't find me. If Alex didn't come soon, would his ex-wife take Tanya and ride the bus back? Lee couldn't risk that.

She scanned the street again. Still no Alex. She scowled at

Bubba, grabbed the door handle and yanked it open. "I'm going to call the police, and you can bet I'll give a good description of you.

"Bitch," Bubba muttered and grabbed for her. She pushed her way through a crowd of people and scurried past them. Inside she stood behind a large man and peeked out a window. She held her breath as Bubba stood there, looking in. She wished he'd get in his Camaro and zoom off.

Why hadn't he left town? Did he think he was smart enough to elude the cops?

Shivers ran down her spine. She marched to the counter and explained to a husky clerk with a bushy beard why she needed to call the police. By standing next to the clerk, she hoped Bubba wouldn't dare try anything.

By the time police dispatcher answered, she was shaking so badly, she could hardly get the words out. "Stay right there," said the officer. "We'll send someone by."

That's all she needed. Alex might grumble if they insisted on a long interview, but if they nabbed Bubba, it would be worth it.

The shuffle of feet filled the station as passengers milled around. She'd better not seek out Kathy and Tanya until she was sure Bubba had left, but sounds of crying drew her attention.

"I want my daddy," a little girl wailed.

Near the ticket counter reddish blonde curls bobbed as Tanya sobbed and clutched a small teddy bear with one hand. Her other hand was held tightly by the bottle blonde who looked about sixteen.

Tears dribbled down onto the front of Tanya's pink and blue playsuit. The blonde chomped on a wad of pink bubble gum and leaned over. "Your daddy will be here any minute. If he's not, I'm going to sit you on the counter so the nice clerk can keep an eye on you. I haven't got all day."

This was Alex's ex-wife?

Tanya took one look at the clerk's bushy beard, and scrunched up her little face. More tears rained down. "He's big. I'm scared of him."

Red-gold curls bobbed as tears ran down the little girl's face and dampened her pink and blue playsuit.

Lee hurried over and knelt in front of the little girl. "Your daddy's coming. He's going to take you on a picnic at a lake. Won't that be fun? He'll be here in a minute. My name's Lee. What's yours?"

Between sobs, the cherub blurted, "Tanya. I'm hungry. Mommy gave me candy. I eated it."

A chocolate smear on her cheek showed the truth of that. Tanya looked up at Lee with big brown eyes. "I want a hot dog...with cheese on it."

"Are you Kathy?" Lee asked.

The young woman shook her pony tail. "Shoot, no. I'm Debbie. Kathy paid me ten dollars to bring the brat here and deliver her to her jerk of an ex-husband, 'cept I don't see him yet." Debbie looked Lee over. "You with him? Kathy said he'd pick up some broad in a hurry."

Lee frowned. "He went to get Tanya's car seat. He should be back any minute."

The girl shoved Tanya toward Lee, and then handed over a tote bag. "You take her. I haven't got all day to stand around this dump. I'm supposed to meet a friend and go to the lake."

"Tanya, would you like to stay with me until your daddy comes?" Lee waited, hoping there wouldn't be another flood of tears.

"Are you a stranger?"

Lee smiled. The moppet had been taught well. "Not exactly. I'm a friend of your daddy's."

"Oh." She looked a little dubious, but let Lee take her hand, still smeared with chocolate.

"Will you come with me to wash your hands?"

Tanya looked at the babysitter. "You come too."

Debbie shook her head. "See you later, baby. I'm out of here."

Tanya's eyes filled. "She called me a baby. I'm not a baby."

"No, dear, you're not." Lee led her over to the clerk. "If a man named Alex Brandon asks, tell him I've taken his daughter to the ladies room." She looked the man in the eye. "Make sure he shows you some ID before you tell him anything."

The clerk looked up from making change at the register and rubbed his beard. "Smart thinking, ma'am. Can't be too careful these days."

As Lee headed toward the ladies room, she glanced around some people to the station window. Bubba stood there, peering in. Grabbing the small girl's hand, Lee hurried her into the restroom, hoping Bubba hadn't seen them. Where were the damn police?

After sponging chocolate off Tanya's playsuit, Lee lifted her up to wash her hands, then set her down. As Lee reached for a towel for her own hands, she heard little footsteps and turned. Oh, no, Tanya was opening the door.

Dropping the towel on the counter, Lee ran to catch her and caught a glimpse of Bubba's back. Damn, she'd hoped he'd given up and left.

Lee yanked Tanya back inside and pushed the door shut. She swooped the little girl up and ran back as far as she could get from the door. As Tanya struggled to be free, Lee whispered in her ear. "We can't open the door. There's a bad man out there, and I don't want him to see us." She hoped that wouldn't make Tanya afraid to use public restrooms, but she couldn't let her open the door.

The little girl's eyes opened wide. "Will he hurt us?"

"Shhhh. Not if he doesn't see us. We must be very quiet until he goes away."

Lee set her down, but kept hold of her hand. Lee's heart pounded. She looked at her watch. Where the hell was Alex? She didn't dare phone him with Bubba standing right outside.

Lee knelt beside her and raised Tanya's little hand to her mouth. "Keep your hand there so no words can come out. I'm going to peek out the door and see if the bad man is still there, but you must stay against the wall and be very quiet."

Tanya stood plastered against the wall. Her eyes big as quarters, she quivered.

Lee hurried to the door and cracked it open. Not more than ten feet away Bubba leaned against the wall. His head swiveled from side to side. He was looking for her. The harsh smell of his cigarette made her nose wrinkle. Why hadn't the police come yet?

Alex marched into the station and looked around. Not knowing what Bubba would do, she dared not call out to warn Alex.

She left the door open a crack. Alex strode to the ticket counter. "Have you seen a little girl about five years old arrive with a woman?"

"Do you have some ID?" the clerk asked. Alex showed him his driver's license. The man pointed toward the restroom.

Lee held her breath. What if Alex came to the door and called her name?

She let the door close softly. She had to think.

Alex's voice sounded loud and clear. "Thought the cops would have found you by now."

"It's a free country, an' this here's a public place, you know," Bubba said. Then he gasped. "You can't pull a gun on me in here," he whined. "Someone will call the cops an' you'll be the one they haul in."

Alex's voice was low, but determined. "If I hold it to your back, no one will see it, but it will poke against your kidneys just the same. And if you don't move fast enough to suit me, I just might shoot you once we get outside if the cops aren't here by then."

"You ain't got the guts."

"Try me. You'll wish you hadn't."

Sounds of scuffling came through the crack in the door. Tanya tugged on Lee's skirt. "Is he going to hurt my daddy?"

"Hush," Lee whispered. "I told you to stay against that wall."

"But I want to see," she wailed.

Lee picked her up and carried her back toward the wall. "Your daddy is big and strong. He won't let the bad guy hurt him. I called the police. They should be here soon."

As Tanya snuggled against her shoulder, now smelling of soap and faintly of chocolate, Lee hoped she was right. If Alex got hurt, heaven knew what she'd do with Tanya. She checked her watch and listened. It sounded as if they were still struggling, but other noises made it hard to tell. Seconds dragged.

She dared not open the restroom door. Bubba might pull her out and leave Tanya here all alone. Poor kid would be scared to death.

Finally, Lee couldn't bear it any longer. She opened the door a crack. She couldn't see either of them. People milled about and talked in loud voices. She opened the door wider. The place smelled of dust and unwashed bodies.

A siren shrilled, then ceased. Thank goodness the cops were coming.

Bubba's voice rang out. "Damn broad musta called the fuzz. They cain't pin nothing on me, you know."

Loud footsteps sounded in the sudden silence. People made way for a uniformed officer.

"Arrest this guy," insisted Alex. "He's the one who broke into my girlfriend's apartment last night and pulled a gun on her. However, he got away when the police chased him."

Angry tones from Bubba and Alex were interspersed with calmly spoken questions from the policeman. Lee could only catch a few words here and there.

Onlookers parted like the red sea before Moses as a

policeman hustled Bubba out the door. Alex followed, holding onto Bubba's other arm, no doubt to be sure he didn't bolt.

Tanya tugged on her arm. "Where's my daddy going? Will he come back?"

Lee put her arm around the child's narrow shoulders. "I'm sure he will, Honey." Holding tight to her hand, Lee followed the onlookers to the bus station's front window. Outside, Alex stood watching as the cop spread-eagled Bubba, frisked him, then barked, "Get in." He turned to Alex and said something Lee couldn't make out. Alex shook his head and pointed toward the bus station. The cop shrugged and slid behind the wheel.

Minutes later as the police car drove off, Lee drew in a deep breath. It was over — for now at least. Alex strode though the doorway, a worried look on his face.

She waved to Alex. "Over here. I've got Tanya."

The little girl raced to Alex, who picked her up and hugged her.

"Did Kathy leave already?"

Lee shook her head. "She didn't come. She sent Tanya with a teenage babysitter."

He frowned. "You mean the sitter just handed her over to a perfect stranger?"

"The girl was only too happy to let me take her. Said she was planning to meet a boyfriend."

Alex sighed. "Thank goodness you were here." He rubbed the back of his neck. "When I saw Bubba, but didn't see you or Tanya or Kathy, I didn't know what to think. Did he threaten you?"

"Not really. He was trying to bribe me to go back to Sheldon. When I told him I was calling the police, he walked away. I thought he was going to leave, but he didn't."

"I could kick myself for leaving you alone. I thought you'd be safe in a public place."

"I'm hungry," said Tanya.

He kissed her cheek. "We'll get you something to eat very soon." He turned to Lee. "Let's go out the back door. I parked the car there."

Still carrying Tanya, he pushed open a door beside the ticket counter, stepped through and held it open for Lee.

She followed him down some steps and out a back door into an alley. Alex handed Tanya to her. "I put the car seat in the back. See if you can buckle her in."

After sliding the little girl into the car seat, Lee tried to fasten the belt. Tanya squirmed and giggled. Finally Lee fastened it and climbed into the front seat.

Alex put the top up. "Would you fasten it down on your side?"

Lee fastened it on her side. "It's a shame to put it up on such a nice day".

Alex barked, "Don't you remember what happened last night? It could rain."

Lee frowned. "Of course. I was just talking."

He pulled onto the highway and gunned the motor. The car shot forward, squeezing the seat belt against her stomach, but Lee didn't complain. For all she knew the cops might let Bubba go for lack of evidence. The faster they got away from here, the safer she'd feel. She didn't breathe easier until the car zoomed past the city limits sign. She turned to Alex. "I'm surprised they didn't insist you go to the station."

"They wanted me to, but I was worried about you and Tanya. I gave them my cell phone number. If they have any questions, they can call me."

"I'm hungry," said Tanya.

Alex pointed to the glove compartment. "Should be some Lifesavers in there."

Lee opened the compartment and fished around, looking for the candy.

A panel truck zoomed around them. Alex slowed to let it pass.

Tanya squealed. "Look Daddy, someone drawed pretty flowers on it."

Alex nodded. "Must be a florist delivery truck."

Seated close to the window, Tanya squirmed to look behind. "Daddy, why black car not have flowers too?"

Lee glanced back. A black Camaro tailed them. Surely, Bubba hadn't been released so soon.

Chapter 8

"Oh, no." Lee groaned. "Not again."

Alex jammed his foot on the accelerator. The car shot forward. He raced up a hill and down the other side. Why did he always seem to be protecting a woman? Only this time his daughter's life was at stake too. He took a deep breath. Couldn't afford to come up short this time.

Tanya bounced in her booster seat. "Oh, goody. We gonna have a roller coaster ride, aren't we Daddy?"

His fingers gripped the wheel so tightly his knuckles turned white. He didn't have the heart to tell her this might be more dangerous than fun.

He heard Lee whisper to Tanya. "Stop talking so Daddy can concentrate."

Alex flew down the highway toward Middletown. The black car kept a steady course behind like a torpedo locked on its target. In the sun's glare he could barely make out the outline of the driver's big body hunched over the wheel. Was it Bubba?

Lee asked. "Can you park in front of the police station in the next town? Maybe he'll leave us alone."

He frowned. "Not smart. He could stay out of sight until we leave, then follow us."

"Oh, I didn't think of that." Her voice sounded subdued as if he'd criticized her. He guessed he had, but one couldn't be too careful.

She turned to look behind. "What if you can't shake him?"

He frowned. He would if that was the last thing he did. The thought chilled him.

The road widened to four lanes. The black car gained on them, pulled alongside.

Alex held his breath. What if the guy had a gun?

The driver, pudgy, but not Bubba, thank the lord, leaned out the window and pointed toward their left rear bumper, then pulled on ahead.

Alex let out the breath he'd been holding and released his tight grip on the wheel. Now he could feel the Jaguar pulling toward the left. Tire must be going flat.

Twenty-five minutes later, after changing the tire, Alex hunched forward over the wheel and pushed down on the accelerator. Good thing Carl's place wasn't much farther. Probably need a good massage by this afternoon.

❦

Lee glanced at Alex. He looked tired, but he seemed to be more relaxed. She hoped the danger was over for the time being.

Trying to distract Tanya so Alex could concentrate on driving, Lee asked her, "Do you know the letters of the alphabet?"

Her answer was to sing the ABC song.

Alex grinned. "Smart for almost five, isn't she?"

Lee nodded. "Okay, Tanya, let's look for letters on the signs we pass. You tell me when you see an 'A,' then look for a 'B.' Let's see who can find all the letters of the alphabet first."

By the time they found a 'P,' Alex said, "We're almost there." He turned off the highway and drove along a road lined with summer homes.

"This guy, Carl, is he a good friend of yours?"

Alex nodded. "I knew him in high school. His dad was an alcoholic, and his mother divorced him."

"Sounds like his childhood wasn't much fun."

"His idea of fun sometimes got outrageous. Once he talked me into driving way out to the country on Halloween and tipping over someone's outhouse. We had to run from a farmer with a shotgun. That was scary."

Alex slowed the car and turned onto a dirt road grooved like a washboard. The car's vibrations jarred her as the Jaguar bumped along the road. He grimaced. "This isn't good for my car's undersides."

"So, what happened to Carl when he grew up?"

"After his dad left, he ran around with a rough crowd. Luckily, he seems to have matured since then, at least I hope so."

Lee caught a pensive look on his face. Was there more to their relationship than Alex was telling her?

Alex stopped at a large cream colored cottage. A sign swaying in the breeze proclaimed, 'Precisely So.'

Lee turned to Alex. "What a strange name."

Alex laughed. "Fits Carl to a 'T.' He keeps everything in its place. Has a maid come twice a week to keep it that way."

Lee raised an eyebrow. "What about his wife?"

"He's not married. Claimed he couldn't find anyone just right. Guess he'd rather play the field." A frown flashed across his face so quickly Lee wondered if she'd imagined it.

As she stepped out of the car, the aroma of grilling burgers wafted over her, making her mouth water. On a table plastic knives and forks lay in a perfectly straight line. Ketchup, mustard, and mayonnaise were lined up in a row. She remembered Alex's neat trailer. He, too, was picky about everything being in the right place. She'd have to watch that working in his office.

Carl, stocky and a bit shorter than Alex, grasped their hands in a hearty shake, then clapped Alex on the back. "Buddy, it's great to see you again." He smoothed back windblown red hair. "Heard you retired from the CIA. What's the matter, too much excitement?" He laughed. "Bet you're glad to be back in the good old U.S.A. What are you doing now, writing a book?"

"You kidding? English was my worst subject. I'm setting up a travel agency. This is Lee Marshall. She's my new secretary."

Lee accepted his handshake. His gaze dwelt too long on her breasts, but she pretended not to notice.

Alex pushed his daughter forward. "Tanya, can you shake hands with Mr. Carson?"

The little girl lifted her left hand. Carl leaned down to grab it. "You're a pretty little girl. How old are you?"

She giggled and held up five fingers.

Carl patted her shoulder and turned to Alex. "Cute kid. You'll have to bring her out here again."

Carl introduced them to five other couples and two single men, most of them already in swim suits, then took them inside.

Alex followed Lee into the house. "Wow, you've sure changed this place. It looks great."

"Got the couch and loveseat delivered two weeks ago. Made by Broyhill. Got a great deal."

Golden cords held back heavy draperies framing a view of the rippling lake. Lee ran her hand over the matching gold striped couch. Something about the brand of furniture here nagged at her memory. Hadn't that truckload of furniture Sheldon couldn't find an invoice for been made by Broyhill?

"Looks great," said Alex. "You get a raise?"

Carl grinned. "No, but I got a great deal on the furniture."

Lee turned to face Carl. "Bet you don't let people in wet swim suits in here."

"My deck's enclosed. People in damp suits can sit out there." He led them through the French doors. A gentle breeze sifted through the slats of the glass jalousies.

After showing them around, Carl led them back outside.

Lee whispered to Alex, "All that must have cost a bundle."

"Looks like he's reached his goal. Before I married Kathy, I told him about my CIA job. Later he couldn't wait to tell me he had landed a government position. He claimed he'd move up faster in the ranks than I would."

"But wasn't the CIA where you wanted to be?"

Alex nodded. "Traveling in different countries and gathering information—that was more exciting than shuffling papers on a desk. Eventually the pay increased so Kathy and I could swing a nice home in Austin, but I had to talk her out of a mansion in the exclusive Tarrytown development."

Later, as Lee savored a juicy hamburger, a tall, lean man rose from the lake and headed their way. He looked vaguely familiar. When he combed his damp blond hair back with long thin fingers and put on thick glasses, she recognized Joe. What was her contact with the U.S. Marshal's office doing here?

She'd called to tell him where she was going. Did he sense a threat from anyone here? She glanced at the people around her. Should she be more watchful?

Carl introduced him as Johann Berg. When he met her gaze, he shook his head slightly, but all he said was, "Nice to meet you." He immediately moved away and joined two men deep in discussion.

After they ate, Carl said she could change in his bedroom in the cottage. Inside Lee shut the door, then pulled on the bottom of her suit. She stepped into the adjoining bathroom, leaving its door open and struggled to fasten the back of her bikini top.

"Can I help you with that?"

Carl's husky voice startled her. She must not have heard the bedroom door open.

He grinned. "I could tie those straps behind your neck for you."

"No thanks." She grabbed her dangling straps and tied them.

Standing in the now open doorway, he ogled her. He

hooked the thumb of one meaty hand into the waistband of his slim fitting shorts as if to call attention to his attributes.

Remembering he was her host and Alex's friend, she glared at him, but swallowed the retort that came to mind. She slid into her flip-flops and pushed past him.

When Lee stepped outside, Alex, already changed into trunks, lifted one of Tanya's pink bathing suit straps to smooth sun burn cream over her shoulders. He fingered a reddish blond curl. "Do you have a life preserver to fit her?" he asked Carl.

Carl nodded and went inside. He returned with one just her size. He knelt down and smiled at Tanya. "Would you let me buckle you up?"

She nodded, and he fastened the straps. "You're a real cutie, do you know that?" He asked. She giggled but said nothing.

Alex took Tanya's hand and led her down to the water. She pulled back, but after a little coaxing, she was splashing water on her dad and laughing.

A petite brunette with a little boy in tow waded toward them. Alex grinned. "Jean Walker, great to see you." He turned to Lee. "She was my sister's best friend."

Jean put her hands on her son's shoulder. "This is Bobby. That your daughter? She looked hesitantly at Lee.

Alex grasped his daughter's hand. "Her name's Tanya." He nodded toward Lee. "This is Lee, my new secretary. Kathy and I are divorced."

"Sorry to hear that." Jean pointed to a tall guy playing horseshoes. "That's my husband, Robert. If you want to swim, we'll be glad to watch her." She turned to Tanya. "Would you like to come help us build a castle in the wet sand?"

When Tanya nodded, Alex said, "Thanks. We won't be out too long."

He held out his hand. "Come on. The water's great."

He led her out to deeper water, and they paddled around for a while. Alex walked out a little farther, then headed back toward her. Lee was watching a heron on the far shore when someone grabbed her legs, stuck a head between them, and stood to toss her backwards into the water.

She came up sputtering. "I'll get you, Alex," she shouted, then looked into Carl's grinning face.

"Go ahead. I dare you." He stood there waiting.

She shook her head. "I thought you were Alex. I'm getting cold. Think I'll go in now."

"Chicken," Carl taunted, but she turned and walked toward shore.

Alex walked beside her. "Quitting already?"

She said, "I want to sit in the sun and warm up."

He shoved back his dark hair, splattering droplets on his muscular tanned shoulders. "I'll join you."

After stepping onto Carl's manicured lawn, she dried herself with a towel, then spread it on the grass and sat. She beckoned Alex closer.

He plopped down beside her.

She whispered. "Your friend, Carl, keeps hitting on me. Would you mind if we didn't stay much longer?"

"I'll tell him I'm your boyfriend. Then he'll lay off." He grinned. "Now that's a role I can get my teeth into." Seconds later his arm circled her waist, and he pulled her closer. "You'd better act the part. How about an adoring look?"

She smiled, then gazed into his blue eyes, flecked with amber highlights.

His look said, 'I can't wait to get you alone.'

She swallowed. What would he act like if this were real? His warm caressing fingers at her waist made her wonder how his hand would feel on her breast. Now where had that thought come from? She met his gaze. Heat rose from her chest to her neck.

With gentle fingers he lifted her chin. His face inched closer. His mesmerizing gaze could melt a stone. She couldn't take her eyes from his face. Hell, he could melt a whole pile of stones.

He took hold of her hand and pulled her closer. He was going to kiss her in front of everyone.

Alex's lips, full and appealing, hovered a breath away. Heart pounding, she squirmed on the towel. What had she got herself into? "I—I didn't mean we had to act crazy in love," she whispered.

His smile held her spellbound. "Shhh. You'll spoil the effect." His lips met hers—soft, sensuous and so much more. She closed her eyes as his warm mouth welcomed hers. She sank into it. The intensity of his kiss seared her all the way down. If he could do a pretend kiss like this, what would it be like if he really meant it?

He pulled her closer until she felt his chest pressing against her breasts. His lips clung, roving over hers as if he'd been away for ages and wanted to re-explore every nuance of her lips. Just when she couldn't hold her breath any longer, he released her.

She opened her eyes. Something in his gaze held her spellbound. "Did you need to...uh, go overboard in front of everyone?" she whispered.

"My pleasure," he said. Grinning, he smoothed a lock of hair from her forehead and pressed a soft kiss on her temple. Merriment danced in his eyes. He whispered, "Carl considers himself a Romeo." He slid his arm around her waist, pulled her close and winked. "But I think he'll leave you alone now."

She gulped. "So will everyone else."

His gaze met hers. "So is there someone special?"

"No, but with kisses like that, you could almost make me forget some other guy," she whispered.

He grinned. "Only almost."

She smiled. "Well, maybe for a month or two."

His smile grew broader. "Keep that up, and I'll swell too big for my britches."

Lee glanced around. No one seemed to be paying any

attention now — or perhaps they were looking the other way on purpose.

Tanya skipped over and tugged at Alex's hand. "I saw you kissing her. Are you going to marry her?"

Uh, oh. Lee hadn't thought about Tanya. His tantalizing kiss so absorbed her she hadn't thought about anything or anyone else.

Alex's Adam's apple moved convulsively, but he spoke in even tones. "No Tanya. I'm not going to marry anyone right now."

"Why do you always yell at Mommy and make her mad?"

Alex brushed sand from the towel and smoothed it out. "Honey, sometimes grownups don't agree about things. Mommy and Daddy have to live in different places so we won't say mean things to each other."

"Oh." Her little face puckered up in bewilderment.

Alex pulled her into his lap. "But don't you worry. I'll always love you."

Tanya snuggled in his lap. "I'm hungry."

Alex set her down, then stood, and took her hand. "Let's see what we can find. There may be some brownies left."

Lee watched them head for the picnic table. He took short steps with his powerful legs so Tanya could keep up. His daughter could worm her way into your heart — and make you want a child of your own — well, almost. Remembering how her mother had died in childbirth, leaving her and Libby motherless, Lee blinked back tears. She'd never go down that path.

Libby might as well have been her child instead of her sister. Maybe when Sheldon and his henchmen were locked up in prison, she could spend some time with her only sibling and introduce her to Alex.

If her sister ever saw him gazing at her with those bedroom eyes, she'd beg Lee to tell her all about him. Lee hugged her knees, her gaze straying to his marvelous sexy mouth.

He swung his daughter up in the air as if she were a rag doll.

Tanya giggled. "Do it again, Daddy." Up she went again, chortling with delight. His daughter trusted him completely, never fearing that he would let her fall or get hurt.

Somehow Lee knew Alex would do all he could to keep Lee safe, too.

Carl walked up, a big grin on his face. "You folks want to go for a boat ride? I have a canoe and a speedboat."

Still holding the brownie, Tanya jumped up and down. "I want to ride in the canoe, Daddy. Can I?" She took a bite and looked up at her father.

Carl shook his head. "This is a pretty big lake for a little girl to go out on. Maybe when you get a little bigger, you can."

Tanya started to pout. Alex ruffled her hair. "Carl's right. Let's see if Jean will keep an eye on you while we go. He led her over to Jean.

"Be glad to watch her," Jean said and took Tanya's hand.

Carl walked up to Alex and Lee, holding a life preserver. "Sorry, I only have one dry life preserver left. I offer that to the lady."

He held out the orange vest to Lee, and then turned to Tanya. "Would you and Bobby like to see my new puppies?"

"You've got puppies?" Tanya squealed. "Where are they?"

Carl took her hand and led her over to a cardboard box wedged in a nook under the deck extending from the cottage. She knelt beside little Bobby and patted the animals under the watchful eyes of his mother, Jean.

Lee buckled the life vest on. The sun peeked from behind a large cloud, making the lake sparkle. A cool breeze sprang up, stirring the damp ruffles on her suit.

After Alex and Carl carried the canoe down to the dock and set it into the water, Carl held out his hand to help Lee into the boat. She didn't want to take his hand, but it would look ungracious to refuse. He grasped her hand and her arm, steadying her as she stepped down. Then, before he let go, his thumb rubbed suggestively over her palm. She yanked her hand away and lowered herself into the seat. Grabbing the gunwale, she glanced up to meet Carl's knowing grin.

Would she and Alex have to put on more shows of affection? She glanced at Alex, but he was busy pulling a paddle out from under the middle seat.

Carl stood on the dock, watching her. She wished Alex would tell him to lay off.

"Carl, can you come here for a moment? Joe yelled. Carl headed toward the U.S. marshal who'd set her up with a new identity as Alex pushed the canoe from the dock.

Brisk paddling soon brought them to the center of the lake. Alex set his paddle down and faced Lee. "Look, there's a blue heron standing on the shore over there."

Lee felt cold water oozing up between her bare toes. She glanced down at the slatted floor boards. The water almost reached the top of the slats. She gasped. "Alex, the canoe's leaking."

He bent his head. "I didn't see any water in the bottom when we started. We need to head back. Paddle hard as you can. We should be able to make it." He dipped his paddle in the water and pulled with a powerful stroke. The craft shot forward.

She gripped her paddle. Dip and pull, dip and pull, became a rhythm. Muscles she hadn't noticed began to ache. She ignored them. The boat seemed to be filling awfully fast. She pulled harder. They didn't seem to be that much closer to shore. The wind blew, rippling the surface of the water.

Now water covered Lee's toes, chilling them. She put more effort into each pull, but the canoe didn't seem to go any faster, and the wind wasn't helping.

She took a deep breath and held tight to the paddle. Dipping and pulling stretched her muscles until they ached, but that didn't matter as long as they reached shore.

She put all her strength into each pull. Water sloshed around her ankles. "Will we have to swim back?"

"I hope not. I can't swim very well, and it looks like a storm is blowing in."

Lee gritted her teeth and dipped her paddle. Thunder rumbled. Big fat raindrops pelted her skin and dribbled down her back. The wind chilled her through and through. Lightning split the sky, followed by a loud crack of thunder.

Lee's teeth chattered.

The wind picked up. Little wavelets turned into bigger ones. Their craft wobbled alarmingly. She glanced toward shore. "Why doesn't someone see we're in trouble?"

The answer was obvious. Carl's guests were scurrying around, grabbing stuff and running toward the cottage.

Carl and Joe stood shouting at each other. Joe gestured toward them, and then ran down to Carl's speedboat. Carl followed.

The roar of the motor rose above that of the wind. The boat headed toward them, but made slow progress in the strong wind.

Lee's muscles cried out for relief, but she kept working the paddle.

The speedboat came alongside, rocking with the waves. Joe grabbed the gunwale of the canoe and pulled the two crafts together.

Alex grasped the side of the speedboat, but a wave lifted the canoe, pulling the larger boat from his grasp. The other boat veered away, widening the distance between them.

As it came close again, Lee grabbed the speedboat's gunwale with both hands. She fought against the tug of the wind and waves, but couldn't pull the canoe alongside.

"I need a rope," said Joe.

Carl reached down, grabbed a rope, and tossed the end to Joe, who handed the end to Lee. "Throw it to Alex and hang on."

She did and watched Alex tie the rope to the oarlock. When Alex finished, Joe tied the other end to a metal ring on the speedboat. Alex and Joe finally managed to get the two crafts lined up alongside each other.

As they clambered over the side into the bigger boat, Alex shouted. "Carl, why the hell did you let us take this sieve out?"

Carl gunned the motor. "Can't hear you. What did you say?"

Alex scowled. "Never mind."

Holding the leaking canoe against the side, they finally reached shore. Alex stepped up on the dock, and then held out his hand for Lee. "Sorry this had to happen. Can you take Tanya and get her dressed? I need to talk to Carl."

Lee picked the little girl up and hurried toward the house.

Behind her the three men's angry shouts peppered the air.

"We could have drowned," shouted Alex.

Joe said, "Letting them go without checking the boat was irresponsible."

"Criminal," added Alex.

Lee shut the door on their arguments. She grabbed Tanya's clothes and hurried her into a bedroom. Even after her playsuit was on, the little girl shivered, and her teeth chattered. Shivering herself, Lee shooed Tanya into the living room, grabbed a folded afghan from an end table and wrapped it about Tanya.

Not wanting to risk another encounter with Carl, she hurried into the bedroom, shut the door and dressed as fast as she could.

The minute she emerged from the bedroom, Alex eased Tanya off his lap. "It's time we left." He rose and grabbed Lee's hand.

After thanking Carl for inviting him, he waved good-bye to the others, and rushed Lee and Tanya out to the car.

When they were all seated, Lee realized she'd forgotten

something. "I need to get my purse." She hurried back inside and bumped into Carl.

He grabbed her shoulders and smiled broadly. "Come to thank me for rescuing you? I'll take a hug and a kiss."

She swallowed and squirmed out of his hold. "No, but thanks for coming for us." Her eyes raked the room, spotted her purse on the couch. She grabbed it and pushed past Carl. "Bye."

He caught her wrist. "Come again. I wouldn't count on Alex if I were you. He may have second thoughts about leaving his ex-wife. I think he's even slept with her occasionally since then, but the welcome mat here is always out for you, even without Alex."

She tugged free. "In your dreams."

Clutching her purse, she scrambled into the car.

"What was that about?" Alex asked.

She turned her face away. "Nothing." She struggled to fasten Tanya's seat belt. As it clicked, she glanced out the window to see Carl grinning. Looking back she saw Tanya was waving to him.

Chapter 9

Lee swallowed. She wouldn't let Alex bring her here again, not with that lecher, but she wasn't sorry Alex had posed as her boyfriend. That kiss — wow — it had left her so weak a gentle breeze could have knocked her down.

She glanced at his mouth, pursed as he concentrated on driving. His lips, warm and enticing, had made her forget all the people watching. Of course that was probably his intent, but it would have been nice to be kissed like that with just the two of them alone — and know he'd meant it for real.

He looked at her and grinned. His smile warmed her heart like a spring day. What could have gone wrong between Alex and his wife? She shouldn't trust the reactions of a man who'd just gone through a divorce, but he sure was tempting.

Tanya tugged against the seat belt of her car seat. "I want to sit in your lap."

"No, dear. If you stay buckled up, that will keep you safe from getting hurt if we have an accident." How it would feel to have a child of her own snuggled in her lap? As long as Sheldon and his goons were alive, she dare not bring a child into the world and risk its life.

Just having a baby was dangerous enough. She couldn't forget Daddy's anguished voice as he tried to explain why her mother couldn't come back from the hospital. He'd tried to tell her she should love the baby sister who'd taken her mother's life.

Tears streaming down her face, she'd told Daddy to take the baby back, that she didn't want it. For weeks she'd cried herself to sleep, wishing for her mother's sweet kiss instead of her father's rough whiskers that brushed her cheeks when he kissed her good night.

Once, when she asked him to sing her to sleep, he'd looked at her strangely for a moment. He sang some funny song. She'd giggled but she'd still missed her mother's sweet lullabies.

Why had her mother been so foolish as to allow a pregnancy to continue despite the doctor's warnings against it? It took time, but after a while she'd come to love her sister, Libby. Now Lee feared she'd inherited the same condition her mother had, one that would make pregnancy dangerous for her, too.

Alex glanced at her. "You're awfully quiet."

"I was thinking about my sister. Her birthday's coming soon. I don't dare visit her. I can't bake cupcakes, but maybe I can send some cookies."

"Won't they get broken if you mail them?"

"Libby won't care. She's used to crumbly cookies. I never was much of a cook, but that was the best I could do when she was growing up. In our school all the kids brought treats on their birthdays. I didn't want her to spend her birthdays like I did so I baked cookies for her birthdays."

Remembering brought a lump to her throat. "All my classmates had home baked cupcakes to share and a mother to smile proudly and help pass them out. The year after my mother died, I asked my father to bake cupcakes for my birthday. He gave me packs of chewing gum to take to school. The kids teased me. It was embarrassing. My birthday is five days after Libby's but I never mentioned when my birthday was after that."

"So when is Libby's birthday?"

"Tomorrow."

"How are you going to get cookies to her by tomorrow if you can't go near her?"

"Guess I'll have to send her a cookie gram instead."

"So did you ever bake cupcakes for your sister's birthday?"

"Once. When she was in kindergarten. They were a disaster. They were burned on the bottom. I had to cut the bottoms off, turn them upside down and slather them with frosting. Thank goodness kindergarteners aren't particular. After that I made cookies. Slice and bake I can manage."

"And I bet they tasted just fine."

"The kids seemed to like them. I wish I could go see her." She crossed her fingers. "I only hope Sheldon doesn't send his goons after her."

Alex glanced in the back. "Tanya's asleep. Probably too tired to stay up for fireworks. She's really taken to you."

"She's a sweet kid. Are you taking her back to your place?"

He nodded. "I don't have to take her back until tomorrow."

"She can sleep in your bed with me if she likes." That would solve one problem. He wouldn't cozy up to her with his daughter there. That was what she wanted, wasn't it?

Alex smiled. "I'm sure she'd like that, but she'll be fine on the hide-a-bed with me."

When they reached the mobile home, Tanya was still sleeping. Lee picked her up and carried her to the steps. Alex unlocked the door and took the sleeping child from her.

Inside, Tanya stretched and yawned. "I'm hungry."

Alex smoothed back her reddish-blonde curls. "How about a hot dog?" Soon he had boiled several wieners and warmed buns in the microwave while Lee set the table.

After supper, she tried to coax the little girl into taking a shower by herself, but Tanya insisted on having Lee bathe her in the tub. All her splashing soon dampened Lee's clothes, making her blouse cling revealingly.

As Lee was drying her, Tanya looked up. "How come you

don't have big boobies like Mommy? Don't you eat your vegetables?"

Lee didn't say anything, but she heard Alex's muffled chuckle. Turning to see him standing in the bathroom doorway, she tried to pull her damp shirt away from her breasts and felt heat rise to her face. He probably preferred women who were well stacked. After all, he'd only kissed her thoroughly to make Carl leave her alone. She didn't need to get any serious thoughts about him.

She'd work as his secretary until fall when Joe said he'd transfer her to another town. Then she wouldn't see Alex or Tanya any more. She'd have a whole new group of people to make friends with. That was something to look forward to, wasn't it?

She glanced up at him as she dried Tanya's toes. His smile flowed over her like warm sunshine. Somehow, leaving didn't seem near as appealing as it had before—before his kisses turned her inside out.

They tucked Tanya between the sheets on the hide-a-bed. Alex kissed his daughter goodnight. Then Tanya held out her arms to Lee. Bending down, Lee pressed a kiss on her soft cheek which smelled of soap.

Tanya smiled and snuggled under the covers. "Daddy, kiss her goodnight too, like you used to do with Mommy. He doesn't stay at home now, so he has to kiss you instead."

Lee's cheeks grew warm. She looked at Alex and waited for him to explain.

He grinned. "Not a bad idea. I need the practice."

Yeah, right—like birds need to practice flying.

He slid an arm around her waist and pulled her close. "Goodnight, Lee." He kissed her with finesse and a touch of hunger. Her pulse quickened, but he released her immediately.

She opened her eyes to meet his intent gaze. His blue eyes sparkled. Had he wanted to kiss her for herself or just because Tanya expected it?

Tanya lay beneath the sheets, her brown eyes drifting closed. Alex squeezed Lee's hand. "That's should be enough for a goodnight kiss, for now at least," he whispered.

She swallowed. It was enough and yet not enough.

He still held her hand. His eyes met hers. Time for her to pull away. After all, he'd only kissed her at his daughter's insistence. He tugged Lee toward the door. "She's out like a light. Let's go look at stars. It's almost meteor season. Maybe we'll see a few tonight."

She glanced at the sleeping child. "Shouldn't we leave the door ajar? She might wake up and be frightened."

"Of course." He let go of her hand, opened the door, and propped a chair against it. "Come on." He led her down the steps.

The sidewalk was just wide enough for them to walk side by side. His hip and thigh brushing against hers sent a warm tingle spiraling through her. His smile said he enjoyed her company. It was surprising how good that made her feel.

A warm breeze ruffled his hair. Glancing up at him, she had a sudden urge to run her fingers through it. Wouldn't do to encourage him. Caught by his gaze, she wondered how he felt about being trapped into playing her boyfriend.

He grasped her forearms and turned her to face him. "This one's for you," he whispered. His sexy mouth came closer. He kissed her, slow and gentle at first. Then he deepened the kiss, sending shivers of delight down her spine.

His hands cradled her face as his lips pressed against hers, asking for a response. Now her mouth was the one that roved, tasting his lips. She hugged him tightly. Her fingers crept into his hair, and she gave in to the urge to tousle his dark waves. His hair was thick and springy, but surprisingly soft.

His blue eyes twinkled, and his smile melted her heart. "My mother used to do that. But you don't make me feel at all like a child." He grinned.

His hand slid up from her waist. His thumb brushed the

underside of her breast. Her nipples firmed into tight buds and tingled with wanting. Helpless to move, she moistened her lips with her tongue. Arching toward him, she swallowed. What was she letting herself in for? Getting mixed up with a newly divorced man was crazy.

His mouth met hers again. He teased her lips with his tongue, then slid it between them. After a quick exploration, his tongue began thrusting. A hardness pressed against her body, hinting at his desire to thrust elsewhere. When at last his lips left hers, he inhaled deeply.

She too, took a deep breath, feeling as if she were coming up for air from the depths of a deep lake.

Grasping her shoulders, he caressed them with his thumbs. His eyes said, "I want to make love to you," but as if sensing she wasn't ready to go that far, he didn't say anything.

She wanted him with an intensity that surprised her. But she couldn't and wouldn't get in so deep. She'd let him protect her while she was here, but soon she'd be gone to a place where she didn't have to keep looking over her shoulder. He might be divorced, but he still could be tied to his family.

His hand tugged at hers, then placed it over his heart. "Come inside."

When she said nothing, he edged her toward the door of the mobile home. "Let's go where we can be close."

Uh, oh, there it was, the invitation. A soft breeze teased her hair as if to say, go on. She couldn't. She shook her head. "We can't. Tanya will hear."

"She's all tuckered out. She won't wake till morning."

She tried not to think how it would feel to lie beside him, skin to skin, with his fingers continuing their intoxicating exploration of her body. "You said you signed the papers. If you haven't gotten a copy of the divorce decree, we can't be sure you're not still married. It doesn't seem right for us to— to—."

"Ha. You think my wife pays any attention to that? For all I know she's been shacking up with someone all along. His bitter laugh tugged at her heartstrings.

"But that doesn't make it okay for us."

He sighed. "My marriage is over. She called me to gloat after I sent the signed decree to her lawyer. Your hesitation won't keep you warm the way I can." His hands roved over her breasts, caressing and squeezing until she could hardly think straight.

She swallowed. "It isn't as if—as if I don't find you rather appealing." She dropped her gaze. She hadn't meant to admit that.

He looked hurt. "Only rather appealing?"

Heat rose to her face. "All right, very appealing."

He grinned. "That's better. I was afraid I was the only one who—"

She watched his expressive lips, remembering his kiss. "How could you not know—how you make me—"

His gaze met hers. "Make you what?"

"You know."

He grinned. "Make you want me?" he whispered.

Ashamed to admit it, she looked away.

Alex tipped her chin up and looked her in the eyes. "If I could give you a copy of the decree to look at, would you say 'yes'?"

She shrugged. "I'm not sure. I hardly know you. And besides, Joe, my U.S. marshal contact, will probably be moving me far from here in a day or two."

"I know it's soon, but I hoped—I hoped you weren't one of those women who give away kisses that don't mean anything."

"I'm not. But you—you've taken me by storm. When I make love with someone, I want it to be someone I'm more than friends with, someone I feel very close to."

He grinned broadly. "That's what I like about you. You're honest." He pulled at her hand. Come inside."

She stepped away. "If you're still suggesting—we can't. Not with Tanya here."

Alex sighed and dropped her hand. "I've only got Tanya today because Kathy told me she had a hot date. I'll take her back in the morning." He wasn't ready to give her back, but he'd promised.

Kathy had sounded excited when she asked him to watch Tanya. He tried to ignore the resentment lurking inside. The guy must be loaded. Money impressed Kathy. She returned gifts he bought her, claiming she needed a different size, but she always exchanged them for something more expensive.

Later, she didn't even make excuses. She'd just take them back and get something else. He'd felt like not buying her any more gifts, but that would have set off World War III. He just made sure he picked the best quality he could find.

He glanced into Lee's eyes, saw the fire within. His body still pulsated with need. But Lee was right. He couldn't let this go on, especially if she were going to stay at his place for only a few days and then move on. She'd said she didn't believe in casual sex. He had to respect her for that.

He'd have a hard time staying away from her after he took Tanya back, but it wasn't just sexual attraction that drew him. He admired Lee. She hadn't complained once about all the material things she'd had to leave behind. She obviously loved her sister, and she'd been good with Tanya even though she'd been in danger from Bubba.

He caught her gaze on him. He'd better reassure her about his intentions, even though they warred with his desires. He held the door open for her. "Don't worry, I won't pressure you into anything you don't want. Besides, I have to get up early to drive Tanya back to Austin."

Lee started up the steps. Alex stood inside holding the door for her. She mounted the top step and stopped. "We need to get one thing straight."

"What's that?" he whispered, taking a step closer. His seductive grin almost unnerved her.

She backed away. "Just remember I'm your secretary, nothing more."

Alex knew he should move away now for sure. Instead he stepped closer, pulling her against him until his mouth was only inches away. His lips met hers with a gentle hunger.

❧

Unable to break away, Lee cursed herself for being weak. She snuggled in his arms, enjoying the feel of his hands caressing her back and pulling her hard against his firm body. If she had any doubts about his ardor cooling, the hardness pressing against her swept them away. She was really in trouble now.

When at last he moved his mouth from hers and took a deep breath, she wrenched herself away. "I don't want to play a tease, but we mustn't," she whispered.

His eyes spoke of need, of longing to be loved. "You don't know how hard you're making it. He pulled her against him to underscore his meaning, then let go. "But I won't ask you for more until you're ready."

He sure was taking a lot for granted. She squeezed his hand, and then pulled away, but his gaze held her spellbound.

A cry jolted them. "Mommy, Mommy."

Alex rushed to the hide-a-bed. Lee followed. He picked up his daughter and cuddled her. "It's all right baby, Daddy's here."

Tanya blinked. "Where's Mommy. Where is she?"

"She went out dancing."

"All by herself?"

"No, pumpkin. With a friend, a man friend."

"Oh. Does that mean I'm going to get a new daddy?" Her little face puckered up. "I don't want a new daddy. I want you and Mommy to stay with me in our house."

Alex smoothed a reddish-blond lock from her eyes. "I'm sorry, baby, but I can't stay there with you anymore. Mommy and Daddy fight and argue too much. But I still love you. I will come get you whenever I can. I promise."

"Can't you promise not to fight Mommy?"

Alex sighed. "Mommy doesn't like me anymore, but we both love you very much. Now, try to sleep." He laid her down, covered her up, and kissed her goodnight.

Moving away, he whispered to Lee. "I'd like to sit outside with you and look at stars, but I think I'd better stay with her. And I'm not letting you go outside by yourself."

"But Bubba's been arrested. I should be safe here."

"I can't guarantee that. I'm going to bolt the door and stack the coffee table against it. Guess we both better get some sleep. You take the bathroom first. You wouldn't agree to share the shower, would you?"

Visions of touching him skin to skin teased her, but she shook her head. "I'll hurry." But she couldn't help imagining his wet slick skin against hers and his caressing hands exploring her body.

"By the way, I have to take Tanya back first thing in the morning. Sleep late if you like. I should be back by ten a.m. at the latest. I don't think anyone will bother you before then, but if someone knocks on the door, don't answer."

Lee resolved to wake early and set the table for breakfast. She hoped there was dry cereal in the cupboard. She didn't want to make Alex and Tanya suffer through eggs with broken yolks.

However, she was so tired, she slept soundly until Tanya's giggle awoke her. She looked at the clock—quarter to six. She stumbled into the tiny kitchen. The table was set, and Alex was pouring orange juice for Tanya. They'd been so quiet, she hadn't heard sounds of Alex dressing Tanya or setting the table.

"Morning, sleepyhead," he said in a cheery voice. He was definitely a morning person.

She joined them for breakfast. She'd sleep more after they left.

Tanya grabbed her hand. "Are you coming with us. I can show you my house, and you can talk to Mommy."

Lee swallowed. Her hair was a mess, and she hadn't brought anything suitable to wear. She shook her head. "Maybe some other time."

"It's time to go, Tanya," Alex said. "I'll be back soon. I don't think Bubba will find you before I return, but keep the curtains closed and bolt the door after we leave."

Tanya pulled at her arm. "Kiss me good-bye."

Lee picked her up and pressed a kiss on her cheek. Tanya's red-gold curls bounced as Lee set her down. "You're a sweet little girl. I hope I see you again soon."

"Me too." Her grin was adorable. "I like you."

As soon as they left, Lee dressed. The urge to go back to bed had flown. She might as well get the rest of her things. She called a cab and left a note for Alex. When she'd worked for Sheldon, she'd never known Bubba to come to the office before ten. Even if the cops had released him, surely he wouldn't venture out to hunt her this early. Or would he?

Chapter 10

The sign said, 'Grandville – five miles.' After the long drive to take Tanya back to her mother and the ensuing argument, Alex was stewing. Kathy had called him a poor excuse for a man. He couldn't imagine Lee ever saying that. He'd slammed down money for child support and stalked out.

As he pulled into the trailer park, he was looking forward to being with Lee again. He glanced into the rearview mirror. A black Camaro was following him into the mobile home park.

The sun glared off the windshield of the other car so he couldn't see who was behind the wheel. He swallowed. Could it be Bubba again?

Better not take any chances. He drove past his place to the end of Primrose Lane, turned onto another street and meandered through the park as if looking for an address.

He parked in front of a mobile home without a car. The Camaro passed and stopped in front of a home down the street.

Slowly, he drove past. Strains of Claire de Lune drifted out of the window. Didn't sound like Bubba's kind of music. An elderly couple got out. Taking her hand, the man escorted her to the door and unlocked it. They went inside.

Relieved, Alex headed back to the trailer, looking forward to spending the rest of the day with Lee, even though she'd accused him of being too macho. Well, maybe he had ordered her around at times, but it was for her own safety. Today he'd ask if she'd like to visit a museum or art gallery in Fort Worth. He hoped she'd say yes.

He tried to remember when he had looked forward to spending the day with Kathy. Seemed like eons ago. All he could recall was how he couldn't wait to take her to bed. He'd been surprised and delighted at the novel ways she'd teased and stroked him. Claiming she'd read up on sexual moves, she rambled on about how nice it would be to have a May wedding with all her girlfriends as bridesmaids.

He wished he hadn't let her rush him into marriage before he'd learned what she was like. When she'd had morning sickness on their honeymoon, he realized why, but hadn't been sure he was ready to become a father. Now Tanya was his pride and joy.

Parking the car in front of number five, he sighed. He wouldn't make the same mistake again. Oh, he'd watch out for Lee and keep her safe. And if the Witness Security Program couldn't keep her out of danger—well, he'd threaten to go to the media and cause heads to roll, but he wouldn't get personally involved with her.

Who was he kidding? In the CIA he made his own rules, made things happen. Here, he could only hope his threats might make the U.S. Marshals more vigilant.

He retrieved his gun from the glove compartment. Just to be on the safe side, he undid the safety before getting out of the car. The air was strangely still as he strode to the door and yanked the handle.

It was locked. "Lee," he called. She didn't respond. He sucked in his breath and called again. Still no answer. Had Bubba gotten to her? Frantic now, he unlocked the door. A sudden gust of wind blew it open. He listened carefully, but didn't hear any unusual sounds. Cautiously he stepped inside, called her name.

Silence met him. He checked everywhere, hoping against

hope he wouldn't find her body. Seeing some of her clothes, but no signs of a struggle, he drew in a ragged breath.

He slumped in a chair at the kitchen table. Where could she go? She didn't have a car or friends she could call, at least none he knew of.

He dreaded the thought of tracking down her sister and telling her Lee was missing and maybe dead.

Through the open door came the sound of the wind ruffling leaves in the trees. Something rustled beneath his feet. Looking down, he spotted a piece of paper and picked up a note from Lee.

He read it, then slammed it down on the table. How could she be so foolish as to go alone to pick up her stuff at the apartment? He'd told her to stay here. What the hell was wrong with her? Did she have a death wish?

Slamming the door on the way out, he prayed she hadn't met up with Bubba or another of Sheldon's goons. Burning rubber, he drove his car from the trailer park like a lost soul fleeing Hades.

❧

Inside the closet in Lee's apartment Bubba fiddled with controls on the device he held. Lucky for him, Sheldon's lawyer had gotten him out of jail early this morning.

He grinned, looking forward to the bonus Sheldon had promised for taking care of her. He could almost feel those G notes between his fingers. He rubbed his sore arm. She'd winged him. Now he'd get even in spades.

He'd like to hang around and see that spitfire stuffed into a body bag, but that wouldn't be smart. He couldn't chance being found anywhere near here.

She'd been here half an hour — almost discovered him once. He'd huddled behind some discarded blinds stacked in the corner of the closet when she yanked her clothes from the hangers. He worked on the controls. Had to get the thing set properly. It would take about two minutes to get out that window — better allow four. He'd loosened the screen, but it still might stick.

When Laura Lee went into the bathroom and shut the door, he pushed the button to start the sequence. Seconds later, he was out the window and tearing down the alley.

⌘

In the living room of her small apartment, Lee wiped perspiration off her brow. It had taken half an hour to get all her things packed and stacked on the front porch. She'd already called a cab, so she hurried out and locked the door. The cab driver pulled up.

After picking up her things, she noticed the bedroom window screen had fallen off, and the window was open. If it rained and got the carpet wet, the landlady would make her pay for the damage. Lee stepped over to the cab. The meter was ticking. "Can you wait a minute" There's something I have to take care of."

Deciding it would be quicker to shut the window from outside, she hurried around to the side of the building, grabbed the screen and reached to pull the window down.

⌘

Despite his sporty car, it seemed to take Alex an eternity to cover the distance to town. After reaching the apartments where she'd stayed, he pulled up behind a waiting taxi. Damn fool woman — why had she risked coming back here alone?

He jumped out of his Jaguar and strode toward the door. There was her stuff piled on the front step. He'd dismiss the cab, help her carry her things out, then rush her back to his place before anyone else saw them. No point in having someone trace his car and find out where she was staying.

Blam! The loud boom nearly deafened him. Dust flew everywhere. Stunned, he watched the small apartment building crumble. Flames crackled somewhere inside.

Oh lord, she must still be in there.

He sprinted to the front door. Piles of debris blocked the entrance.

Should he climb over it or hunt for another way in? He needed help. The taxi driver would have a phone. He turned.

A man with olive skin and dark wavy hair stood behind him. "I called 9-1-1."

"Thanks." Alex rubbed the back of his neck. "A woman with long hair — did you see her before — before it blew?"

The driver nodded. "She told me to wait a minute — said something about closing a window, but she didn't go in." He pointed. "She went around the building."

His heart in this throat, Alex ran around to the side of the building. Footsteps behind him told Alex the driver was following. A window — what used to be a window — was now only a gaping hole in the wall.

Lee lay motionless on the grass amidst jumbled shards of glass.

The taxi driver bent over her. "You okay, miss?"

"Don't move her," Alex shouted. "There's broken glass all around, and she might have broken bones."

"Ohhhh," she moaned.

Alex let out the breath he'd been holding. She was alive, but blood oozed from a cut on her face. An ugly scratch ran several inches down her arm. She was breathing slightly faster than normal. Running his hands over her arms and legs, he saw no signs of broken bones or swelling.

"Lie still. There's broken glass everywhere." Tossing pieces of glass right and left, he cut his hand in the process. "Damn," he said, but kept at it until he'd removed all the pieces nearby.

After wiping his bleeding hand on his jeans, he knelt beside her. "Does it feel as if you broke anything?"

"No," she said in a hoarse whisper, "but my head hurts."

She started to get up.

"Don't move," Alex said. He whipped out a clean handkerchief and wiped blood from her cheek, careful not to touch the cut itself. He took her hand. It felt cool in his, too cool. At least her eyes didn't have a glassy look like someone in shock. "What happened?"

Dazed, Lee rubbed her head, then groaned as her headache intensified. "Shouldn't have done it."

"Done what?"

"Touched the window. Tried to shut it—bomb went off." She shuddered. "If I'd been inside—I'd be—be dead." She could hardly believe Sheldon had gone to such lengths.

"I told you not to leave my place. Now see what happened."

"But—I needed my things. Didn't think Bubba would come...so early."

"Your assumptions almost got you killed. It's a miracle you weren't. Now maybe you'll listen."

She frowned. "Hey, I uh...I appreciate your help, but do you have to talk to me like—like you would a two-year-old?"

"If that's what it takes to keep you safe."

A siren sounded, getting louder by the second. Gently, he smoothed a lock of hair from her face. "The ambulance is coming. Let them take you to the hospital so a doctor can take care of you."

"Okay, but I'm not staying overnight. And I don't want to be carried on a stretcher. I can walk."

Lee tried to rise, but wasn't sure her wobbly legs would cooperate.

He pushed her shoulders down, pinning her to the ground. "You crazy? You need to be checked for internal injuries and broken bones."

He sounded so cold and professional. Apparently she was

only a responsibility to him. Well, that was how she wanted things, wasn't it? She rose up on her elbows and opened her mouth to speak.

Alex frowned. "Don't argue, at least not until after you get to the hospital."

A paramedic came and waved at Alex to move.

She felt Alex's touch on the top of her head. She opened her mouth to complain that she didn't want to be patted on the head like a little kid, then realized it could have been a kiss.

They lifted her onto a stretcher and carried her into the ambulance. Just before they closed the doors, she heard more sirens. The police must have arrived.

The ambulance siren filled her ears. Inside, Alex's gaze met hers as the medic continued to check her over. She was glad Alex had insisted on riding with her—she didn't want to be surrounded by complete strangers.

Alex's eyes never left her face. "Stay with me, Lee. I don't want to lose you."

She shivered. Maybe she was worse off than she thought.

Alex remained with her until they carried her into the hospital and laid her on a bed. Then they pulled a curtain around her and asked him to step outside.

She winced as a doctor poked and prodded. She could hear Alex pacing in the corridor. Then she didn't hear him for a while. She caught her breath. Surely, he wouldn't leave her here all alone. What if Bubba found her?

Finally, they finished checking her over, put antiseptic and bandages on her cuts, and told her she could leave in an hour if Alex would promise to wake her up periodically to be sure she wasn't unconscious. She was still dazed, but didn't want to stay. Seeing Alex walk back in the room, she felt relieved.

He smiled, then took her hand and squeezed it. "Feeling better now?"

She nodded. "A little."

"I went back and got your stuff. The police came to the

hospital and asked me about the bombing. I told them what I'd seen. They wanted to talk to you, but I told them you weren't up to it yet. Do you want to tell them what's behind it or just what happened?"

"Think I'd better call Iceberg, I mean Joe, and see what he thinks, but I don't feel like talking to the police now. Let's get out of here before they come back."

"You want them to catch Bubba?"

She nodded.

"Then you've got to tell them something. And call Joe, as soon as you can."

She frowned. "There you go, telling me what to do again."

"Hell, Lee. It's only common sense. If you want to catch a criminal, you don't wait until he's had time to get far."

She frowned. "Okay. As soon as we get in the car, I'll call on your cell phone."

After they released her, Alex helped Lee into his car and headed toward his place. She dialed Joe's cell phone number. An operator spoke in a monotone, saying all circuits were busy. Then she called the police, related what happened, and described Bubba. They promised to look for him. She called Joe again and left a message.

Alex pulled up in front of the mobile home and parked the Jaguar. He got out, unlocked the door to the trailer, then came around and opened the car door. She hoped her legs wouldn't wobble. She'd probably have to lean on him to walk inside.

Suddenly, she felt his arms around her back and under her knees. He lifted her with strong arms and strode toward the door. His firm shoulder felt warm against her cheek. Somewhere nearby a mockingbird warbled a song, then changed its tune. The breeze rippled through her hair and brought with it smells of barbecuing hamburgers and children's laughter.

Sighing, she rested her head on his shoulder, wishing she

felt up to running and playing like the children.

It must be afternoon by now, she thought as she snuggled against him. He might be bossy, but she had to admit he'd been there when she needed him.

After he settled her into a chair, his gaze met hers. "Feel up to getting ready for bed?"

She didn't, but made her way to the bedroom on shaky legs. It helped to hold on to furniture on the way.

Later, standing in the bedroom and sorry her nightgown was transparent, she removed the robe. She caught his gaze on her breasts, well outlined by the clinging material. Meeting her eyes, he quickly averted his gaze, but his smile told her he liked what he'd seen. After slipping beneath the sheets, she yanked the covers up to her neck.

He stepped close and took her hand. "Lee, I'm sorry you got hurt. I shouldn't have spoken so sharply when you'd just been knocked flat. If I seem overbearing sometimes, it's only because I want to keep you safe."

"Only sometimes?"

"Hey, I want to keep you safe all the time." His fingers caressed the back of her hand. He grinned. "I like having you around."

He lifted her hand and pressed warm lips to her skin. She met his gaze, catching a look that said he really cared what happened to her.

She smiled and wondered about his ex-wife's side of the story. Maybe Kathy had seen an ugly side to Alex that she hadn't. She shouldn't be encouraging him until he received that decree signed by the judge. She needed his protection, but as far as expecting anything else, she'd just have to cool it.

She tried to pull her hand away, but he wouldn't let go.

He cleared his throat. "I can't help but admire you. To leave your family and all your friends and start a new life, let alone defend yourself against a killer, that takes guts."

She smiled. "I didn't have much choice."

"Maybe not, but some women wouldn't have faced it as well. They would have retreated from life or let fear control them."

His thumbs caressed her arm, sending a delightful warmth throughout. Then he moved away. "Lee, I can't promise you a thing, except I'll try to keep you safe."

Her hand still warm from his touch, she kept her gaze fixed on his eyes. Could he just miss touching a woman—any woman? She didn't want to be a stand-in for an ex-wife that might decide she wanted him back. What little he'd said about Kathy suggested he didn't want her back, but Lee couldn't be sure. She nibbled her lower lip.

He reached in his pocket and pulled out an envelope. "I forgot to give you something. Someone left this at the front desk of the hospital. It's addressed to you."

A lump formed in her throat. Who knew where she was except Joe and maybe Bubba?

Her hand shook as he gave her an envelope. His warm fingers lingered on hers for an instant afterwards.

She sat up to read it, and the sheet dropped to her waist. Noting where his gaze strayed, she tucked the sheet around her breasts and studied the writing on the envelope.

The large letters looked as if someone had scrawled them in a hurry. She held her breath, tore open the envelope, and read it.

Her mouth dropped open. "I can't believe this." Covering her face with her hands she dropped the letter. Oh, no. They can't do that."

"What does it say?"

Her throat choked up. She couldn't answer him.

He snatched it up and read the words aloud.

"We've got your sister. Call the number below if you want to see her again."

Chapter 11

Lee gasped, trying to catch her breath. "Oh, my God! They've got Libby. It's not fair. My sister's done nothing—" She brushed tears from her eyes. "Nothing to deserve that. Today's her birthday. What a horrible way to spend it."

Lee imagined Bubba torturing Libby. Shivers ran down Lee's spine as she squeezed her eyes shut. Her insides twisted in knots. They might even kill her sister if she didn't do what they wanted. Her heart raced. "She's all I've got—I can't let anything happen to her. You've got to help me get her back."

"Put the note down. They may be able to pick up fingerprints from it."

She dropped it as if it would burn her.

Alex took her hands in his. Warm and steady, they imparted a comforting strength. She looked up. "I hate to get you involved, but I need you. I can't decide what to do."

He sat on the bed, a serious expression on his face. "Let's think. What are our options?"

"Well, we could call the police. I can call Joe and get the U.S. Marshals involved, or," she shivered, "we can call Bubba and see what he wants."

Alex's gaze met hers head on. "You know what he wants. To keep you from testifying even if he has to get you out of the picture." His chin had a determined thrust. "I'm not letting you near him."

His bossiness might be annoying, but she was lucky to have Alex in her corner. "Bart Sheldon seemed so charming when I started working there. But if he wanted something done right away, he was like a steam roller. I'll never forget the steely look in his eyes and the way he shouted at me the day he was arrested." She shuddered. "Poor Libby."

The ticking of the old-fashioned clock on the wall was the only sound she heard. The hands seemed to move with terrifying speed. They had to do something—and do it fast. Heaven only knew what Bubba was doing to Libby. She looked at Alex. "What do you think I should do?"

He handed her his cell phone. "Call that marshal, Iceberg, or Joe, whatever he's called. Tell him what's happened."

With shaking fingers, she dialed the number.

"Sorry, that customer is not available at this time," came the message.

"I can't get through. Now what?"

"Wait five minutes and try again."

"I can't wait. Even now Bubba might be doing something horrible to her." Lee didn't even want to think about rape, that fat slob tearing her clothes off, looking at Libby's naked body.

The clock on the wall ticked. Now the hands moved with agonizing slowness. Shadows outside grew longer.

After four minutes, Lee couldn't wait any longer. She tried again and got the same refrain. "Libby frightens easily. She'll do anything, tell them anything. I'm afraid for her."

"Does she know where you are?"

Lee shook her head. "Only that I'm somewhere in Texas. Each time I send a letter to her, I mail it to Joe in another envelope so no one will see the Grandville postmark."

"That won't help now. Bubba probably figures you're still somewhere around Grandville."

She twisted her fingers together. "I'm sure he does."

"Call Bubba at the number he gave you. And insist on speaking to Libby. Don't even try to negotiate unless he lets you talk to her. And don't take too long. If you hang up after only a few minutes, he can't trace the call." He handed her his phone.

"Unless he's got caller ID."

Alex shook his head. "I've got that blocked. Besides, my number's unlisted. He can't get my address."

Lee dialed the number. She held the phone away from her ear so Alex could listen also.

"Hello," came Bubba's nasal drawl. "Whatcha want?"

"I want to talk to my sister."

"Suppose she's not here."

"I'm not making any deals unless I can talk to her and hear for myself that she's all right."

Clunk. He must have dropped the phone. Then she heard Libby's voice.

"It's me, Laura Lee." Her voice sounded thin and strained as if she were close to going to pieces. "He's got me tied up, but he hasn't hurt me...at least not yet." Her voice quivered.

"Hold tight, Libby, Alex and I will get you out of there."

Bubba came back on the line. "You talked to her. Now talk to me."

"What do you want?"

"I want—Sheldon wants you to tell the cops it was all a mistake, that you kept separate books because you were embezzling."

"What? I never did any such thing. Besides, if I do that, I'll go to jail."

"Not if you get a good lawyer."

"Why can't Sheldon's lawyer handle that for him?"

"It would sound more convincing if you signed a paper saying you were embezzlin', you know."

"I'm not going to sign a confession for something I didn't do."

"You want your sister back in one piece?"

Alex whispered in her ear, "Go along with him."

"If I do that, will you let Libby go?"

"After you sign an affidavit fixed by Sheldon's lawyer, we'll let her go. That way you won't have to show up in court, you know."

Lee tensed, held her hand over the receiver. "Alex, he wants me to go to his lawyer's office. How do I know it's safe to show up there? Some sniper could blow me away."

"Use your head. It would make Sheldon look bad if you suddenly turned up dead in his lawyer's office. He won't want that."

She took her hand from the mouthpiece. "Why did you blow up my apartment?"

"You needed to know Sheldon means business. And if you happened to get killed, it would have looked like an accident. Look, do you want to see your sister or not?"

"Okay, tell me what time the paper will be ready and give me the address. And I want to take Libby with me when I leave the law office."

"Can't promise that. She's our insurance that you'll do as we say."

"If I don't keep my word, your men could kill me anytime. That's your insurance."

"Sheldon won't like it, you know, but I'll see if I can talk him into it. Be on the fifth floor of La Paloma Plaza in downtown Dallas at 4:45 tomorrow. It's that building where Akard and Ervay join together. Don't bring in the cops or you won't see your sister alive again."

"Wait a moment. Where on the fifth floor?"

"Don't worry 'bout that. Just wait by the elevator. We'll find you."

"The fifth floor at 4:45? What if we—what if I get caught in rush hour traffic?"

"You want to save your sister, you better be on time."

Alex scribbled something on a piece of paper and held it up.

The note said, 'make it the second floor.'

"Can't we meet on the second floor?"

"Why?"

Alex grabbed the phone from her. "Because there's a restaurant there and lots of people. We don't want you trying anything funny." He listened for a moment, then pushed the button to end the call.

"What did he say?"

"He insisted on the fifth floor."

She bit her lip. "What do we do now?"

He handed the phone back. "Try Joe again."

She did and got the same response she had earlier.

"Don't you have an office number for him?"

She reached for her purse on the end table and searched inside. Finally she pulled out a piece of paper with a number on it.

He frowned. "Why do you have it on such a small piece of paper? You could lose it."

"Joe said to do it that way, in case someone else found it. That's his direct dial number. Without a name, no one could trace it to the office of the federal marshals. They keep a low profile."

She dialed. This time he answered.

"Joe here."

She explained about Bubba threatening her and setting off the bomb and then the note about her sister, then told him what they planned to do.

Joe interrupted her. "Why the hell didn't you call me sooner?"

"I tried, but I couldn't get through."

"Look, Lee, if you don't let me handle things like this, you'll be dropped from the Witness Security Program. You can't second guess those guys. Hold off until I can get there."

"Okay, I'll wait. Alex is still keeping me at his place out from town to protect me, but I'll keep you informed from now on."

"If your apartment was bombed, Alex wasn't doing a very good job of protecting you," Joe grumbled.

"I went there by myself, so he couldn't have stopped Bubba."

"You should have asked me to pick up your stuff. You could have been killed."

"Okay, I made a mistake, but I need help getting Libby rescued."

"I got the picture. Don't bring the police in on the kidnapping yet. I'll recruit another marshal to help. We'll meet you in the restaurant on the second floor at four o'clock, and I'll fill you in on our strategy."

"I'll bring Alex, the guy who brought me to the picnic at Carl's house. He's ex-CIA."

Annoyance colored Joe's voice. "Why bring in someone else? Two marshals should be enough to handle the situation."

"But what if they have guns?"

"I don't think they'd shoot up a public building with security guards."

"They might. Sheldon must be getting desperate to kidnap Libby."

"A show of force wouldn't hurt. Okay, bring Alex. Be sure you leave Grandville in plenty of time. Traffic is thick in Dallas after four."

Lee hung up, handed the phone to Alex and told him what Joe said.

"At least he's got a plan." He gripped her forearm. "And it had better be a good one. Just in case it isn't, I'm making one, too."

❧

The next afternoon Alex wriggled his shoulders, trying to get the kinks out. Downtown Dallas with all its one way streets was tricky and congested.

He'd suggested Lee nap on the way, but she kept fidgeting and looking out the window. He wished he still had a sister to worry about. She should have lived long enough to give him more nieces and nephews instead of dying in childbirth after a car crash.

Her son, Danny, was all he had left of his vivacious sister. The lively toddler seemed to be following in her footsteps. He was getting to be a handful for Alex's mother.

He gripped the wheel, hoping Joe and his associate would get there early enough to include him in their plan of attack. Now if he were doing this alone, he'd enlist the police. This wasn't like assignments he'd handled overseas. There you could shoot the enemy, in fact, often had to before they wiped you out.

Here, if he winged someone, they'd probably arrest him. He glanced at his watch. Traffic was crawling on Stemmons Freeway. It was almost as bad on Ross. He was glad to see the La Paloma Plaza looming ahead. Getting here had taken longer than he figured. Nearing the building, he wished he could leave the Jaguar in a parking garage, but they needed to be able to get away quickly.

He stuffed quarters in a parking meter on a side street. If he got a ticket, he'd worry about it later. After walking around his car, he opened the car door for Lee. She looked pale. She stood there, smoothing down her skirt and tucking her blouse in.

He frowned. "Come on. We're not here to impress anyone."

She worried her lip with her teeth. "I don't want them to know we're planning anything. What will they think if they see you?"

"I'm supposed to be your boyfriend, remember."

"So what are you going to do?"

"I'll have to talk with Joe first. It's his call. Let's go. We need to get there before Sheldon's men do."

She hesitated. "Do you have a gun?"

"Of course. Did you bring yours?"

She nodded and patted her purse.

"Well, be careful. If they take it away, they could use it on you."

She scowled. "I won't let them have it."

"If things go bad, you won't have a choice, now come on." He started walking.

She hurried to catch up. "I can take care of myself."

"I'm sure you can handle a gun, but you probably haven't dealt with rough types like this. I have." He held open the glass and chrome door to the La Paloma Plaza building.

Once inside, they rode the escalator to the second floor and stood beside the entrance to the restaurant. The place looked deserted. He glanced at his watch. "Joe and his backup should be here by now to meet us. I hope they haven't gotten stuck in traffic."

He touched her arm. "We need to check out the offices on the floor where we're supposed to meet them. We'll take the elevator to the fifth floor."

After emerging from the elevator, Alex scanned the area. He didn't relish a confrontation in the elevator hallway. No hiding places. Walking down the hall to some office would leave them exposed to gunfire. They walked down to the second floor to wait for Joe.

By four-thirty Lee was pacing the pink and tan marble floor. She drew a deep breath. "I don't like this."

"Neither do I. We need a back-up plan."

"I'll ask the security guard at the desk on the first floor to come up to the fifth floor."

Alex frowned. "I worked as a security guard once. About all they're trained to do is call the police."

"Even that would be a help. I'll hurry." She walked down the escalator to the first, then strode to the counter.

Behind it hung a huge tapestry scene, reminiscent of life in a slower paced world. A man in a navy sports coat stood at attention and smiled. "What can I do for you, miss?"

"Are you security?"

He nodded. "Is there a problem?"

She explained the kidnappers' demands, then said, "I hope you have a gun."

"You'd better call the police."

"The men who have my sister said all I had to do was to sign some papers in a lawyer's office on the fifth floor."

"There's no lawyer with an office on the fifth floor."

"Well, maybe they're only meeting us there. Is there a lawyer's office on a nearby floor?"

"We have lots of law firms in the building. I don't know much about the law, but if they force you to sign something, you probably don't have to go through with it. That's called duress."

"I don't intend to stand by those papers. I'll just sign them so they'll let my sister go."

"Let me call the police for you." He reached for the phone.

She grasped his arm. "No, don't. They might hurt my sister if the cops rush in before I sign the papers. And even if the cops chase them away, they might try it again later. Please, could you just come up to the fifth floor with your gun in plain sight and look authoritative?"

He scratched his head. "I still think I ought to call the cops."

She glanced at her watch. "Oh, my gosh. I have to go." She ran for the escalator and took the steps two at a time. She wove around the two stationary riders and reached the top just as Alex strode to meet her.

"It's 4:37. Come on." He grabbed her arm and practically dragged her to the elevators. Scowling, he jabbed at the button. "Where the Hell are Joe and his back-up man?"

"Probably caught in traffic. I don't think we can count on much help from the security guard.

"Told you so," said Alex as the elevator door sprang open. His hand on her back urged her in. He pushed a button. The elevator creaked, but began to rise.

Inside he turned to Lee. "I'll get out first and see who's there."

"Okay." Adrenaline surged, but didn't seem to help her think. She needed to help Alex come up with a plan. Maybe he already had. She was about to ask him when the car came to a stop at the fifth floor.

Alex grabbed her and kissed her hard. "That's for luck."

Still reeling from his kiss, she could feel her heart pounding. Was he afraid they might not live through this? She clenched her hands into tight fists, hoping they could rescue her sister without one of them being killed.

The door opened. Her pulse racing, she stepped forward.

"Wait." He shoved her behind him and pulled his 357 out. Gun ready, he stuck his head out and looked both ways. He stepped out and motioned for her to follow. "I don't see anyone. Of course, they could be holed up in an empty office somewhere."

"The security guard said there were no lawyer's offices on this floor." The elevator slid closed behind them.

He frowned. "This is off to a bad start."

"Is there such a thing as a good start for a kidnapping?"

"Shhhh. I need to listen."

She held her breath and concentrated on listening.

Was that footsteps on carpet?

A man rounded the corner. Alex reached for his gun.

Lee grabbed his wrist. "Don't. That's the security guard I talked to."

"Any trouble, miss?"

"No. This is my — my boyfriend. He's here to help me talk those men into letting my sister come with me."

The guard's gaze raked Alex. "You sure you don't want me to call the cops, miss?"

"Not unless you hear shots."

The guard looked around. "Don't see anyone. Maybe they aren't coming. Still think you should call the police.

I'm not supposed to unless it looks like there will be trouble."

She smiled. "Thanks for coming up. What's your name?"

"My friends call me Robbie."

"Can I ask one more favor? Could you come back in about ten minutes, just to check?"

"I have to get back to my post. If I can find someone to watch the phone for a few minutes, I might be able to stop by here later." He walked around the corner. The sound of his footsteps grew fainter, and then dissolved into silence.

For an instant, Lee thought she heard a muffled cough, but she couldn't be sure. Perhaps it was the air conditioner coming on.

Alex looked at his watch. "It's 4:43. Why aren't that damn Joe and his cohort here? The nickname Iceberg is appropriate. He's probably so cold he doesn't care if his being late makes you scared spitless." Alex wasn't ready to admit, he was a little apprehensive also. "We can't wait."

"Can you come up with a back-up plan?"

"When they lead us to a room, I'll stand outside in the hall. You insist they leave the door open so I can see what's happening. Refuse to sign anything unless they agree to that. And make sure they untie Libby before you sign. She may have to make a run for it."

Lee swallowed. Alex's plan made sense. She hoped she could be firm. Right now she'd do anything to get them to let Libby go.

She straightened her shoulders. She had to be strong now.

Footsteps sounded. She looked at her watch. It was time.

Chapter 12

Alex glanced at the marble tiled floor beside the elevator bank. The place had class. But would those orange, pink, and tan squares be streaked with his and Lee's blood before the day was over?

He sucked in a deep breath. Mustn't let fear shatter his concentration. He'd been shot before, and lived through it, but he dreaded facing a replay of what happened overseas. He couldn't let that happen. He had to make things go right.

Lee or her sister mustn't get hurt—especially not Lee. It was bad enough she'd been injured by the bomb blast. He couldn't bear to see her hurt again. That would almost kill him. She'd come to be such an important part of his life that he'd rather do anything than see her get hurt.

He swallowed, and then checked his gun again. Still no sign of Joe, the coward. Alex straightened his spine. He'd have to run this show alone.

He stiffened and turned to Lee. "Looks like it's you and me. We can't let fear paralyze us. Be ready to act at a second's notice. Watch, and take your cues from me."

She nodded, her face pale. "Okay. What's the plan?"

"First, we negotiate. Get them to bring out your sister and hand her over. Then sign the damn papers and get her out of here. Oh, and back your way into the elevator so they can't shoot you in the back."

She shuddered. "You think they'd actually open fire in a public building?"

"If Sheldon is as ruthless as you say he is, I wouldn't put it past them."

He watched her swallow, watched the movements of her slender neck, hoping she'd still be alive by evening when he could dare to smooth his fingers over her soft skin. He couldn't think about that now. Everything depended on him. His pulse raced, and his adrenaline surged.

The elevator doors clanged open. He jerked around, his hand on his gun.

Bubba and another much thinner man emerged. The other guy had a scar on his face that curved around one side of his jaw. Bubba's beefy arm reached toward Lee.

She stood her ground. "Where's my sister?"

Bubba chuckled. "We got her up on another floor. Ain't that right, Floyd?"

The other man nodded. "Yeah. She's waiting for you up there." He pushed the elevator button and held the door open. "Are you coming?"

Bubba stared at Alex. "What's he doing here?"

"I brought my boyfriend along to be sure you didn't put anything over on me."

Floyd sneered. "He some hot-shot lawyer?"

Alex shook his head. "Name's Alex. I'm a businessman, and Lee's my friend."

Lee leaned forward. "Take me to Libby. I'll sign your damn papers if you'll just let her go."

Bubba grinned. "Now, you're talking. Come on." He pointed to the open elevator.

Alex shook his head. "Don't like elevators—too closed in. Can't we take the stairs?"

Bubba frowned. "Jeez. You'd think I hadn't taken a bath in a week."

"I ain't doing no stairs," Floyd said. "You want the girl,

you'll come." He sidled farther back into the elevator. Bubba shrugged and backed into the car.

Alex beckoned to Lee. "Come on." He didn't like this set up one bit. Inside the elevator he backed up against a wall. He tensed as the door closed. So far they hadn't pulled any guns, but no doubt both men were armed. Seconds later, the door opened. Bubba and Floyd stepped out.

"You coming?" Bubba asked.

Alex squeezed Lee's hand, then dropped it. They followed the men down the hall and around the corner. Eyes alert, he listened for sounds of activity—nothing. Had the occupants of this floor all left for the weekend? Not good. His heart beat a tattoo against his ribs. He'd been in situations like this before, but he'd been alone. The stakes were higher now. For Tanya's and Lee's sake, he mustn't fail.

Bubba waddled down the hall to a solid wooden door and pushed it open. One with a window would have been better. Alex dropped Lee's hand and nodded to indicate she should go inside. He leaned against the door, holding it open.

A petite blonde sat in a chair, her arms tied behind her. A lock of hair that had escaped from her pony tail hung down one side of her pale face. Lee gasped and ran to her. "You okay, Libby?"

She nodded. "But I can't say much for the company I've been keeping."

Floyd clapped a hand on her arm. "Watch it, sister. You're not in a position to bitch."

"Yeah, we could have roughed you up, you know." Bubba grabbed some papers from the desk and thrust them at Lee. "Sign these, and we'll let her go."

Lee reached for the papers. Alex stepped inside the door and grabbed her arm. "Not so fast. Wait until they free her."

Lee shook off his arm and straightened her shoulders. "That's right. Untie her first."

Alex moved back and leaned against the open door.

Floyd shoved some papers toward Lee. "Sign them now or we keep your precious Libby."

Lee's lip quivered. Alex's pulse raced. Not for a moment did he think they'd honor their promises. If she caved in to their demands, they didn't have much chance of getting Libby out. He waited. Surely, she'd see that.

She reached for the papers.

He stepped forward. "Lee, don't give in."

She frowned, but pulled her arm back. "You're right. Untie her or I won't sign."

Bubba scowled, his face resembling a grizzly bear's. "You don't sign, she don't get loose. Now, what's it gonna be?"

Alex watched and wondered how long she'd hold out.

She inclined her head to the right, and then reached in her purse. "I've got to find my pen." She glanced at Alex, inclining her head once more.

He got the message and reached for his gun. As she pulled hers out and leveled it at Bubba, Alex pointed his at Floyd. "Okay, untie her."

Floyd didn't move. "What are you gonna do if I don't. Can't kill me in a public building and get away with it."

Alex moved closer. "If I shoot you in the leg, and you run for it, you'll probably bleed to death. Of course, I'll call an ambulance...after ten minutes or so that is. If you die, I'll say it was an accident or maybe self-defense."

Bubba scowled. "Shouldn't have let them get the drop on us, you know." He rubbed his arm. "I wouldn't mess with her. She'll shoot."

Alex stepped closer. "Now, is one of you going to untie her or do I have to nail someone to show I mean business?"

Floyd edged behind Libby and pulled at the ropes binding her hands. As soon as her hands were loose, she rubbed her wrists.

Bubba edged toward the door.

Lee adjusted her aim. "Oh, no you don't."

Bubba leaned against a desk, striking a nonchalant pose. Alex was glad to see Lee keeping her eyes on the guy. He turned to Floyd. "Now untie her feet."

Floyd stepped around the chair. "You better not shoot me in the back."

"I won't as long as you don't try anything funny," Alex said.

The man stooped down and began unwinding rope from Libby's ankles.

Out of the corner of Alex's eye, he caught a movement. "Watch him, Lee."

She stepped closer to Bubba. "Get your hand away from your pocket or I'll shoot your other arm."

Bubba grimaced. "Hell, my arm's still sore from the last time, you know."

Finally the ropes dropped from Libby's ankles. Libby stood and took a deep breath. "Laura, I owe you two my life. She rushed forward to hug Lee."

A rustle to one side alerted Alex. He turned and pointed his gun at Bubba, who now sported a 357 magnum.

Bubba's laugh grated on Alex's nerves. "We could just shoot it out, an' maybe both end up dead, but I want to hang around, you know."

Alex shifted so he could see both men. Floyd grabbed Lee's arm, the one with the gun, and twisted it behind her. She struggled. Her gun clattered to the floor.

Floyd snatched it up. "Now we got two guns to your one. That puts us ahead, wouldn't you say, Bubba?"

"Yeah, but I'm not takin' no chances." Bubba waved his gun at Alex. "Okay, Buster. Put the gun down, nice and easy."

"What's to stop me from shooting one of you instead?"

"I could shoot Laura Lee."

"You don't want her dead before the trial. That will make you look guilty."

Bubba pointed his gun at Alex's chest. "Wouldn't mind plugging you though. Rid the world of your ugly puss."

"At least I don't have a nose like a pig."

Bubba's hand moved toward his nose, then dropped. "Leave my nose out of this."

Alex lunged forward, knocking the gun from Bubba's hand. Grabbing Bubba's arm, he pulled him off balance, shoving the big man to the floor. Alex kicked his head, making it bounce. One "Ooof" from Bubba, and he was silent.

Alex straightened just in time to see Floyd's gun pointed at him. As it went off, he swerved to one side. The explosion jarred his eardrums. A searing pain burned its way across his left arm.

He aimed his gun, but Floyd was holding Lee in front of him.

Libby rushed in front of Lee. What was she trying to do— get herself killed? She grabbed Bubba's gun off the floor and pointed it at Floyd. She held it in both hands. "Let go of my sister, or I'll shoot."

Floyd held his gun against Lee's back. "You do, and your sister gets it."

Libby's hands trembled. She hesitated.

Alex moved sideways. Floyd pivoted just enough to keep Lee at risk if Alex fired. She struggled, but the man held on.

From the floor Bubba gripped Alex's left leg. Alex tried to shake loose.

Lee broke free. Alex aimed low. He didn't want to kill Floyd, just disable him. He squeezed the trigger. The blast was deafening in the small office.

Floyd cursed, grabbed his leg with one hand, and then swung the gun in Alex's direction.

Alex tensed and shot again, hitting Floyd in the side. Floyd dropped the gun and grabbed his side. The gun skittered along the floor. Lee wrenched loose and grabbed the gun.

Alex felt Bubba grab him around the middle in a vice-like grip.

124

At the sound of footsteps, Alex jerked his head. Lee had her gun back—must have snatched it from Libby.

She faced him and Bubba. "Okay, let him loose or I'll let you have it."

"You know, I believe you would." He swung Alex in front of him. "Want to chance killing him?"

Lee stepped to the side, but Bubba moved too. Alex struggled, but couldn't shake the heavier guy. She aimed the gun down.

"Lee, keep that gun trained on him."

Lee pulled the trigger. The blast nearly deafened Alex, but the python-like grip loosened. He broke free.

Bubba's face contorted. "You hit my foot." He cursed. "You should have died in that apartment explosion. I'd have been long gone and wouldn't have to explain that to the cops."

Lee pointed the gun at Bubba's chest.

Floyd's arm crooked around Libby's neck. "Don't you try anything or I'll hurt her."

Libby swallowed convulsively and moaned, but raised her foot.

Alex clamped his mouth shut as Libby slammed her heel down on Floyd's foot, then pivoted and kneed him in the groin.

Floyd doubled over in obvious pain.

Lee poked her gun into Bubba's flabby middle. "Move. Sit in that chair."

He scowled at her but edged toward the nearest chair.

"Well done," came a voice at the door. Joe strode in, followed by an Arnold Schwarzenegger type. "Looks like you didn't need us Marshals after all. We'll take these scumbags into custody so they won't annoy you anymore." He pulled a pair of handcuffs from his pocket and marched toward Bubba. The other Marshal grabbed Floyd.

"About time you got here," said Alex. The jangling of the cuffs and the following snaps were welcome sounds. Alex leaned against a desk, suddenly exhausted.

Joe cleared his throat. Joe Berg at your service. "I'll read them their rights, just in case the police forget." He turned to Lee. "Pay attention. I may need you as a witness."

He recited the Miranda phrases. Then the two of them marched Bubba and Floyd toward the hall. At the door Joe paused. "By supper time they'll be locked up in Lew Sterrett Jail."

"Wait a minute," said Alex. "How come you took so long to get here? Don't tell me it was traffic. We got here in plenty of time."

Bubba cut in, "Hey, you can't drag us off to jail without seeing to our wounds. They shot Floyd, too. Cripes, we could be bleeding inside, you know."

"Shut up," Joe barked. I'm sure they have bandages where you're going." He yanked a cell phone from his pocket and punched in some numbers. "This is Joe Berg of the U.S. Marshal's office. I have two kidnappers in custody. Send two policemen to La Paloma Plaza to pick them up."

Joe and his companion walked the two thugs out the door. "Keep an eye on them," he told his partner. Then he stepped back into the room. "For your information, my boss insisted on briefing me on proper procedure for this situation. Took longer than expected. Sorry, I wasn't here sooner." He glanced at Libby, and then lowered his voice. "Take her to a hotel." He handed Libby a card. "Call me in the morning. I can arrange something for you by then if you think you need it."

After they left, Libby hugged Lee. "I was so scared we'd all die." She looked at Alex. "You were wonderful. Are you Lee's bodyguard?"

He shook his head. "No, just someone who rescues her from dangerous men and friends with more on their mind than friendship." He glanced at Lee and winked. "Name's Alex by the way. Alex Brandon. Pleased to meet you." He stuck out his hand. "Sorry, guess I'm supposed to wait until you offer yours. I'll never get the hang of this politically correct stuff."

Libby shook his hand. "That's okay. You saved Laura Lee and me. I'm glad to know you."

After Alex scrubbed his arm in the men's room, Libby gave him directions to the house in Dallas that she and Lee had shared before Lee went into the Witness Security Program.

On the way they passed a bakery. "Stop," Lee said. "I need to get something."

"Can't it wait until we get back?" Alex asked.

Lee shook her head. "I should have taken care of this yesterday, but with Libby being in danger I forgot."

Alex frowned, but stepped on the brakes. The car jerked to a stop. "Okay, but be quick about it."

"Can I borrow ten dollars? You can take it out of my first paycheck."

He frowned, but yanked out his billfold and handed her a bill.

Lee ran into the bakery. "Can you write letters to spell Elizabeth on a dozen cupcakes real quick?"

The pudgy young clerk wiped her hands on the white apron enveloping her, then nodded and set to work, holding her mouth in a tight line.

By the time the girl got to the letter 'T,' Alex was honking the horn. Lee stuck her head out of the door and said, "Just a minute."

The clerk squirted rosettes on the last three cakes and packed them in a box.

"Thanks," Lee said. She took the box and plunked down the ten dollars. "Keep the change."

Lee hurried back to the car, yanked open the door, and saw Alex's frown.

"What took so long?"

"I had to get something." She handed Libby the white cardboard box. "Happy Birthday."

Libby opened it. "Oh, sis. You remembered."

Lee grinned. "It's not much after the horrible way you spent the day. Maybe you can munch on these instead of dwelling on what happened."

When they reached the house, Lee held the box of cupcakes while Libby got out. Then she opened the door and handed the box to her sister. Lee stepped out to hug her shoulders.

Libby whispered, "That's some guy. Hang onto him."

"He's just looking out for me. I'm going to work as his secretary—until he can get his travel agency started. Except I'm afraid I've kept him pretty busy protecting me from Bubba."

Libby looked at her quizzically. "I saw the way he looks at you. Why else would a guy starting a new business spend all this time helping someone he doesn't care about? Sure there's not something between you?"

"Can't be. I may have to leave at a moment's notice. And he's just gone through a divorce. He hasn't even gotten a copy of the decree yet. I hope she doesn't think I'm the other woman."

Alex honked the horn, and the window slid down. "Libby, would you hurry up and pack? Lee and I have a long drive ahead."

Libby leaned down to talk to Alex. "Sure you don't want to come in and get some antiseptic on your arm?"

He shook his head. "For all we know, someone may have followed us here."

Lee looked around. "I don't see anyone."

"A good tail would park around the corner and stand behind a tree or a bush to watch."

Lee marched around the car and pulled the door open. "It won't take a minute to swab your arm." She grabbed his wrist. "Come on."

"Now, who's being bossy?"

"It's only common sense to disinfect a wound."

"Since when have you used common sense? If you'd stayed put and waited until I returned to get your things before going back to your apartment—"

She frowned. "And we might both have been killed." She dragged him toward the house.

At the door he asked, "This where you grew up?"

She nodded. "My dad died last year. He willed us the house."

In the bathroom she ran the water until it was warm. Taking his arm, she marveled at its muscled hardness. The tangy scent of his aftershave made her intensely aware of his nearness. Sponging away crusted blood, she tried to be as gentle as she could. He didn't even flinch.

She pulled out some mercurochrome. "Sorry, this is all I can find." With a Q-tip she applied antiseptic until his arm sported a large orange splotch.

"Now that you've branded me, can we go?"

She shook her head, got out a large gauze pad and fastened it with adhesive tape. "Hope that doesn't ooze."

"It wouldn't dare. Not after you've taken such good care of me." He squeezed her hand and gave her a look that made her heart zing. He kissed her, his lips lingering on hers. Then he met her gaze. "Thanks for the fix-up, but we need to get going."

In the hallway he paused at the doorway of a bedroom. "This your room?"

"Yes, or it was—before I had to leave."

"Anything you want to take with you?"

Inside Lee glanced at the picture of herself and a date at the senior prom. That seemed eons ago. "Just a few things."

She grabbed a small tote bag from her closet. As she picked up a matching black bra and panty set made almost entirely of lace, she heard him behind her and turned.

He grinned. "I can't wait to see you in that."

"If you think I'm going to parade around in your trailer in these, you've got another think coming."

He sighed. "A guy can hope."

"Forget it. I appreciate your protection, but—look, you've

got a business to set up, and a daughter to take care of. And I don't want to stand between you and a possible reconciliation."

He shook his head. "No way. It's over, and we both know it."

Seeing his scowl, Lee dropped the subject. Giving in to impulse, she stuffed the little white bear with a red ribbon that her father had given her in her tote bag. His head with black glass eyes peeked out the top. "Okay, I'm ready," she said, hoping Alex wouldn't tease her for bringing it.

Libby stood at the front door with an overnight bag. Lee hugged her sister. "I'm sorry to make you leave home, but I can't let Sheldon get away with this."

"It will only be until the trial, and I'm sure your marshal friend will take care of me." Libby grasped Alex's hand. "Thanks again for rescuing me."

Alex smiled. "According to Lee, you're worth it. Come on, Lee. Sheldon may have some other goons hanging around."

They let Libby out in front of a Courtyard Marriot. Alex and Lee followed them inside. Alex insisted on checking the place out.

Lee waited in the doorway but kept an eye on the hall. She'd sure caused Alex a lot of trouble. Knowing he had to get his business going, she felt a little guilty for delaying him. She'd put him in danger rescuing Libby. And Tanya would tell her mother all about their day at the lake and that he'd kissed her at least twice. No doubt that would cause an ugly row.

Remembering the intensity of their last kiss in the elevator, she could have sworn Alex cared about her. Had he been letting her know he cared in case he got killed? He very well might have been. She shuddered.

Back at the car, Alex slid behind the wheel and glanced her way. "Are you cold?"

She shook her head. "Just thinking about what might have happened if Joe hadn't come along."

He frowned. "I thought I had the situation pretty well in hand."

"You mean we had the situation pretty well in hand."

He didn't say anything.

"Aren't you going to say you couldn't have done it without me?"

"I'm sure I could have."

"Men."

He reached out and took her hand. "Okay, you helped some. What's important is that you and Libby got out safely."

Alex stared straight ahead, his hands gripping the wheel. "Joe sure had a half-baked excuse for taking so long to get there."

"I remember him telling me that his boss is very meticulous about details and proper procedure. Maybe Joe had to explain his plans for every possible scenario."

"I'm glad he wasn't my boss. In the CIA they give us credit for figuring out what to do. In tense situations, we didn't have time to confer with anyone stateside or otherwise." He shook his head. "Can't figure out how those U.S. Marshals get anything done."

Alex didn't say much on the ride back to the trailer park. By the time she emerged from taking a shower, he was in his robe. Royal blue and knotted about his waist, it hugged his hips and thighs—like she wished she could—bad idea—she needed to leave soon so he'd be safe.

He smiled and patted her arm. "Good night. I'm going to bed."

The sky was clear and covered with stars but he hadn't even mentioned going out to look at them or suggested kissing her good night. Either he was more disciplined than she—or he really didn't care that much. If he did, he probably had just as hard a time resisting her as she did staying away from him.

She crawled between the sheets of his bed. If only the trial would be over soon so she could move back home. But what if they didn't convict Sheldon? She gulped. They had to. With the testimony she'd give, conviction should be a sure thing—shouldn't it?

A chill cascaded down her spine. She and Libby might never be able to be safe in their house. She couldn't stay with Alex forever. Snuggling into the pillow, she wished for his warm sandpaper cheek against hers instead of the cool percale pillowcase.

❦

Lying on the hide-a-bed, Alex rubbed his aching shoulders. He couldn't get comfortable. Maybe a walk outside would help. He threw off the sheet, slipped out of bed and tiptoed to the door of the bedroom. Hoping Lee wouldn't wake, he rummaged in his drawers by the light of the moon for a pair of pajama bottoms and yanked them on.

Lee lay curled up on one side of the bed, the sheet awry, covering her only to her waist. Her cotton nightgown strained against her breasts which moved with each deep breath. He wanted to slide in behind her, put an arm around her waist, and feel her bottom close against him.

Kathy never wanted to cuddle in bed. Oh, she'd take part vigorously when they made love. Afterwards she'd scurry to the shower as if she couldn't wait to wash off the feel of him. And later all he'd gotten were excuses—she was too hot, or too tired, or too sleepy.

He wanted Lee with an ache that was more than just physical. And he wanted her to want him the way he hungered for her. He'd failed at one marriage. Could he ever be successful with another woman?

A sigh from Lee pulled his attention back to her. She turned over and shivered, but didn't waken. He grasped the sheet to pull it up.

The bodice of her nightgown slid open, revealing a creamy expanse of one breast. He took a deep breath and tried to still the desire stirring in his loins. His fingers itched to touch her enticing curves.

She'd be shocked if he gave in to his impulses and pulled her into his arms. She'd probably push him away, but what if she didn't?

Chapter 13

Standing by the bedside, Alex leaned closer and inhaled her delicate scent. Perhaps if he kissed her, gently at first...her lips might meld with his and hopefully with hot kisses.

Surely, she couldn't deny the sparks that zinged whenever they got near each other. She kept trying to evade him, but her kisses gave her away. No woman had ever stirred him like she did.

He imagined sinking into her warm velvet softness, feeling her arms around him as she met his surges. Some day maybe they could share a life together...yeah, in his dreams. He sighed.

He should leave now. He dropped the sheet over her shoulders, but couldn't resist giving her a gentle kiss on her cheek.

Still feeling the softness of her cheek against his lips, he tiptoed out the bedroom door. He needed a breeze to cool off.

Outside he paced, and then circled the mobile home. Stars twinkled and crickets sang in the deepening blackness. A dog howled at the moon. Loneliness washed over him. In the CIA, adrenaline spurred him on whenever he ferreted out secrets or tracked his quarries through teeming crowds and steamy jungles. That was a high like no other.

The thrill of the chase made clambering up rocky mountainsides easy. By the time he flung himself on a bed in a mountain chalet or hotel room, he'd been too tired to be lonely.

Kathy had complained bitterly about his being away so much, but she'd had Tanya to keep her company. And the sex, when they had it was over too soon and somehow not as satisfying as before. Had she been pulling away, and he hadn't noticed it?

Now if his new business weren't successful, he'd have to sell the lake cottage his uncle willed him. He winced at the thought. He'd like to take Lee there, even if only for the day.

Why hadn't he met Lee first, instead of Kathy? But then he wouldn't have had Tanya, or enjoyed her freckle-faced enthusiasm when he took her swimming or riding in a boat. He would have missed the satisfying way she snuggled up against him when he read her bedtime stories.

He cursed himself for spending so much time away from Kathy and their daughter. Poor Tanya must be all mixed up by now, wondering if he were going to present her with a new mom. Or if Kathy were going to spring a new dad on her, or worse, a series of 'uncles.'

❦

Inside, Lee stirred. She'd been dreaming that Alex was saying goodbye to her, that he'd decided to try to patch up his marriage. His gentle good-bye kiss on her cheek had felt so real.

Something rustled. She rose, padded to the bedroom door, and opened it a crack. Moonlight streamed in the open door to the mobile home. Alex was nowhere to be seen.

Lee pushed the bedroom door open wider and peered into the living area. The swath of moonlight from the open door pierced the darkness. A cool breeze fanned her face. Traffic hummed from the highway a mile or so away. From somewhere close came the soft hoot of an owl.

Where was Alex? And why was the front door open?

Something rustled. Her heart pounded as she peered into murky darkness. There was that sound again. She held her breath. Was someone out there?

She tried to filter out the buzz of katydids and crickets. Outside a twig snapped—or was it the click of someone cocking a gun? Had Bubba or another of Sheldon's men found them?

Her senses sprung to alertness. Again she stared into the dark shadows. Nothing moved. Her imagination must be working double time.

Before she lost her nerve, she slipped into her robe and tiptoed to the open doorway, her pulse pounding. A breeze chilled her.

Shielded by the lacy shadow of a mesquite tree, Alex sat in a plastic lawn chair. She let out a sigh of relief, but was she really safe here?

It wasn't fair. She'd tried to do the right thing by offering to testify. She wanted to topple Bart Sheldon's small time mafia operation, but look where it had gotten her. Now that she'd met a man who appealed to her, she couldn't ask him to share the dangers she faced. And though she adored children, she couldn't chance having one traumatized like Libby had been by the loss of a mother. She squeezed her eyes shut, tried to block out the memory of Libby slumped in a chair, her hands and feet bound.

Alex had been wonderful, but from now on she needed to keep their relationship strictly business—not think about how appealing he was. Besides, even if she were not putting him in danger, she mustn't dwell on that kiss in the elevator, the kiss that had seared her lips, set her heart thrumming, and made her wish things could be different.

She had a new life to look forward to in the fall, new challenges, and new friends. But if she stepped outside, Alex would consider that an invitation. She had to remember he was only her employer — and her protector — and only for the time being.

The scrape of a chair on concrete spurred her to hurry back to bed. She scrambled under the covers, pretended to be asleep.

Footsteps sounded, then a knock on the open door. "Not so fast, Lee. I know you're not asleep." His deep seductive voice pulled at her resolve.

She squeezed her eyes shut and burrowed into the pillow to blot out his tempting voice. His footsteps came closer. He grasped her wrist and pulled her to a sitting position.

The sheet slipped away, and her robe parted. Cool air seeped through her thin gown. His dark soulful eyes seemed to devour her, bringing a disturbing warmth to her breasts. She jerked free and tucked the sheet under her arms.

"Relax," he said. I'm not going to move in on you. That's not my style." His brows drew together. Fingering the sleeve of her robe, he said, "Looks like you couldn't sleep either." He sat on the bed. "Let's talk."

She swallowed. He was so near she could smell the citrusy tang of his aftershave. His breaths feathered the hair at her temples. "Talk? About the business?"

He shook his head. "About us."

"There is no 'us.' There can't be."

"You're right. I'm not exactly free. Kathy said she gave the divorce decree I signed to her lawyer, but I've yet to receive a copy. Besides, I've a kid that depends on me. About that kiss in the elevator. I don't want you to get the wrong idea. It won't happen again."

"Are you...are you saying you don't like kissing me?" Now why had she blurted that out?. Her face grew hot.

"Hell, no." He took hold of her hand and caressed her palm, sending a delightful warmth through her. "It's all I can do to leave you alone." His face took on a serious look. "I've faced a lot of tense situations where I had to block out my emotions. That time in the elevator...I was afraid they'd kill one or both of us. I wanted you to know someone cared just in case—well, just in case."

His words warmed her heart. She smiled and squeezed his hand. Could he tell how wonderful that made her feel?

He let go of her hand. "Even if I were sure my divorce were final, it's not fair to lead you on. You deserve more than a rebound romance."

"So, we're going to work together and pretend we're...not—" she swallowed, "not attracted to each other?"

"Right." He stood, his body ramrod straight, his chin jutting out at a determined angle. "It will be easier that way. Just forget I ever kissed you."

No way could she do that. The memory of his hungry mouth on hers, the way she'd felt cherished and desired washed over her. Why couldn't she control her emotions like he did? She didn't want to forget that kiss. She met his gaze. Something in his sea-blue eyes said he didn't want to forget it either.

His voice softened. "I'm going to bed, but first I'll check outside. Sleep well." Seconds later the front door slammed.

She went to the window and peered out. He was pacing outside. She shed her robe, crawled back into bed, and snuggled against the pillow.

She wouldn't dream of him, wouldn't imagine his lips pressed against hers, wouldn't think about his hands caressing her shoulders, or pulling her against his hard body. Turning over, she squeezed her eyes shut. She tried to visualize herself in a sunny meadow, leaning against a tree and listening to the birds.

He slipped into her vision, sliding an arm around her waist, kissing her on the mouth. She licked her lips. This was no good.

She tried counting sheep. First one jumped over a fence, then two, then four. But they all had Alex's face. How absurd, she thought, as she smiled and nestled into the pillow.

Early next morning, the phone rang, startling her. She

threw the covers off, and tried to guess where the sound came from.

Alex rushed in and grabbed the phone from under her robe on the bedside table. "Hello," he said and stepped into the hallway.

Oh no, not another argument with his ex-wife. His "Hi, Mom," reassured her. She pulled the covers back up and shut her eyes.

It seemed like only a short while later he was shaking her shoulder. She opened her eyes to bright sunlight. She felt as if she'd only slept two winks. Groggy, she slid out of bed. Noticing his appreciative glance at her clinging gown, she turned her face to hide a smile as she grabbed her robe.

His expression was all business. "Get dressed. I—we have to go pick up Danny, and I'm not leaving you here alone."

"Who's Danny."

"My sister's kid."

"Why are we going to pick him up?"

"Mom's working at a church bazaar in Ennis until some time tonight, and can't find a sitter. I didn't want to explain about you or why I can't leave you here alone. Now get dressed."

He was ordering her around again. She frowned but held her tongue. She did need to get dressed.

Later, he held open the car door. "That green blouse looks good on you."

"Thanks," she said, smiling as she slid into the Jaguar's seat.

On the drive to Ennis, he didn't say much. Finally, he glanced her way. "Sorry if I seem to be ignoring you. I've got some decisions to make."

"But it's Saturday. You don't need to be a workaholic."

"In the CIA I had to make thorough plans and back-up ones as well. My missions depended on it."

"Planning well is good, but you need to have a life, too."

He looked at her and grinned. "And you want to see that I have one, is that it?"

"Well—I'd like to see you lighten up a bit."

"Okay, for the rest of today, I'll try to forget about the business."

"Good."

"I found your suggestions about the business helpful, by the way."

She smiled. He'd actually paid her two compliments in less than an hour.

An hour later they arrived at a church bustling with women getting ready for a bazaar. Alex entered a room and brought out a wriggling toddler, who was just learning to walk. His big blue eyes and wavy brown hair resembled Alex's. The boy took off down the hall toward a fountain.

After stumbling over his feet, he picked himself up and looked around. Obviously conscious of Lee and Alex hurrying toward him, he whimpered. "Hurt."

Lee started toward him to pick him up, but Alex held her back. "I've seen him jump right up without crying when he thinks no one is watching. He'll be all right."

She glared at him. "A little comfort won't spoil him." She picked him up, brushed off his knee and kissed it. "That will make it well."

Danny's smile melted her heart. "Down," he begged.

Lee set him on his feet, and he took off again, only to stop when he got to the water fountain. "Dink, dink," he said. Alex picked Danny up and held him so he could drink.

After a hamburger and fries at a McDonald in Ennis, Lee suggested they take Danny to the park. "It's Saturday, and there'll be plenty of people there. Surely, Bubba and Floyd won't be able to get out on bond this quickly."

Before getting out of the car, Alex scanned the area. Adults pushed swings in the warm breeze or helped little ones climb to the top of the slide. After they stepped from the car, Danny walked to an empty swing and grabbed the chain. Alex set him in it and pushed him for a while.

Later a soft breeze lifted Lee's hair as she pushed Danny in the swing. The fresh smell of green grass wafted by. Danny's chortles of glee played counterpoint to the ever changing tunes of a mockingbird and a nearby gurgling brook.

She thought she saw a face, one with a scar that she recognized, but the man turned and walked away. She tapped Alex on the shoulder. "I think I saw someone from Sheldon's business. It looked like Floyd. He's the one who helped Bubba abduct Libby."

Instantly alert, Alex plucked Danny from the swing. "We need to leave."

She grabbed the diaper bag. "Then you'll take us back to the trai—"

He frowned and placed a finger to his lips, then leaned closer and whispered, "Don't mention where we live. Someone may be listening."

She looked for the man she'd noticed earlier. He was gone.

At the car Alex strapped Danny into a car seat, and then got behind the wheel. "Watch for someone following." Their drive back was laced with twists and turns for the car and for Lee's neck as she craned it to watch for a tail. She hoped her neck wouldn't be stiff later.

By the time they reached the trailer, Danny had fallen asleep. She carried him inside. If she bore Alex a son, he might look like this. Now why was she thinking about that? She and Alex had no future together, and she didn't intend to have a baby and worry about it being in danger.

Danny yawned and snuggled his warm body against her. How warm and trusting he was—and how good it felt to hold him. If only things were different....

Inside she heated a can of soup. When she tried spooning warm soup into Danny's mouth, he kept grabbing the spoon. Finally she let him have it and listened to the wind slapping the tree branches. Intermittent thunder followed lightning flashes. The sky grew even darker. Hating storms, she shivered.

Danny's eyes drooped as she sponged soup from his face.

"Sing," he begged sleepily as his head slumped lower.

Alex smiled and gently ruffled the toddler's hair. "He likes to have his grandmother sing him to sleep. It would be easier to drive him back if he's sleeping. Maybe the thunder and lightning won't make him cry."

"He'll fall asleep sooner if I rock him." After picking Danny up, she settled in a rocking chair. He snuggled against her shoulder, his plump form somehow comforting.

Danny pulled on her arm. "Sing."

She leaned close to his ear and sang quietly. "The itsy bitsy spider climbed up the water spout."

His face broke into smiles, but soon his eyelids drooped. He snuggled in her arms. He felt so warm and cuddly. What would it be like to hold Alex's baby close? She laid him on the sofa, surprised to miss the toddler's comforting warmth. Then she moved a chair alongside so he wouldn't fall.

"Alex," she whispered, "can you keep an eye on him while I wash my hair? If I don't start now, there won't be time for it to dry before bedtime."

He looked up from a magazine. "Sure."

Dressed in her robe, she was rubbing her hair dry when Alex knocked on the bathroom door.

She opened it a crack.

Alex said, "Get dressed. We've got to take Danny home now or Mom will worry."

"I don't want to meet your mother with my hair like this."

He smiled. "It will dry by the time we get there."

"Can I just stay in the car while you take him inside?"

"Probably not. My mother will insist on meeting you."

"Can't I just stay here"

"I don't want to leave you alone."

"Surely, I'll be okay until you get back."

He frowned. His phone rang, and he reached for it.

"Hello," he said, then listened. "I'll be right there." Clicking the phone off, he turned to her. "Someone called from the hospital. A buddy I worked with overseas is there recovering from plastic surgery. Someone sneaked in his room and shot him. Sam's a tough old bird, but they're afraid he won't last much longer. I have to go see him tonight. I'll be back soon."

"Will you—will you be in danger? What if the shooter comes back to finish the job?"

"Not likely. They called the police. Don't think you and Danny will be in danger either, not in the short time I'll be gone. It's not dark yet, and there are neighbors around."

He pulled her into his arms. Crushing her breasts against his firm chest, he kissed her, setting her mouth and her insides on fire.

She ought to break away, but she felt so good in his arms she couldn't bring herself to. Good thing he was leaving. She didn't know if she could resist him if he wanted more.

He drew a deep breath and broke away. "I wasn't going to do that again." But his eyes said he didn't regret it. "Lock up after I leave, and don't let anyone in."

She bristled. "You think I'm stupid?"

He strode toward the bedroom, his brisk footsteps echoing from the hallway. He returned with a cordless phone and thrust it into her hand. He scribbled on a piece of paper. "This is my cell phone number." He stuffed it in her jeans pocket. "Use it if you need me. I'll be back before you know it."

He yanked the door open. "When I come back, you're coming with me when I take Danny home."

His gaze burned into hers, as if he were trying to tell her how much he wanted to find her safe when he returned, but couldn't or wouldn't say the words. Then he waved and shut the door behind him. Heavy footsteps marked his stride to the curb. His car roared away, leaving an empty silence.

She stood there, her lips still burning from his kiss. Sam

must be a very good friend. Alex hadn't said as much, but she was sure he'd been looking forward to spending the rest of the evening together as much as she, even if all they did was talk.

A wail from Danny drew her attention. She picked him up and rocked him until he went back to sleep.

By seven Alex still hadn't returned. What could be keeping him? Outside, the sky darkened and thunder rumbled. The wind whistled and dashed the branches of the half-grown sweet gum tree against the thin walls. She hoped a tornado didn't come by. She'd heard mobile homes didn't stand up to the force of the wind. Frequent glances out the window didn't reassure her.

Restless, she picked up a magazine and sat on the end of the couch. Something bumped against the outside wall of the mobile home. She froze. There were no windows on that side of the room.

Couldn't be Alex. He had a key. Could Bubba be out on bail already?

She picked up Danny, grabbed the phone, and tiptoed to the bedroom. Once there, she laid the sleeping Danny on the bed and looked toward the window. A shadow moved past it. Scrunching up against the wall, she yanked the piece of paper from her pocket, and dialed.

"Alex here. That you, Lee?" Static made him hard to hear.

"Someone's walking around outside the trailer. I'm afraid he'll try to break in."

"I'm five minutes away. Dial 9-1-1." The line went dead.

With trembling fingers she dialed 9-1-1, and was rewarded to hear a dispatcher's voice. In a whisper she explained what was happening.

The dispatcher made her repeat it louder. She kept her voice low, hoping the man outside wouldn't hear, and then said she didn't know the address.

"That's okay, we have it," the woman said.

Someone knocked. She hoped he'd give up if no one answered. She waited and tried to still her trembling.

The sound of someone jiggling the doorknob outside made her heart pound. Why hadn't Alex or the police gotten here by now?

She couldn't let anyone hurt Danny. Where could she hide? Her eyes raked the bedroom. This place was so small—no nooks to hide in. Was the closet big enough?

Hoping she wasn't visible from the window, she edged along the wall to the closet door and opened it. She grabbed Danny. Still asleep, thank goodness. She held him tight and slid inside. She pulled the door almost shut. Danny's warm breaths washed over her cheeks. Her heart pounded fast and furiously.

Outside a twig snapped. Sounded like someone scraping by between the bushes and the side of the trailer.

She held her breath, listened. Her pulse raced. How could she protect Danny if that guy broke in? Wriggling around in the tiny space, she laid the child down. Prayed he wouldn't wake. Hoped Alex got there quickly.

She peeked through the crack in the door, saw a face at the bedroom window. Heart pounding, she swallowed a gasp. What if he broke in and took them hostage? How could she escape with a baby to carry?

The shadowed head looked thinner than Bubba's. Was that Floyd she'd caught a glimpse of in the park? Or just a run-of-the-mill burglar? She hoped the guy didn't have a gun. What if he were an escaped prisoner? She shuddered.

The shadow disappeared. She let out her breath and waited to hear footsteps leaving.

The front door handle jiggled again. Her insides knotted. The sound of breaking glass jolted her. She stifled a scream.

Chapter 14

From the closet where she hid, Lee heard glass crashing onto the floor. The next thing she heard must be the front door creaking open. She held her breath. What if Danny cried out? That guy would be on them in seconds.

Heart pounding, she listened for footsteps, heavy breathing, a cough—anything to tell her where the intruder was. Should have grabbed the phone before she crawled in here.

One footstep sounded, then another. Something fell with a clunk. Her throat constricted until she could hardly breathe.

Something rustled. What was he looking for?

More noise followed, then heavier footsteps. Were there two of them? Clenching her hands into fists, she strained to hear.

"Hold it right there."

Alex! Thank the Lord. But could he subdue the burglar?

"Let go, damn it," another voice snarled. She let out her breath. Alex was back, but would the burglar be intimidated?

"Let go, damn it," the intruder said. "You're gonna break my arm."

"Don't move, or I'll shoot."

She laid Danny on the floor, edged from the closet and moved to the door of the bedroom, hoping she could peek without being seen. But when she got there, she couldn't see either of them. Alex didn't need distracting. She ducked back.

Someone dragged something heavy across the floor. She hoped that wasn't Alex.

She heard a click. It sounded like a safety being released or a trigger readied. Which was it?

She held her breath.

"Lee," Alex called. "I have him subdued. Call 9-1-1."

She hurried into the living room.

The intruder was Floyd, the man she'd seen in the park. He must have gotten out on bail. Perhaps Bubba was, too. A shiver rolled down her spine.

Alex had Floyd in a choke-hold. The scar curving around his cheek stood out. "The phone's over there." Alex angled his head toward a phone on the wall in the kitchen area. She grabbed it and dialed. Three tones sounded. At least the line hadn't been cut.

She heard scuffling behind her and turned. Thank goodness, Alex still held Floyd in a tight grip.

"Hold the phone to my ear," Alex said. She did.

Alex listened, then said, "I want to report a break-in. I'm holding the guy now. Send someone to pick him up." He looked at Lee. "Stay on the line with the dispatcher and answer any questions she has."

A distant siren sounded. Could Alex hold the burglar until they came?

The siren's wail grew louder.

A car screeched to a stop. "That can't be the police already. There hasn't been time."

Two sets of footsteps approached. Someone knocked.

She crossed her fingers, hoping the new arrivals were cops.

"Police. Open up."

She rushed to let the two uniformed officers in. "How'd you get here so fast?"

"We were cruising by when the dispatcher alerted us to your situation," said the taller cop. "Now, which one of you reported a break-in?" he asked.

"I did," Alex said. "My name's Alex Brandon. I caught this guy searching my place. He was arrested for kidnapping Lee's sister, but he must have gotten out on bail."

The shorter cop grasped their skinny intruder by the arm.

"Mr. Brandon," the cop barked, "do you have some ID?"

Alex pulled out his wallet and flipped it open to show a driver's license.

The shorter officer holding the other man said, "Okay, bub, what were you doing in this man's trailer?"

Floyd shoved a greasy lock of hair from his eyes. "Lost my key. Thought this was my place."

"The hell you did," said Alex.

"You're under arrest for breaking and entering," the cop barked.

"You have the right to remain silent...." The officer continued reciting the Miranda spiel.

Following the snap of handcuffs, Lee let out a sigh of relief as the two officers marched Floyd out.

Sheldon had sent Floyd this time, but he could have several people on the outside working for him. She might not recognize the next person who was a threat. She shuddered. Would she ever be safe?

"Lee," Alex called. "Is Danny okay?"

She nodded. "He's asleep on the closet floor."

"Why in the closet?"

"I was hiding there with him after I heard noises."

"Thank goodness you're all right. When I didn't hear you, I was afraid I'd find you unconscious—" he swallowed, "or dead. Thank the Lord, I got here when I did."

He drew a deep breath, then hugged her.

She leaned into his strength. "I shudder to think what would have happened if he found me and Danny."

He squeezed her again, and then leaned against the wall. "I never should have left you alone."

A shiver ran down her spine. "I was so scared he'd find us."

He slumped in a chair, his head in his hands. "Guess keeping you here wasn't such a hot idea."

He rubbed the back of his neck. He looked miserable.

Lee swallowed. "You couldn't help it if Floyd came here."

His head shot up. "Damn it, I didn't see anyone following when we left the park. That Floyd's sharp when it comes to loose tailing. You'd better ask Joe to find you another place to stay. Will he find you another job if he moves you?"

She shook her head. "That's not what the Witness Security Program does. I have to find one on my own. But don't worry. I'll manage somehow. I'm sorry Floyd smashed the window in your door, but I don't think he broke anything else. He didn't have much time to search before you came."

Alex looked around. "The only things messed up are some papers I have lying around. Have you ever seen him before he helped kidnap your sister?"

She nodded. "He came into Sheldon's office once or twice. I'm sure he was the man I saw watching us in the park. I was supposed to be moved to another town in the fall, but I guess that can't wait."

He frowned. "You expected me to spend all this time breaking you in, and then you'd run out," he snapped his fingers, "just like that."

"Well...I could train a new secretary for you."

He scowled. "Why didn't you tell me before?"

"I figured I was being paranoid about someone coming after me." She looked away. "I was going to tell you, but I just hadn't gotten around to it."

"But I thought that maybe after the trial was over, you and I...." He rested his head in his hands. "I don't know why I haven't received a copy of my divorce decree yet. I'm afraid Kathy might have changed her mind again. It took forever for us to agree on dividing our stuff, but I'm paying generous child support. I love my daughter. I want her to have everything she needs."

"Everything except a home with a mother and a father?"

He frowned. "You speak your mind, don't you?"

"Is there a chance you and Kathy might patch things up? I've heard it's better for the children if couples stay together until they're grown." She had a new job to look forward to in a different town. Reconciliation would be good for Alex and Tanya, but now she wished she hadn't mentioned it.

His eyes looked sad. "Kathy and I—we can't talk for five minutes without arguing. It wouldn't work."

Going back with his ex-wife might be better for Tanya, but from what he'd just said about Kathy, it couldn't be the best thing for him, and besides, she wanted to be the one to make him happy.

"Get dressed. We need to take Danny back, and this time you're coming with me."

"My hair isn't dry yet."

"I won't take you in to meet Mom unless you want to."

"Okay."

Alex glanced outside. "The storm's blown over. Grab your bathing suit. I know a place where we can go swimming on the way back."

"Where?"

"You'll see."

He picked up the sleeping toddler and carried him to the car. He barely came to when Alex fastened him in the car seat and promptly fell asleep as soon as they were on the way.

During the ride Alex was silent. She tried to think of a safe topic of conversation—one that didn't touch on their relationship—or rather, non relationship—it just wasn't possible.

She sighed. Too many things were working against their being together. She had to steel herself not to think about it. No use stewing about something that couldn't ever happen—but wouldn't it be nice and cozy if she and Alex could live safely in a little house somewhere with Tanya.

After they arrived at his mother's home, Alex wanted Lee to meet his mother, but she stayed in the car while Alex took Danny inside.

On the way back she found herself watching the sure way he handled the car, how his hands held the wheel with just the right firmness. One hand caressed the soft leather covering the wheel. She imagined those fingers warming her skin. She shouldn't let it happen. They had no future, but she was finding it harder and harder to act as if she weren't attracted to him. She cleared her throat. "When will you see Tanya again?"

"I'm supposed to get her for the month of August." He sighed. "I wish I could see her more often."

Half an hour later Alex turned off on a dirt road. The Jaguar took the washboard road in stride, but not without jarring her.

By the time he stopped at a cottage, she noticed it was getting quite dark. A light illuminated the sign hanging beside the door. It said, 'Ne'er a Dulmo.'

"Ne'er a Dulmo? Why is it called that?" Lee asked.

"It means, 'Never a dull moment'—we used to have a bunch of friends out here every weekend I was home. Lately we didn't come out here much."

He sighed. "Kathy got tired of cooking for a crowd. She preferred going out to a restaurant, the kind where they expect you to wear a suit and tie and charge you plenty."

He fingered his chin. "However, we did have some good times here. We'd dip Tanya into the water. She'd kick and giggle—so much fun to watch. I can still bring her here, but it won't be the same."

"Bet you miss those times."

Lee stepped out of the car. By the light of a full moon, she walked to the edge of a terrace. "I can really see the stars out here." A soft plop could have been a fish jumping. A bird added its warble to the sound of crickets and katydids. In the distance a train whistle sounded.

Alex came up behind her and slid his arms around her waist. She leaned back until her cheek touched his, hardly daring to breathe. She should remind him they'd decided not to give in to their attraction. She would…in a moment.

His cheek was warm and slightly rough. A breeze plastered a lock of her hair to her cheek. He smoothed it away. After turning her in his arms, he grasped her hand and placed it over his heart. The look in his eyes caught her in his spell.

Then he kissed her.

She quivered all the way to her toes. He cradled her face in his hands and planted kisses on her cheek, her forehead, and even her nose.

Laughing, she laced her fingers behind his head to pull his face down for another kiss. She couldn't seem to get enough of his sensuous mouth. She let her mouth say how she felt, say the words she couldn't, that he was beginning to mean a lot to her — that she didn't want to leave him, not now, not ever.

His hand strayed to her breast, caressing and squeezing. "Oh, Lee," he murmured. "I wish — "

She leaned into him, savoring the touch of his hands. His eyes seemed to burn with hunger, hunger for her. Knowing he desired her made her heart swell with joy. How she wished she could give herself to him, here and now — but she mustn't — they mustn't. How had Kathy managed to turn off such a passionate man?

Thrilled she was the one he seemed to want at the moment, Lee threw her arms around him and hugged him. His answering grip was so tight she could hardly breathe.

Then he grasped her arms and pulled them away.

Taken aback, she stared into his eyes, trying to read him.

He stepped back. "This is crazy. We've got to stop."

He was right. She'd draw danger to him, or to any man who got close. She sighed. "You said we could go swimming."

He nodded. "I-uh could use a dip to cool off."

He unlocked the cottage door. "Go change. Come out when you're done. Then I'll go in and put on my trunks."

Was he afraid to be alone in the cottage with her? She grabbed her tote bag and hurried inside. The moon lit the comfy living room enough so that she didn't need a light. Instead of going in the tiny bathroom, she dressed in the dark where she could look out the big picture window and see moonlight shimmer on the water.

She pulled up her bikini bottoms. The straps of the top were still knotted from the last time she went swimming. She stepped closer to the window to see better. Damn, the straps to go around her neck were knotted really tight.

*

Outside Alex strolled down the terrace steps and turned to pull up a thistle growing beside the steps. Rising, he glanced toward the picture window and caught a glimpse of Lee fiddling with her bathing suit top. Didn't she realize how visible the moonlight made her?

He stood there, taking in the vision of her soft round breasts, creamy white in the moonlight, her peaked nipples calling him like a beacon. His pants became unbearably tight.

He wouldn't compromise her, wouldn't lead her on. Hell, even if he had received that divorce decree and knew for sure he were free, he couldn't offer any promises. He'd be lucky if he managed to keep her safe until that damn marshal dragged her away to another town. He didn't want to think how drab his life would be without her.

She stepped closer to the window. Lord help him, he wanted to rush in, wanted to hold those lovely breasts in his hands and pull her close to feel her softness against his chest. More than anything, he wanted to sink into her warmth and make her his.

Inside, she slammed the top against her thighs, then pulled

it up. Apparently, she had given up on the knot. After tying the loose straps behind her back, she tucked the knotted ones inside her top.

Standing here watching her was madness.

Taking the steps to the terrace two at a time, he hurried to the car. After grabbing his trunks from the back seat, he yanked off his pants and briefs and pulled on his swim suit. Good thing the bushes hid him from prying eyes. Going down the steps, he unbuttoned his shirt, tossed it on the grass, and raced into the water. The cool water merely tamped the heat burning inside. He surged forward until he was deep enough to submerge his head and come up dripping.

Lee called from behind. "Why didn't you wait for me?"

Her pert breasts, now covered by her swim suit, shook slightly as she ran to the water's edge. He caught his breath, remembering their creamy whiteness. He'd thought submerging in the cool waters would dampen his feelings.

He was wrong.

He moved toward shore until he could take her hand. He led her out until the water reached her neck, then headed back. When he reached the place where the water was waist high, he noticed her shivering. "You're cold."

She nodded.

He put his arms around her, trying to infuse some of his heat into her body. She felt so soft and willing in his arms. She snuggled against him. He was getting aroused again. He drew a deep breath. Staying away from her was getting harder and harder, but he couldn't let desire rule him. She deserved better than a man who'd failed at marriage.

She sighed. "I'm going to get dressed." She jerked from his arms as if his touch burned her. His fingers caught in the straps behind her back, and the top gave way, baring her enticing breasts just as the moon emerged from behind a wispy cloud. His breath caught in his throat. She was even more beautiful up close in the full moonlight.

Hearing a rustle on shore, he pulled her to him. "Wait. I heard something."

She struggled in his arms, her soft breasts rubbing against his bare chest.

As she pulled away, a flash of light blinded him.

She screamed. Seconds later, another flash lit up the water around them. She ducked down in the water. He surged toward the shore, cursing the water for slowing his pace. A sinister laugh echoed across the water, followed by a man's voice. "Nice knockers."

A third flash came, then the sound of running footsteps.

Fists clenched, Alex raced after the guy. He had to catch that photographer, find out who sent him. Kathy wouldn't be likely to pay for surveillance after he'd signed the divorce decree, or would she? Must be someone Sheldon sent. That could be even worse.

Alex sprinted over sharp stones that hurt his feet and raced across the grass. His wet feet kept slipping on the short-cropped lawn. He reached the road in time to hear the thud of the man's rear against a motorcycle seat. Its motor roared to life, and the guy vanished into the darkness.

He cursed. With all the roads criss-crossing the lake area, he'd never find the guy even if he took off in the Jag. Besides, he couldn't leave Lee unprotected. He shook his fist after the guy.

Still scowling, he trudged down the slope. Lee sat on the dock, her top back in place and her arms clasped around her knees.

"He got away." Alex cursed himself for being careless. "Must have missed a tail on the way here." Was he losing his grip? He didn't think he'd been out of the CIA long enough to lose his alertness, but passion must have blinded him. "Are you okay?"

She nodded and stood, her shapely legs outlined in the moonlight. He couldn't help remembering the soft loveliness of her bare breasts. She was shivering. He needed to take her somewhere warm and safe. "I'm sorry that happened. We'd better get dressed." He stepped closer and held out his hand.

She gripped it tightly. Her eyes met his as if seeking reassurance or was it something more? He put an arm around her shoulders and led her inside. She headed straight for the bathroom. He retrieved his shirt and trudged to his car for the rest of his clothes.

A few minutes later, clothes in hand, he opened the door to the living room as she stepped out of the bathroom, her hair combed and her lipstick refreshed. Those ruby lips looked so kissable. He hurried inside the bathroom and dressed quickly. When he came out, she was standing by the large window, her creamy shoulders and long shapely legs straining his good intentions as well as his pants. More compelling was his worry about who sent that photographer and why.

"We'd better get back," she said, "before someone else catches us on film."

"I don't know who sent that photographer—but we can't stay here, Lee," he said, not sure if he should put his speculations into words. "What if it's someone Sheldon sent?"

Her face took on a strained look. "Why would he want pictures?" she asked as he locked the cottage door.

He opened the car door for her. "Maybe to give them to another man to track you so he'd recognize you."

She froze, half in and half out of the car. "You mean, I'll have to watch everyone I see.?"

"You should have been doing that already."

"Think I ought to call Joe?"

"Yes, but it's late. I should be able to protect you until tomorrow." Even as he said it, he felt as if he'd failed her. Why hadn't he seen that tail?

❧

Lee looked back at the cottage as Alex pulled away from it. Her heart still pounded. "I see why you like this place. If I had a hideaway like this, I'd come as often as I could."

On the drive back the wind whipped Lee's hair about. Why should she worry about mussed up hair? There was no future in their attraction, not with who knew how many men hunting her. For all she knew, her future could be measured in days. She shuddered.

With his hands on the wheel, Alex's eyes seemed glued to the path illuminated by his headlights. Once they got to the mobile home park, he glanced her way and grinned. "You look like you had a nice long roll in the hay, except there's none sticking to you."

His words conjured a picture of the two of them naked in a straw-filled loft, lit only by moonlight. With Alex making love to her, she'd probably never notice if the hay were scratchy. She sighed. Mustn't think about things like that.

She cleared her throat. "Alex, I can't imagine how you managed to live in constant danger when you worked for the CIA."

His serious gaze met hers. "I had to be on the lookout for trouble at all times."

"Would you take another spying assignment if they offered you one?"

He shrugged. "Maybe. I don't know. I used to take mostly short ones so I could be with my family more — but things are different now."

"But you still can have Tanya visit, can't you?"

"Only once a month." He scowled. "Her damn lawyer saw to that." He unlocked the door and insisted on checking the place out before letting her go in. "I scanned the decree before I signed it, but I must have been so hung up on who got what, that I didn't catch the part he stuck in about changing to once a month visitations if I lived over a hundred miles away. I need to call a lawyer to get that changed."

By the time they entered his place, Lee felt exhausted. After taking a nice hot relaxing bath, it felt good to crawl in between the cool sheets of his bed. It would feel even nicer to curl up beside his warm body, but that wasn't in the cards, at least not until after she'd testified, and Bubba and Sheldon were behind bars. And maybe not even then. Would she ever be sure she wasn't in danger?

She was dreaming about Alex when a strange noise awoke her. Light streamed in through the small high window. Must be morning. She heard him talking.

Alex's cell phone must have rung.

"Someone's broken into my office?" he asked. "I'll be there as soon as I can."

A few minutes later he walked down the hall and into the bedroom. "Lee, the police called. My office has been vandalized. I've got to go there. Can you get dressed real quick and come with me?"

She yawned. "I'm not really awake yet. Can't you go without me?"

"I don't like to leave you alone."

"When will you return?"

"I shouldn't be long." He grabbed a note pad and wrote on it. "Look, here's my cell phone number and Carl's in case you need anything before I get back and can't get in touch with Joe."

"I'm not calling Carl unless I can't get you or Joe or 9-1-1. He—well, you saw how he acted at the picnic. He won't need any encouragement."

"Hey, we were best friends in high school. Just tell him you and I are engaged and will probably get married soon. That should keep him at bay."

He didn't kiss her, just gave her the paper. His warm fingers made her long to grasp his hand and pull him closer. But maybe he wasn't as interested in something more permanent like she was.

"Lock up behind me, "Alex said as he headed down the hall. Minutes later the door slammed.

Yawning, she padded to the door and locked the bolt. Still sleepy, she crawled back in bed. Thank goodness that burglar was in jail. Alex should be back soon. She shouldn't have to worry.

Chapter 15

Not sleepy anymore, Lee was reading a magazine when she heard the noise—it sounded like a locomotive. She'd heard train whistles blow in the distance, but she hadn't seen any railroad crossings nearby. The sky was much darker, and she could no longer see the moon. Tree branches blew back and forth. Bushes shook in the wind. Her heart pounded. A tornado?

Rain pelted the roof or maybe it was hailstones. She stepped to the window. The wind whipped trees about like they were tall weeds. Across the street a large sycamore tree split in half and crashed to the ground, barely missing the trailer there.

Out front stood a tree tall enough to fall on this place. Her pulse raced. Tornadoes—weren't you supposed to open all the doors and windows? She rushed around, opening windows, wishing she were in a regular house.

When she opened the door, rain and debris blew in. Over the tops of the trees she saw it—a twister—heading her way.

Omigosh! If she were in the bathroom, the only interior room, the roof and walls might collapse and pin her down. Her heart pounded. Should she stay inside or throw herself in a ditch?

What if the wind pulled the trailer off its foundation like Dorothy's house in the 'Wizard of Oz.' She grabbed a sweater and ran outside. She picked a spot in the ditch away from any trees and flung herself down with the sweater over her head.

The ditch had mud — soft now, it would be soup soon. Rain soaked her clothes, plastered her shirt to her back. Cold and wet, she shivered.

The roar of the wind was deafening — like a loud thunder crack, but lasting longer. The wind tore through the trailer park, whirling leaves, sticks, small branches, and debris about. Twigs and leaves fell on her. Afraid to rise up, she let them lie. When the noise subsided, she sat up, shook off the debris, and peeled her soaked shirt loose. Rain wet her face'

She listened carefully. The twister was gone — she hoped. She took a deep breath. She'd survived, thank the Lord. Rain fell in gusts, sluicing down her face and neck. She must look like an otter that had been playing in the mud.

Looking around, what she saw took her breath away. All that was left of the trailer across the street were pipes and part of a wall swaying in the wind. The home next to it was a crumpled mass.

Alex's trailer still stood. Part of the roof had blown away, and rain was slashing in. Her teeth chattered. It was hard to keep from shaking. She wanted to get out of the rain, but was it safe to go inside?

The sky looked gray, but no heavy dark clouds threatened. In the distance she heard sirens. Why hadn't they blown earlier to warn people of the tornado? She probably should be out looking for survivors and helping someone who was injured, but she was shaking too much to do any good.

Lightning still crackled. Between flashes she saw only one car moving slowly down the street. She hoped most of the residents were somewhere else right now.

The sirens grew louder. Minutes later she watched emergency medical technicians down the street push someone on a gurney into an ambulance. An elderly man followed and climbed into the vehicle. The wind tore the back door from the medical technician's hand, slamming it shut. He raced around and got in. The vehicle took off with sirens blowing'

All the homes across the street were wrecked, including the one where the ambulance had stopped. Down the street a couple loaded two suitcases in a Sport Utility Vehicle and drove away. The mobile homes on her side of the street had only minor damage. A twisted metal door lay strewn in the yard of one. A large branch lay stuck in the groove it had made in someone's roof.

She couldn't seem to stop shaking. She kept telling herself the danger was over, but her pulse still raced. Her heart was beating rapidly. She found it hard to catch her breath. She'd hyperventilate if she stayed here much longer. Why hadn't Alex come back by now? She had no car, and she didn't want to walk anywhere.

Maybe another ambulance would come. She could beg to ride with them to the hospital. She'd be safe in a sturdy building like a hospital. And she could get warm. But the medical technicians wouldn't welcome someone on the verge of hysteria. They'd be trying to keep patients stable. She might be cold and wet and dirty, but she wasn't really injured. However, if she stayed here in the ditch, she'd go crazy.

Listening carefully for another twister or return of the relentless wind, she stood, braced to throw herself down in the mud again. Like thick soup, the wet soil held onto her shoes. Her feet finally came loose with a sucking sound. Mud, leaves and twigs clung to her shoes.

After stumbling to the trailer, she leaned against the wall beside the open door. Still shaking, she took one last look at the sky, and then stepped inside. Now, if only she could find Alex's cordless phone. She headed down the hall to the bedroom, taking a quick detour into the bathroom to grab a towel to wipe her face, dry her hair, and scrape some of the mud off her clothes.

A gaping hole in the bedroom roof loomed over a wet floor.

Water dripped from the fringe of the chenille bedspread. Still shivering, she yanked it off and snatched a blanket from the bed to cover herself. It was soaked too. She threw it down' She grabbed Alex's robe and wrapped it around her. After snatching up his cordless phone, she rushed to the closet. Here the roof was still intact, sheltering the area from the downpour.

She dialed Alex's cell phone, but couldn't get through. Dialing 9-1-1, only got her a busy signal. She tried again and gave up. From her pocket she pulled out the paper with Carl's number. She didn't want to call him. Instead she dialed Joe's number, heard it ring and ring. Had the marshal gone somewhere and left his cell phone behind? She dialed the office number. No one answered. Of course not—it was the weekend.

A piece of the roof fell onto the bed. She couldn't stay here. Her hands shook as she dialed the number for Joe's cell phone again. Still no answer. She stepped toward the window and looked out.

The wind had died down, but rain still fell from darkened skies. What if another tornado came through? She pressed her hands to her temple, trying to calm herself. The trailer might not fare so well if there were any more wind gusts. And if she went outside, a tree might fall on her. She shuddered.

With unsteady fingers she dialed Carl's number. Fending off a few passes was better than staying here. Glad the noise of the wind had subsided enough to hear him, she said, "It's Lee. A tornado struck here. Can you come get me?"

"Where's Alex?"

"Don't know. Someone broke into his office and he's down there straightening things out. I tried his cell phone. He didn't answer."

"Maybe the roads are blocked. Have you tried calling Iceberg?"

"How do you know about Joe? Did Alex say something?"

"About you're being in the Witness Security Program? I'm Joe's boss, or didn't you know?"

"No, I didn't." No wonder Joe had been at Carl's party.

"Okay, where exactly are you?"

She gave him directions from the highway. She hoped Alex would show up soon, but she couldn't bear to stay in this flimsy structure a minute longer than she had to.

"By the way, Lee, I wouldn't count on Alex if I were you. He fell apart when his wife filed for a divorce. If you need a friend, I'd be happy to advise—or take you out for a nice hot dinner. I bet you could use one about now."

"If I can just get away from here until things quiet down, I'll be okay, but I'll keep trying to call Alex."

"If you're afraid of being seen by one of Sheldon's men, you could stay here. We could rent a movie."

That's all she needed—a cozy get together with him. "I think you should know—Alex and I—well after his divorce is final, we're getting married."

"You've got to be kidding. Alex isn't the type to settle down with one woman. Look what happened with him and Kathy. I went to high school with the guy. As quarterback on the football team, he made a wide sweep."

"What do you mean?"

"The girls fell all over him."

"So."

"He was wild in those days. I'm surprised he didn't knock one of 'em up. He hasn't changed much. Bet he only hinted he'd marry you to get you in the sack, right?"

"That's none of your business." Steaming, she almost hung up on him. Outside, a large tree branch cracked. It fell with a resounding crash. The wall on that side of the trailer shook. That was close. Would another one fall on the trailer and perhaps crush her in its path? Her breaths came rapidly.

"Lee, I asked if you'd be outside when I got there. Didn't you hear me?"

"I—uh, I may be out back lying in a ditch if the wind doesn't die down." Now that she had time to think, calling him hadn't been a good idea. She might be better off with the wind. Then she imagined being tossed about. Her heart still pounded. She had to get out of here.

"Hang tight. I'm on my way."

"But—" The line was silent.

She rested her head in her hands. He didn't seem to take her lie about being engaged seriously. She'd better keep trying to reach Alex and think up some good moves in case Carl got fresh.

The wind whistled, sending shivers down her spine. Rain came in gusts. She watched the skies. She hoped if another twister came, she'd see it in time to take cover.

Realizing she still clutched the phone, she dialed Alex again. No answer. She tried Joe. Still no answer. Afraid to shut the door, she sat cross-legged beside it and hoped the wind wouldn't hurl debris at her.

❦

Several miles away, Alex surveyed the mess that was his office and shook his head. He couldn't even figure out what was missing until he straightened things out. A low rumble sounded outside. He went to the window. It was darker, much darker than it had been earlier. The wind howled, and rain splashed against the window. Damn, he'd left the top down again. And Lee was alone. Hadn't she said she was afraid of storms? He rushed out, barely remembering to lock the door.

Outside, rain dampened his shirt as he ran to the car. Rain came down in torrents. By the time he got the top up and climbed inside, he was soaked. The radio crackled so he could barely make out the announcer's comments. The word 'tornado' slammed his gut. Lee—if his trailer were caught up in the twister, who knew what could happen. He gunned the motor and headed out of town.

165

He hadn't gone more than three miles when he saw the police cars, lights flashing, blocking the highway.

Damn, the road to the trailer park was just over the hill. Now what?

A cop waved at him to turn around. He stopped the car and got out. He had to get through.

The cop frowned. "Turn back. There's an overturned eighteen wheeler and several wrecked cars just over the hill. The road's completely blocked."

"How long?"

"Can't tell. Find another way, but watch out. We've had reports of a twister touching down nearby."

Alex's gut roiled. "What about the trailer park? Did it get hit?"

The cop shrugged. "Don't know. Tornadoes can rip those places apart. There may only be bits and pieces left."

Alex caught his breath. "My place is in that trailer park, and I left my girlfriend there. Is there another way to get through?"

"Afraid not, sir. The road to the park is just beyond the wreck. Nobody's getting through until the ambulances and the rescue teams get through here. They're going to have to cut the truck driver out of his cab."

He had to find Lee, see if she were all right. He moved his car to the shoulder and parked. He was walking around a police cruiser when an officer yelled, "Stop. Unless you're a doctor, I can't let you through."

Alex scowled. "Look, I won't bother the rescue team. I'm walking to my trailer to see if my girlfriend's okay."

"She's probably left. Most of the residents already have. A steady stream of cars pulled out right after the accident. We had to put a man on the other side of the accident scene to wave them on."

The officer looked up at the darkened sky. "You better go back to town. It's not safe out until the wind dies down."

A strong gust blew dead leaves around them in a swirling motion as if to punctuate the officer's words.

"I'll walk through the woods if I have to."

"It's your funeral," the officer said. "Just stay away from the emergency medical teams."

"I will." After returning to his car for his cell phone, Alex tried it. Nothing but static. Damn. He parked the car beside the road, locked it and set off. Striding briskly, he barely skirted the trees at the edge of the woods.

The wind gusted again, slamming twigs against his legs. Rain wet his shirt, chilling him. He hoped he wouldn't find Lee lying injured or worse — he tried not to think of that.

It usually took only a few minutes to drive to his place from the highway, but he must have two or three miles to go at least. Now he wished he'd rented an apartment in town. She'd have been a lot safer there, even with Sheldon's goons hunting her.

He clenched and unclenched his fists. Face it buddy, she'd be a lot safer anywhere else but his place with tissue-thin walls. What had he been thinking to keep her here when she could have gone to a big city where she'd be harder to find and have interesting things to do?

He'd have to find another secretary, but it wouldn't be the same as having Lee near every day, watching her tantalizing body and smelling her perfume. But it wasn't just that. Her brave spirit drew him to her, made him want to protect her and keep her safe.

He sighed. After his disastrous failure at marriage, he had no business getting involved, but he couldn't help worrying. Picturing her lying bleeding, maybe trapped under a twisted piece of wall, he broke into a run. Usually, he liked the smell of damp earth when it rained, but now that wet earth was spattering against his ankles.

Farther up on the highway the eighteen-wheeler lay on its side like some discarded toddler's toy. The rescue team seemed to be taking care of things, so he hurried past. He jogged for a while, and then slowed to catch his breath. He wouldn't be any use to Lee if she were hurt and he was too tired to carry her out.

An ambulance headed out of the trailer park toward the highway, its siren blowing. He thought about flagging it down, but decided against it. Whoever was inside needed medical help immediately. He hoped it wasn't Lee.

He stopped and pulled out his phone. If she were not at the trailer, he'd call the hospital. He'd dial information for the number.

His phone was dead. Damn, the charge must have run out. He stuffed it back in his pocket. Finally he reached the entrance to the mobile home park.

He'd always enjoyed the winding drive through sweet gum, oak, and cypress trees, but now he wished they'd cut the road straight through. He headed down the road to his place. One trailer lay on its side, bent almost in half. He gasped. Too out of breath to run, he walked faster. The tornado must have come down the other side of the street. So far it had barely touched the side his place was on, but he kept his fingers crossed until he could see it.

Even from 100 yards he could see the roof on his trailer was half gone. He broke into a run. Then he saw Carl's purple pick-up truck parked in front. He'd given his number to Lee in case of emergency, but what if Carl were trying to hit on her again? Spurred by that thought, he broke into a run.

❦

Inside the trailer's living room kitchen, Lee faced Carl. She backed under the portion of the roof that was still intact. A twig with leaves dropped through the gaping hole. "I appreciate your coming to get me." She took a deep breath. "I was about to lose it when I called."

"Hey, I don't blame you." Water dripped from the roof onto his red hair and fell to his shoulders. "Man, this place is a mess." He stepped away from the hole, closer to her. The scent of his musky cologne and his intimidating nearness made her edge backwards until the kitchen counter jutted against her back.

"The weather report says the storm has blown over." He smiled. "Come with me to my place. We can sit by the fire and watch the stars come out. I've got steaks to grill, and I toss a mean salad."

"I want to try to reach Alex again. Maybe I can get through now."

"If it didn't work before, it won't now. Come on. You'll be safer in my truck. It's only forty miles to my place." He pointed to the sky. "The storm's gone. By the way, I'm sorry if you think I was out of line on the fourth. I didn't know Alex was interested in you."

"You weren't just out of line, you were rather—"

"Crude? Hey, give me a break. In that bikini, well, I was bowled over by your looks. I'm a pretty cool guy, but as long as you're not formally engaged, well—."

That put her immediately on guard. A breeze shook the part of the roof dangling through the gaping hole. "It's not safe here. I'll go with you, but don't bother to grill a steak for me. As soon as I can reach Alex, I'll have him come get me."

"Now you're talking sense. Come on." He opened the door and held out his hand. When she didn't take it, he let go of the doorknob and grabbed her hand. He pulled her off balance into a close embrace, catching her off guard. With his mouth inches away, she pushed against his chest. "Let me go."

"I saw you kissing Alex at my picnic. You don't know him like I do. His wife threw him out, and he doesn't even have a job. I can afford to take you to the best places if you'll only give me a chance—" His tones turned seductive. "I'm a great dancer, and baby, I can deliver in bed like you wouldn't believe."

Still struggling to get away, she opened her mouth to protest. His lips came down on hers, his tongue shoveling into her mouth like a bulldozer.

Where was Alex?

Chapter 16

Summoning all her strength, Lee wrenched free of Carl's arms and slapped his face. "Your ego's as big as Texas. Even a pig has more finesse."

His face flamed red. "You're a tease and a bitch. You'll be sorry. Alex doesn't know squat about running a business or keeping a woman happy. His business won't even get off the ground. Now me, I'm successful enough to show a woman a good time. I could have really gone for you, but you just poisoned the well."

"Lee," called a voice from outside.

She looked out the doorway.

Alex strode up the walk, stepping over broken branches and panting for breath. "Thank goodness you're all right. Why the hell didn't you call me?"

"I tried, but you didn't answer."

"Storm must have screwed up transmission. Thanks for coming, Carl, but I'll take care of her now." His chin jutted out as he faced Carl. "I'm going to marry her as soon as I get my copy of the divorce decree."

Lee smothered a gasp. The way Alex said it with such conviction—she could almost believe he meant it. She glanced at Carl to see if he bought it.

Carl leaned against the wall—it shook a bit so he stepped away from it. His mocking grin made her want to step back, but she held her ground. He cocked his head to one side and scratched behind his ear. "Wouldn't move too fast if I were you. A divorce isn't final until thirty days after the judge signs the decree, just in case someone wants to appeal. You can't get married again until then."

Alex frowned. "How come you know so much? You've never been married or divorced."

"Just something Kathy mentioned the other day."

She moved closer to Alex and turned to Carl. "Thanks for coming, but now that Alex is here, he can take me somewhere safe." She looked up and down the street. "Alex, where's your car?"

"Had to leave it on the highway."

"How come?"

"There's an accident blocking the road. I was worried you might have been hurt so I left the car and walked here."

Carl nodded. "Saw an ambulance and a fire truck just before I turned in. Should be cleared up by now. I'll drive you both to your car."

"I'd appreciated it, Carl. Lee, pack your clothes. I'm taking you to a hotel."

After they'd both packed some clothes, Alex put his arm around Lee's waist and led her to Carl's truck. He got in first, and then reached out to help her climb up.

Carl slid behind the wheel. "I would have let her get in first."

"But then, she'd have to sit next to you, old buddy."

Lee hardly got the seat belt buckled before Carl zoomed off. After shooting an angry glance her way, he followed the winding road from the trailer park, and then pulled onto the highway. She turned to Alex. "You must have walked at least three miles."

He nodded. "Ran most of the way. I had to be sure you were okay."

A lump constricted her throat. He'd worried about her and rushed here to see if she were safe.

And he'd gone the extra mile by continuing the pretense as her fiancé. That's the kind of man he was. She knew he'd do all in his power to keep her safe. She had to love him for that alone.

Whoa, love wasn't an option in their case. She couldn't get involved and especially not when he had a daughter who could be vulnerable to any danger Lee might face. No, no matter how appealing he was, she couldn't fall for him — or encourage him.

Heat from his body warmed her side as did his arm around her. Each curve the pick-up made pushed her closer to his firm body. His fingers caressed her waist, setting her pulse racing. She had to keep reminding herself it was an act.

"I better call Iceberg, I mean Joe," Lee said. "Carl, do you have a cell phone in this truck?"

"In the glove compartment."

This time Joe answered. "Hear you had a touch of weather over there. Glad to hear you're okay. Tried to call, but couldn't get through."

"High winds wrecked the trailer where I was staying."

"Tough luck. Where are you? I can come get you."

"Carl's driving me to Alex's car. He'll take me to a hotel."

"Good. Then I won't worry about you tonight. They delivered my Corvette today. It's a '93 C-4,' and I'd rather not take it out until I'm sure there's no chance of hailstones. Call me from the hotel. I'll find you another temporary safe place tomorrow."

"I don't want another temporary place. I want a permanent place. I need to get on with my life."

"Sorry, Lee, even if I find you a good place, you may have to move again, maybe in the middle of the night."

"That trial can't come too soon for me. Why didn't you tell me at the picnic that Carl was your supervisor?"

"It wasn't a good idea to say much with all those people there. Since then I've been busy setting up things for another witness. Got to go now. Take care."

Lee hung up. Seeing they'd reached Alex's Jaguar, she

stuffed Carl's cell phone in the glove compartment and reached for the door handle.

As soon as Lee was alone with Alex in his car, she asked, "Why did you tell me to call Carl?"

"I wanted him to protect you if you needed someone."

"I believed you when you said he'd leave me alone if I said we were engaged, but he didn't."

"What did he do?"

"He grabbed me and tried to kiss me. I had to slap his face."

"Damn him. I figured you'd be safe if he thought I was your fiancé."

"I guess you don't know him as well as you thought you did."

"Sorry. If he bothers you again, just tell me. I'll make him wish he hadn't."

Two hours later Alex and Lee followed the bellhop across a glass enclosed passageway over a Fort Worth street to the west side of the Worthington Hotel. Two stories down cars buzzed underneath.

Taking her hand, he leaned close. "I told them we were on our honeymoon when I signed in," he whispered. "That way, no one will bother us." He winked, making her wish she could share a real honeymoon with him.

When they reached the room, Alex unlocked the door, then picked her up and carried her over the threshold.

"Alex, what are you doing?"

"Following tradition, Mrs. Lance." He gave her a tender kiss, then set her down and handed a five-dollar bill to the bellhop, who smiled, unloaded their things, and left.

Lee looked at Alex. "Lance? Where did you come up with that name?"

"Actually, it's mine. Took a lot of ribbing when the kids at school found out my middle name was Lancelot. When I played football, the cheerleaders used to yell, "Use your lance.""

"Why?"

"When I carried the ball, I always straight-armed anybody coming at me."

She looked around the room. "Well, at least there are two beds. Why do we have to pretend we're married? Lots of unmarried couples share a room nowadays."

"Anyone looking for you isn't likely to check out newlyweds."

"Oh." Her stomach rumbled, reminding her it had been hours since she'd eaten. "I'm hungry. Can we order food?"

He handed her a room service menu. "Pick something."

She sank down on one of the beds and shivered. "It's chilly."

"There's none on the menu."

She laughed. "I'll take the Chicken Rosemary."

He sat beside her, grabbed the phone and dialed room service. His arm slid around her shoulders, imparting a pleasant warmth. He ordered two dinners, then looked at her and grinned.

"Now what's funny."

He squeezed her shoulders, then dropped his arm. "I can't seem to stop playing your lover." His smile hinted he might want to go beyond pretending.

She swallowed, suddenly unsure of him. "You don't have to. Carl's not here, and I can't afford to get involved with anyone until Sheldon's behind bars permanently."

"Are you going to put your life on hold forever?"

"I won't ever feel safe enough to marry or have children— not as long as Sheldon's alive."

"That's ridiculous. You're letting Sheldon control your life."

"I won't put you or anyone else in jeopardy."

"What if some man loves you enough to take his chances?"

She took a deep breath. "I wouldn't ask anyone to take that risk."

"Not even to marry and have a family?"

She faced him, clenching her hands into fists to keep them

from shaking. "I don't plan to have a baby. My mother—my mother died giving birth to Libby." She blinked back tears. "I could face the same complications she did."

She swallowed, trying to ignore the knot of fear in her stomach. "It was awful growing up without a mother. I won't subject a child to that."

"Have you asked a doctor about it?"

"Of course not."

"Why not?"

"Because I haven't found a man I wanted to marry so the question never came up." And now, even if she were free to choose one, the man who stirred her soul wasn't really free. He and Kathy could still reconcile their differences and make up.

She couldn't, she wouldn't, fall for him. Who was she kidding? She already had. Any career she took up wouldn't make up for not being with Alex. But she couldn't bear it if he were injured or killed because of her.

❦

Alex turned on the TV. Scenes of devastation wrought by the tornado in the mobile home park flashed on the screen.

"Oh, my gosh," said Lee. "I need to let Libby know I'm all right.? She picked up the phone and called Joe, who relayed the call to her sister's phone. Libby didn't answer, so Lee left a message. She handed Alex the phone. "You had better call your mom and Tanya—they may be watching TV and be worried about you."

Alex picked up the phone. "You're right, Lee." He punched in numbers. "Hello" Tanya, it's daddy."

"Daddy, where are you?"

"I'm in a hotel in Fort Worth."

"What if the tornado hits it? Will it break?"

"No, dear. This is a big, strong building, and it's far away from where the tornado hit."

176

"But Daddy, a tornado hit Fort Worth on my birthday last year. What if another one hits it again? Something might happen to you."

Knowing she was anxious about him touched his heart. "Don't worry, Sweetheart. They don't usually hit the same place twice."

"I miss you. Can you come see me tonight?" In her quivering tones, he sensed tears about to break through.

"No Tanya. I'm not supposed to see you until Thursday night. How about if I take you to Chuck-E-Cheese. We can eat pizza, and you can play games."

"That's fun. But I want you to read stories to me every night. Why can't you stay here with me 'n Mommy? I'll be good and keep my room clean."

Guilt washed over him. Tanya must blame herself for the divorce. She hadn't asked for this. "I can't stay with you because Mommy and I are divorced. Remember we fight so we can't live together. I'll read you a story every night you stay with me."

"But Daddy, at school, when the kids fight, the teacher talks to them in a loud voice and tells them to stop. If I yell at you and Mommy to stop, couldn't you stop fighting?"

Alex sighed, remembering her tears when he took her back to her mother, how she'd cling to him, with her sweet little arms around his neck. Kathy's attorney had promised to send him a copy of the divorce decree as soon as the judge signed it. The marriage might be over, but Tanya was tearing at his heart.

"Honey, it isn't that easy. Would you feel better if I call you every day?"

"Will Mommy get mad?"

"I hope not, dear."

"Tanya, I've got to hang up now. I'll blow a kiss at the phone for you."

Tanya giggled. "You can't kiss me over the phone. I miss you kissing me goodnight, Daddy. I wish you'd come home."

Alex made smacking noises into the receiver, then hung up.

He missed quiet nights in front of the TV with someone to share. He sighed. What would it be like to have Lee sharing his nights? At least she was here for this night. He stood and pulled her into his arms.

A knock sounded. "Room service," said an impatient sounding male voice.

"Must be the food," he told Lee. "Just a minute," he called and kissed her soundly. Her mouth was so sweet, and she felt so good in his arms. Oh to be able to do this every night.

❦

Lee's mouth trembled from his onslaught. She couldn't help kissing him back. All the feelings she'd been holding back, the ones she didn't trust, the ones she didn't want to yield to, poured forth like a raging flood. Hungry to taste him, she grasped his head with both hands and gave back as good as she got.

Beneath her fingers, his hair was springy. Beneath her mouth, his lips were surprisingly soft and his skin slightly rough. Drowning in his kiss, she floated in a whirlpool of swirling sensation. This might never happen again, but she'd never felt so desired, so thrillingly alive.

The knock sounded again.

Alex pulled the door open a crack, then undid the chain. A waiter wheeled a cart into their room and unloaded their food. Alex handed the waiter a tip, and he left.

Lee reached for a chicken leg and bit into it. "This fried chicken tastes delicious, but I can't stop thinking about what you said to Tanya."

Alex hadn't touched his food yet. "I need to get that visitation schedule changed. Once a month isn't enough for a little girl whose whole world has been turned upside down. Maybe if I talk with Kathy, try to reason with her — I won't let her keep me away from Tanya."

Lee slumped on the bed. She'd had only her sister and her

father for a family. Her childhood with only one parent hadn't been easy. And now there were just Lee and her sister. Tanya deserved a chance for a happy childhood with two parents. She swallowed, trying to get the words out, words she didn't want to say.

But she had to. It was the right thing to do — for Tanya if not for herself. "Maybe you and Kathy can still make a family — for Tanya's sake."

Blinking back tears, she waited for his answer. She wasn't sure how he really felt. If he still loved Kathy, he'd want that. But if he didn't —. Ashamed to admit she wanted to hear him say he didn't love Kathy, she waited, twisting her skirt with nervous fingers.

Alex rubbed his neck. "Kathy always hated not being able to tell anyone what I did. Working for the CIA was exciting, but now I just want to run a little business in a quiet town like Grandville, but...."

"You said earlier that she didn't like the idea."

"She wanted me to run for the legislature. She begged me to run for the Texas Senate so she'd be the wife of somebody important. In the CIA I concentrated on being unobtrusive. Being important doesn't mean that much to me."

"But what about Tanya? She needs a mother and a father to take care of her. Maybe if you two saw a marriage counselor —" Her mouth dropped open. She couldn't believe she'd suggested that.

He shook his head. "I don't know. Maybe if we could come to some kind of compromise —"

Lee took another bite of chicken. It might have been tasty if she hadn't been thinking about Alex going back to his ex-wife. That was best for Tanya, but Lee didn't have to like it. She swallowed. Knots grew inside, threatening to twist her in two. Tears filled her eyes. She couldn't let him see. She grabbed her robe and willed her voice not to crack. "I'm going to take a shower."

❦

Alex sat on one of the beds and watched her walk to the bathroom, her hips swaying like a tulip in a gentle breeze. She didn't seem to be trying to entice him now, but the way she'd clung to him and kissed him said she might chance a relationship with him. Except, she obviously didn't approve of his breaking up his family. How could she want a man who'd failed miserably at marriage?

Everything would have been fine if Kathy had just accepted the move to Grandville. With her sense of style and her flair for organizing civic groups, she could be a queen bee there.

Tanya was worth a little compromising, but Kathy probably wouldn't be interested in a reconciliation. And he didn't want to give up Lee. Might be different if he hadn't met her and come to care about her. He liked her spunk and optimism. She'd need it to start over again—most likely far from him. Thank goodness he'd been there to protect her from Bubba. By golly, Joe had better be there for Lee when Alex couldn't watch out for her.

If they could be together, he knew Lee would never push him to be someone he was not—but her kisses could inspire him to accomplish something big.

The sound of running water ceased. Might as well get ready to take a shower. He damn sure needed a cold one. After shedding his shirt, he undid the snap at the top of his jeans.

❦

Lee emerged from the steamy bathroom, her robe tightly belted, and saw Alex, bare-chested, lift his bag and throw it on the bed. Muscles rippled, honed no doubt from frequent workouts. No wonder he'd subdued that burglar so quickly.

He'd left the snap undone on his jeans. Was he getting ready to shower—or did he have something else in mind? She ran her tongue over her lower lip. How good it would feel to lie in his arms, to feel his hands stroke her skin, caress her breasts and more intimate places, then thrust deep inside and send her spirits soaring. It would be wonderful. She was sure of that.

If he were going to try to make peace with Kathy—for Tanya's sake, she needed to leave him alone. What had he meant by compromise? Was he seeking a more amicable divorce or would he really try to save their marriage? It didn't matter if the decree had been signed. They could always get married again.

Tanya was a dear. She needed a stable family. Lee didn't want to be the thorn that ripped apart a rosy future for the child, but saying goodbye to Alex would tear her heart to pieces. Except there was a child, a dear child whose happiness depended on it.

Lee unbelted her robe, shed it, and slid beneath the covers. "Good night, Alex," she said and quickly turned away. Snuggling into the pillow, she shut her eyes. Now, if she could only stop thinking about him and fall asleep.

❦

Alex yanked his robe and pajama bottoms from the suitcase and headed for the shower. It took a long time to cool his desire. He kept remembering the feel of her lips on his. She'd kissed him as if she were saying hello and goodbye forever. Then she'd talked about him going back to Kathy. Did she really think that was best?

After finishing his shower, he rubbed his skin with a towel, wishing her hands were smoothing the moisture from his skin, and her body was pressing against his. Hell, he wouldn't care if she were dripping wet, if only he could make love to her.

He had to stop thinking about Lee. He wasn't good enough for her. He toweled his legs vigorously, wishing he could make

Sheldon go away as easily as he rubbed the moisture from his body.

It would take a lot of vigilance and persuasion to calm Lee's fears of Sheldon getting revenge. Someday some strong man would convince her to let go of her fears. He didn't want to think about someone else with her. Why couldn't he be the one?

Then he thought of Tanya with her impish smile and dancing red curls. Her sparkling brown eyes had lit up the last time he'd picked her up. She deserved a happy childhood, and by gosh, he'd do what he could to see her get it. But could he persuade Kathy Tanya's happiness was more important than their differences?

He yanked on his pajama bottoms. That's what he should do. But Lee was the one his heart called to. Hardened by desire, he wrapped his robe around him, hoping that would hide the truth—that she stirred his blood like no other woman, not even Kathy when they were first going together.

His gut twisted. What had gone wrong in his marriage? In the beginning, when he took the job with the CIA, every time he returned home they'd spend hours swimming and lying in the sun at the lake cottage. At night they'd end up making love on a rug by the fireplace. Luckily, Tanya, the product of their love, had never awakened.

The last time he'd suggested it, Kathy said, "That's only for fools madly in love." Even though he and Lee hadn't even made love—and might never do it, Lee responded to his kisses with more feeling than Kathy had lately.

Perhaps he'd been the one in love—in love with a dream of a perfect marriage, one Kathy hadn't shared.

Once Lee was safely settled in a new place, he could stop worrying about her. This mad craving to make love to her would go away if he didn't see her regularly, wouldn't it?

He didn't want Tanya to go through what his friend Carl had when his dad moved out. He and Carl used to do things together, but for weeks his friend hadn't wanted to go swimming or even take in a movie with him.

After Carl took up with a rough bunch, Alex wondered if he'd been involved in the string of robberies of convenience stores. If Carl's father had stayed, he would have straightened Carl out in no time.

Now that Carl had a responsible job and a lake home of his own, he seemed to have matured. Carl had definitely been taken with Tanya. Maybe he'd marry and settle down now.

Alex wanted to be a good father for Tanya. Maybe if he paid more attention to Kathy—like he should have done before, they could make a go of things. He'd introduce Kathy to Grandville's mayor and his wife. Kathy would enjoy mingling with the important folks in the town.

He eased the door open. Lee lay still, her breaths slow and rhythmic, her breasts rising and falling with each breath. He wanted to wake her and entice her to make love. But he couldn't, not until he settled things with Kathy one way or the other. Cursing his conscience, he walked to the other bed and slid beneath the sheets.

Could he ever forget Lee's warm brown eyes, her flushed face after he'd kissed her, and the way she ravished his mouth with a soul-searing kiss. No, he'd cherish that memory in his heart, but he had to think of Tanya.

He wrapped his arm around the pillow, wishing it were around Lee instead. He wondered how she'd react when he told her he planned to take her advice.

Chapter 17

Lee nestled under the covers and hugged the warm form beside her. She shut her eyes even tighter, wanting the night to last forever. She was glad Alex had been the one to make the move to her bed—her conscience wouldn't let her. Hadn't she insisted he try to rebuild his marriage for Tanya's sake?

Lee snuggled closer, surprised to find some softness about Alex's body. Sunlight assaulted her eyes, and the sound of a shower made her wonder why the walls were thin enough to let sounds from the next room carry so easily. Reluctantly, she opened her eyes—she had her arms around a pillow. Darn.

She shoved it away and glanced over at the other bed, hoping Alex hadn't seen. He'd think she was love starved.

His bed was empty. The shower sounds must be coming from their bathroom, not someone else's. It would have been nice to wake up in his arms, but it was better this way. She wouldn't have so many memories to haunt her.

She threw off the sheet and shivered. Why did they always think the air conditioners had to be set on 'frigid' inside a hotel, just because it was hot outside? She grabbed some clothes and dressed. She could wash later when Alex came out of the bathroom. Facing the mirror, she was combing her hair when the bathroom door opened.

"Your turn. I'm afraid the air's saturated with moisture

after the cold shower I took, the second one in twelve hours."

Thinking he had to take cold showers last night and this morning because of her made her feel deliciously wicked. Her conscience stabbed her. She should be encouraging him to go back to his wife, instead of being glad she turned him on.

Any contact from now on she'd have to keep strictly professional—no more midnight drives to look at stars, no more picnics—unless they took Tanya to the park.

He was humming. It sounded like 'Puff the Magic Dragon.'

In the mirror she caught his gaze.

He grinned sheepishly. "That's Tanya's favorite song. I have to sing it to her when I put her in bed at night. Now it keeps going round in my head like a whirlwind."

She imagined Alex with Kathy and Tanya, sitting close together on a couch facing a cozy fire. She sighed. There would never be times like that for her. Might as well get used to the idea. Maybe Libby would have children, and she could be a doting aunt. That is if she dared visit without putting them in danger. If only the authorities could make a strong enough case against all of Sheldon's cronies to put them all away, she could breathe freely again.

But she wouldn't lean on Alex's well-muscled chest again. She'd have to fight temptation. Moisture welled up in her eyes. She brushed it away and straightened her spine. She could handle this. She'd have to, at least until fall. She grabbed her cosmetic bag, hurried into the bathroom, and closed the door. She rubbed at the condensate on the mirror so she could see to finish combing her hair.

A tear ran down her cheek. Angrily, she brushed it away. She couldn't put makeup on wet cheeks. If Alex and Kathy could reconcile for Tanya's sake, they might even recapture feelings they'd had before. She imagined him hugging Kathy, maybe even kissing her hungrily. That sent tears coursing down her cheek.

"Stop it, you fool," she whispered. "He's not yours—never

was." But her heart didn't listen. Hot tears burned her eyes. If only things could be different.

Squeezing her eyes shut to release the last bit of moisture, she scrubbed her face with a towel, and then applied her make-up. She assumed a calm expression. She'd keep it up until this day was over. She'd act so cheerful, he'd never know she was falling apart inside. Taking a deep breath, she opened the door, pasted a smile on her face, and walked out, as gracefully as she could. Alex glanced her way. "We need to get going. I'm glad you're not one of those women who take forever to get ready."

❧

Alex caught her brief smile, but it was soon followed by a poker face.

"Where are we going?" She looked apprehensive.

"To Kathy's house. I've decided to take your advice."

"And you're going to try to make up with Kathy?" Lee turned to face him, her face impassive, as if she didn't care one way or the other.

He studied her expression, wishing she'd look disappointed or say making up with Kathy wasn't such a good idea after all.

"That's what's best for Tanya. After seeing you with her, I can tell you're a great father, especially now that you can spend more time with her."

She turned her back to him and busied herself combing her hair. "Why don't you drop me off in Fort Worth at the Kimball Art Gallery for the day. I hear the Amon Carter Art Museum is within walking distance so I'll have plenty to see."

He frowned. "Oh, no you don't. If that camera man found you, Sheldon can too. I'm not letting you wander alone in Fort Worth."

She perched her fists on her slim hips. "I won't go in the house while you talk to Kathy. I've talked to friends in the middle of their divorces. She won't take you seriously if I come with you. And who knows what she might accuse me of. It could get ugly."

"Don't worry. I'll tell her I only brought my new secretary to babysit Tanya while we talk."

"In her shoes I wouldn't buy that for a minute."

"You can stay in the car, and I could hint you're very plain looking and don't want to get out." Seeing her look of dismay, he hastened to add, "Which you're not, but she doesn't need to know that. I suppose if you messed up your hair—"

"She'd think we'd been kissing up a storm."

He scratched his head. "Hadn't thought of that." He grinned in spite of himself, wishing for another opportunity to do just that. He wouldn't kiss her again he promised himself. Because he couldn't stop at a kiss. "I'm not leaving you here alone. Come on, we need to get going."

Outside in the car, he waited until Lee had buckled up before turning on the ignition. He tried to ignore the sweet smell of her perfume—something light and floral which made her seem innocent and free like a delicate wild flower waving in the breeze.

Traffic claimed his attention until they were out on the highway to Austin. Tanya hadn't asked to be born. She deserved a happy childhood, and if he had to give up the woman he wanted to provide it—well, he'd manage somehow.

He sighed. He loved his daughter. For her sake he'd do all he could to keep his family intact. He tried not to think about living with Kathy again. Even for Tanya, he wasn't sure if he could say the vows again. His heart might not be in it.

How could he leave Lee alone to fend for herself—even if she had Joe to watch out for her? A lot of help he'd been. Alex hoped the guy would keep better tabs on threats to her life than he had so far. Even if Alex married Kathy again, he hoped he could convince Lee to stay on as his secretary. He'd see her every day, be sure she was safe. They could share platonic lunches where they'd discuss interesting things. That would have to be enough.

Or maybe when she was safely established in a job in another town, he could take her to lunch at a nice place occasionally — in public so he wouldn't be tempted to touch her.

He suppressed a groan. Kathy wouldn't stand for that. If she were behind those pictures that had been taken, she'd have him followed again. Most likely Sheldon's men were behind it.

Lee's voice broke into his thoughts. "While you talk to Kathy, I could take Tanya to see the capital building. They should have good security there."

"And they may be shorthanded during the summer. I can't take the chance that either of you might get hurt or kidnapped. When I get to Kathy's house, I'll park in the shade, and then bring Tanya out. Take her in the back yard and push her on the swing."

"What if Kathy makes a scene."

"She won't if you stay outdoors. She won't want the neighbors gossiping. If she invites you in for coffee, refuse. I hope we can figure things out reasonably, but if there are any shouting matches, I want it to be just between me and Kathy."

Lee sighed and opened a book.

An hour later, Lee roused from a short nap. She opened her eyes. They were zooming up the ramp to an elevated expressway. They must be in Austin already. She was interested in seeing his house, but she dreaded meeting Kathy. She hoped Alex would just bring Tanya out, and let Lee keep her entertained until Alex and Kathy got something settled.

Tanya was a dear, and Lee enjoyed being with her. She supposed she should encourage Alex to try his best to talk his ex-wife into getting back together, but she couldn't think of anything else to say. Her heart just wasn't in it. She tried not to think how wonderful his kisses had felt. She wished they could share one last kiss before he promised his loyalty to Kathy again.

It was small comfort to remember he'd seemed to enjoy the

few times he had kissed her. She'd felt as if he were concentrating on her alone—as if no one else mattered. She sighed. No more wonderful kisses. She wouldn't stand in the way of Tanya's happiness.

She wished she had some knitting or crocheting to keep her mind off the impending meeting. What if they talked until lunch time, and Tanya got hungry? It would be hard to convince the little girl not to go into her own house until her parents were through talking. Lee didn't want Tanya to hear any angry comments and get scared they were going to come to blows.

Remembering Alex with the burglar, she wondered if he'd take a swing at Kathy if things got ugly. No, he wouldn't she decided. No matter how mad he got, he'd hold himself in. However, he hadn't shown any restraint when the photographer snapped them.

No other man would tempt her again, not for a long, long time. None could compare with Alex. She wondered if part of his appeal was that he was forbidden. No, she'd want him even if he were free, despite his tendency to be bossy. He'd protected her and cared for her. His kisses hinted he had a hard time resisting her. Any woman would love to have a man feel about her like that.

Alex pulled up in front of a brick house with four white columns. Built in the style of a colonial mansion, it looked spacious and maybe a little pretentious. Without a word, he slammed the car door and strode up the walk. Lee waited, twisting the material of her skirt in her fingers.

The front door opened. A petite blonde stood staring, a frown marring her face. Her halter top showcased her full breasts, and the pencil slim shorts revealed trim hips. Lee gasped. No wonder Alex decided to go back to her. Next to Kathy, Lee might as well be invisible.

Alex spoke to Kathy for a few minutes, then grasped Tanya's hand and headed toward the car. Lee waved to Tanya, who broke loose from Alex's hold and raced toward her.

"Hi, Tanya."

"Hi, Lee. Will you push me in the swing?"

Lee jumped out of the car, grasped the little girl's hand and headed around the side of the house. Lee averted her eyes, but she could feel Kathy's stare boring into her all the way.

Kathy's voice followed them. "Thought you said she was older and plain looking. Why's she wearing such a short skirt? Her legs look like they go on forever."

Tanya asked Lee. "What does 'legs go on forever' mean? Can you walk a long ways before you get tired and stop?"

Lee fumbled with the gate latch. "Uh, never mind."

Tanya looked at Lee. "Mommy asked if you were pretty. I said, 'I guess so.' I bet Daddy thinks so, too."

Struggling with the gate, Lee hoped he did, but that was small comfort now. She urged Tanya toward the swing. Lee settled her in the seat and inhaled the smell of rain-washed earth.

In a nearby magnolia tree a mockingbird sang several different tunes while the aroma of the huge white blooms wafted by. How could the day seem so perfect when her world was falling apart? Lee gave Tanya a shove in the swing, brushed a tear from her cheek and glanced toward the window.

Lee remembered his kiss, how it had felt to be in his arms. A knot burgeoned inside. She had never even shared his bed. He hadn't ever said he cared about her—but he'd risked his life to keep her safe. Would it be harder to give him up if he'd said he loved her?

All she knew was that come fall she couldn't be with him anymore. She wouldn't see the adorable way his hair curled at the base of his neck when he needed a haircut, wouldn't smell the spicy scent of his aftershave, and wouldn't feel his arms around her, keeping her safe in the face of danger. Hardest to bear, was the thought that she wouldn't feel his lips on hers ever again.

She blinked her eyes, and then brushed the moisture away. It wasn't the end of the world. She wouldn't cry in front of Tanya. She had a good future to look forward to, didn't she?

She'd treasure the last few weeks she had to work with him. And if he so much as suggested an affair, she'd be strong and say no. She straightened her spine. Now that she realized what she had to do, she was determined to carry it off.

"Lee, this is fun. Push me higher, please," Tanya asked.

Lee pushed harder. Tanya was a dear. She deserved a chance to grow up with a mother and father at home. Giving her that chance was worth the sacrifice. But oh, how Lee'd miss being with Alex. Not seeing him every day would leave a hole in her life and in her heart.

She'd never been in love before—hadn't realized it could bring you pain as well as joy. Well, the joy had been fleeting. Was it really worth it?

She wouldn't have missed any of his kisses, not even the ones for show, and definitely not the ones he gave her when no one watched. She clamped her lips together.

There'd be no more hand-holding, no more looking at the stars, no hot kisses.

She'd have to do without all that.

She'd save her love for her nieces and nephews if she had any. At least Libby could marry and have children. Alex didn't know how lucky he was to have a daughter like Tanya. Being a parent was something Lee would have to forego.

Alex stood at the front door. His gaze followed Lee and Tanya until they disappeared around the corner of the house. Holding Lee's hand, Tanya was skipping along beside Lee. Alex followed Kathy into the hall.

Her outfit didn't leave much to the imagination. Her body still looked fabulous, but it didn't turn him on like—like looking at Lee did now. He wouldn't go there—mustn't think about Lee any more. He'd brought Tanya into the world, and her happiness was what counted.

Instead of being annoyed he was staring at her figure, Kathy seemed to relish it. She smiled finally, but her eyes still smoldered. What could she be stewing about now? She was the one who'd filed for divorce so many months ago, but could she be jealous of Lee?

He reached out to take her hand. "Kathy, we need to talk."

She pulled her hand back. "Okay, come in and sit down then."

He stepped into the living room. Same cream-colored walls and tan couch he'd seen a hundred times but it wasn't home anymore.

Kathy sat in a chair and gestured to the couch, the one she'd always discouraged him from sitting on because it might look old too soon. She let one shoe dangle provocatively as she leaned forward to show even more of her breasts. "Is this about your tag-a-long?"

He pushed back a wave of irritation. "Lee isn't a tag-a-long. She's my secretary, but I came to talk about Tanya. She needs a family—a mother and father who can work together to bring her up."

"You want to have her every other week, is that it?"

"That's not all I want." He scooted to the edge of the couch and stretched out his hand to take hers, but she held it out of reach. He swallowed. "You're not making this easy."

She leaned forward. "You think raising a daughter by myself while you gallivanted around Europe was easy?"

He leaned back, trying to look more at ease than he felt. "Of course not. You did a great job. I'm sorry I wasn't here when you had to rush her to the emergency room for stitches after she dropped that heavy window grate on her head.

"That was the grating you ordered. It was supposed to keep her from falling into the window well."

"So, how did it fall on her head?"

"Well, she claimed she wanted to look into the basement windows so that's why she lifted it up to climb down there." Kathy glared at him, her green eyes piercing.

He needed to get her in a more conciliatory mood. He cleared his throat, searching for the right words.

She spoke first. "I suppose you want to have the thirty-day waiting period waived so you can marry your current cutie, though I can't imagine what you see in her."

He swallowed. He'd been kissing Lee, and his divorce hadn't even been final. He should have left her alone. "You mean — you mean the divorce isn't final yet? But I thought—"

"Well, my lawyer waited to send it in. He wanted to be sure that was what I wanted. Then the judge took a while to sign it. I just got it back last week. The thirty days will be over by the end of this month, so you can marry your bimbo then unless I have my lawyer appeal it."

"She's not a bimbo. She's a damn good secretary." He wanted to defend Lee, to explain all her good qualities, how brave she was, how she never belittled him — but that wouldn't help now. Besides, that wasn't why he'd come.

He held out his hand. "Kathy, I want is for us to be a family again. I know I spent too much time away from home, but things could be different now. With the rent from this house and my early retirement payments from the government, we should have enough to get by until I get my business going."

She frowned. "And live on hot dogs and beans until then?"

"We won't have to. Besides, it shouldn't take that long for me to make a pretty good living. The economy's getting stronger. More people will want to travel. I can advertise on the web to build up the business. I'll build you a showplace home that will be the envy of those who matter in Grandville. Just wait until you meet the mayor and his wife. They can introduce us to other important people." He watched her face. That ought to impress her.

"You haven't said you love me. Now that I think about it, you haven't said it since we were first married. Other husbands tell their wives that. If you really loved me, you'd say it—every day."

He swallowed, then looked outside, saw Lee pushing Tanya in the swing and heard her squeal in delight. Tanya was worth whatever sacrifice he had to make.

He leaned forward. "Of course I love you. I wouldn't suggest this if I didn't." Even as he said it, he knew it was a lie.

She crossed her shapely legs and leaned forward, her breasts straining against her halter top. That didn't excite him like it used to, but Tanya was what mattered. Still, he couldn't seem to banish Lee's face from his thoughts.

Lee had encouraged him to do this, but her sad eyes had told him her heart wasn't in it. How would she take it when he told her he was actually going back to Kathy?

He shoved his hands into his pockets, leaned back and waited for Kathy's reply. He clamped his mouth shut to keep from blurting out he hadn't meant it. Instead he asked, "If I'd come home more often, bought us a nicer house and resigned from the CIA sooner, would you have still asked for a divorce?"

Kathy rested her hand in her chin.

Lee said he was too bossy. Could that have had something to do with the break up?

Kathy threw back her head and laughed. Her high-pitched tones grated on his ears. How had he ever thought her laugh sounded sweet.

"You've got to be kidding or incredibly stupid. If you think for one moment, I'll take your sorry ass back into my life or let you into my bed—you weren't that great in the sack by the way. Don't know why I let you into my pants that first time—guess I was curious to see how it would feel. Too bad you didn't live up to my expectations. But then I was pregnant, so I married you."

Her words slammed into his gut. She made him feel small and naked. How had he ever thought this could work?

She rose and pointed to the table behind the couch. A manila envelope lay on top. "Since we've got that nonsense out of the way, you can open that envelope."

"Nonsense, huh?" *Doing what's best for Tanya isn't nonsense, but there's no way I'd even consider getting back together now.*

He glared at her, swallowed the vile names he wanted to call her. He rose, marched around the couch and reached for the envelope. "What's in here, the divorce decree?"

She looked smug. "Open it and see."

At last, a copy for him. He reached inside and pulled out glossy 8 X 10s. The camera man had caught it all—their torrid kiss, Lee's beautiful naked breasts—the way they stood waist deep in water, as if they were both naked, the look of surprise on her face, the way he clutched her arms. Alex smothered a gasp.

Kathy looked triumphant now. She ran a red nail over the image of Lee's naked breasts. "Do you want the whole world and especially Tanya to see these?"

Dread wrapped itself around him. She'd put the worst possible slant on things if she showed them to Tanya. Kathy could turn his daughter against him so that she'd refuse to visit him.

He shoved the photos back in the envelope. "What kind of mother would show those pictures to her daughter—would she even understand what they imply?"

"I'm not afraid to tell my daughter what a sorry bastard her so-called father is."

He clenched his hands into fists. He wanted to throttle her, make her see reason. "I don't care what you think of me." He shoved the envelope behind him. "You're not showing these to Tanya."

"I have other copies."

"If you show them to her, you'd be a sorry excuse for a mother. I'll sue for full custody."

She looked smug. "I don't think so. Now I've got the upper hand. I'll appeal the divorce decree, claim adultery and ask for more than half of your assets, like your lake cottage for instance."

He stepped closer, shook a finger at her chest. "You can't do that. The lake property was willed to me by my uncle. It's separate property. And I haven't committed adultery. Even though I thought the divorce was final, we didn't—"

Kathy laughed. "Sure, and the Pope isn't Catholic. I'm sure you've been screwing her to kingdom come behind my back."

"I have not."

"You're a lying bastard." She grabbed the pictures. "Do you want these shown to Tanya and sent to the papers and the judge?"

"The newspapers won't care about them but surely you won't let our daughter see them. How do you think she'll feel? If she thinks I'm carrying on with another woman, she'll feel rejected. She'll feel bad about herself and hate her own father."

"Suppose you aren't her father?"

He shook his fist in her face. "The hell I'm not. You're lying. Why did you drop out of college and insist we had to get married if I'm not her father?"

"I didn't want my child to be called illegitimate."

"What sorry bastard would let some other guy take responsibility for his wild oats?"

Kathy raised her chin. "I'm not about to tell you. With that temper of yours, you'd probably try to beat him up. And he did ask me to marry him, but you looked like you had a better future."

It was all he could manage not to take a swing at her. He wanted the divorce to be final, but no matter what the facts, he loved Tanya, wanted the best for the dear little scamp. And he wasn't giving her up.

"I married you for love, but you've been faking it all along, just for a comfortable living and a name." He'd been feeling guilty about his attraction to Lee, but Kathy was despicable. "You've been carrying on a masquerade as my so-called wife all those years, without telling me who else you were sleeping with, and now you have the gall to blackmail me with pictures and demand outrageous terms." He shook his fist at her.

She backed away a step. "Like I said, I'm not telling you his name because you'd probably go after him with both barrels."

Alex smothered a gasp. Maybe she wasn't bluffing about Tanya. "I might take a swing at the guy, but I'm not a murderer."

"What about all the men you must have killed as a CIA agent?"

He glared at her. "That's got nothing to do with this. Besides, there was only one. He would have killed me if I didn't get him first. It was only a stroke of luck that a car blocked his aim before I shot him."

Facing known assassins hadn't scared him near as much as Kathy's threats. He had to stop her. Kathy would alienate both Tanya and Lee and ruin his life and his daughter's. He grabbed her arm, wanting to shake her into admitting the guy's name. She was stubborn. If she didn't want to tell him, she wouldn't.

He let go of her arm. The way he felt now, he couldn't risk the chance he'd injure her seriously.

He sank onto the couch. How had he ever thought he loved Kathy? She was nothing like Lee.

He hadn't realized how much he cared about Lee until now. No wonder he hadn't wanted to do this. He loved Lee. Loved her wholeheartedly. And she cared for him. He was sure of that. But talking her out of avoiding marriage just because Sheldon was a threat—well he'd have to do something about that.

Except now he had to protect Tanya from her mother. He

wasn't taking this sitting down. Rising, he glared at her. What could he threaten her with?

❧

Outside Lee had just gotten Tanya swinging fast enough so that only an occasional push was needed. She glanced toward the house.

Through the window she could see Kathy shaking her fist at Alex, then pointing at Lee. Through the thin pane came the phrase, "shameless slut."

Lee cringed. She shouldn't have come.

Alex shook his head, then pulled out his wallet and held out some bills. Kathy snatched them and threw them on a table. Folding her arms beneath her sizable breasts, now heaving as if she were taking hurried breaths, Kathy shouted something sounding like 'bastard'.

Kathy stepped closer and slapped Alex. Lee held her breath. Surely, he wouldn't hit back. She could see his murderous scowl and his hands balled into fists, but he didn't punch her. Kathy launched into a tirade, spouting phrases like 'determined devil' and 'ambitionless asshole,' and then 'pitiful excuse for a man.'

Lee could imagine how that must hurt, but he just stood there with a stoic expression. She hoped Tanya hadn't heard.

"Lee." Tanya's anguished cry caught her attention. "I saw Mommy slap him. Are they going to fight? Daddy's bigger. He might hurt Mommy."

"No, dear. He won't hurt Mommy." From the pained look in his eyes, Lee could tell Kathy had hurt him plenty. Maybe not with blows, but her words must have slashed him raw. Regretting she had put Alex through this, Lee tried to imagine how awful he must feel. And worse yet, in the heat of the moment he might blame her for insisting he try to patch things up. Well, if he did, she'd stand there and take whatever he said.

This was her fault. Why oh why had she thought she had the answer to someone else's problems? She should have minded her own business.

The back door opened, and Alex stormed out, a scowl blackening his face. He snatched Tanya off the swing and carried her to the back steps. Opening the door, he practically shoved her inside. "Go play in your bedroom until Mommy feels better."

"Is she sick?"

"No, but she's mad. I'm leaving now. I will come pick you up next month." He leaned down and kissed her forehead.

"I wish you could stay here with me and Mommy."

"I can't, sweetheart." Alex turned to Lee. "Come on, let's go."

She followed him out of the yard. When she stopped to fasten the gate latch, he barked, "Never mind that. We're leaving now."

She had barely shut the car door when the Jaguar lurched away from the curb and zoomed down the street. She hoped no children were playing in the road. In his present mood, he might not see them in time to stop.

"What happened with Kathy?" She had a pretty good idea, but figured he needed to talk about it instead of letting it fester.

"She turned me down."

"Oh." She tried to say, 'that's too bad,' but she just couldn't get the words out. She'd be lying if she did. "Was she behind those pictures that man took?"

Alex scowled. "Oh, she was behind them all right. You should have seen the evil glint in her eye as she handed the envelope to me. She claimed she'd let the divorce go through as long as I agreed to her exorbitant demands and continued letting Tanya visit only once a month after the divorce is final."

"Wait a minute. I thought your divorce was final."

"I did, too. I signed it long ago, but Kathy just had her lawyer finalize it a few days ago. Now she's threatening to appeal it during the thirty-day waiting period after the judge signed it. She claims she'll show those pictures to the judge as evidence of adultery so the judge will give her more than half of our assets, including sixty percent of my pension allotment, all the furniture, higher child support and sole custody of Tanya. And besides that she wants my lake cottage."

"But-but—that's not fair, and we haven't—haven't even— you know." Lee clamped her mouth shut and crossed her arms in front of her chest.

Alex gripped the wheel. Her chin jutted out, and a hurt look lurked in her brown eyes. "I didn't lie to you. After I signed that damn Agreed Divorce Decree, I assumed it would be taken right to court. I don't know why Kathy waited to have her lawyer take the decree to the judge. Maybe she hoped to talk me into more child support than we'd agreed on. Now she claims she'll take those pictures to the judge and have her lawyer appeal. She wants to ask the judge to award her more of my assets."

"Can she really get the judge to give her more than half?"

"She said she'd claim I've been committing adultery for months."

"That's not true. We only met a few weeks ago."

"I know that, damn it, but the pictures may convince the judge otherwise."

"But if the judge has already signed the decree, isn't it final?"

"Kathy claimed if it's less than thirty days since he did, that she can appeal it and because of those pictures, she can ask for more."

"Did she say anything about me?"

"You don't want to know."

"Please, tell me what she said."

He looked straight ahead, his hands gripping the wheel. "She's got it in her head that we are having a mad passionate affair." Kathy had said, 'That slut's got you twisted around her little finger like Delilah did Sampson,' but he wasn't going to tell Lee that. "She called you a slut."

Lee's eyes flashed fire. "I'm not a slut."

He patted her arm. "Of course you're not. But that wasn't the worst of it. She claimed Tanya, my darling daughter, isn't mine."

Lee gasped. "You mean, she could be some other guy's child?"

He nodded, remembering. His gut tightened as if an outboard motor were tearing at his stomach muscles. "She said she'd been with another guy all the while we'd been going together. Then when she got pregnant, she chose me because I had more potential for making money.

"Can you believe that? Here I thought she loved me, not just what I could give her. She claimed this other guy makes more money now and swears he'd always loved her. She probably wants marry him now."

"So did she tell you who the guy was?"

"When I demanded to know who it was, she zipped her lips shut. That asshole didn't have the balls to admit to fathering a child and do the right thing by marrying her. I've taken care of Kathy and her child for almost six years." He clenched the hand that wasn't on the wheel into a fist. "I'd like to knock his brains out. But if she was having sex with both of us, Tanya could still be my daughter."

"Are you going to take a paternity test to find out for sure?"

"As far as I'm concerned, I've been her father for the whole five years of her life."

"So that's why Kathy wouldn't agree to a reconciliation."

Remembering her high-pitched laugh, his gut twisted. "There's no chance in hell I'd go back to her now. She wants to redo the divorce decree on her terms."

"You can't let her get away with that."

"Right now, she'll do anything to get back at me, even risk confusing Tanya by showing her those damn pictures. I wanted to kick the shit out of her, but of course I didn't." He was sorry now that he hadn't made love to Lee already. If he were going to be accused of philandering, he might as well enjoy the fruits—but that wouldn't be fair to Lee. And now that the divorce wasn't final yet, he couldn't.

Things seemed impossible. He needed to find a way out of this dilemma, one that would keep Lee safe and but not turn Tanya against him. He wanted to be able to see her regularly. And he didn't want to let Lee go. But he hadn't the foggiest idea where to start.

Chapter 18

Back in their hotel room, Lee tried to think how to comfort him. She wanted to dance and sing and shout 'Hurrah!' Kathy didn't deserve him. Maybe he could find happiness again—if not with hers, then with someone else.

The thought of another woman in his arms dampened her exhilaration, dumping her back on the stony surface of reality. He was free, but she wasn't. She had to stay away from him for his own safety—and Tanya's. Life was so unfair.

Later, after they'd checked out of the Worthington Hotel, she sat in his car, watching him load their things. From his expression she couldn't tell if he were relieved Kathy had turned him down or still furious with her.

"Where are you taking me?" she asked as he slid in behind the wheel.

He started the car, then reached over and took her hand. "You've been cooped up in that room all day. I'm taking you to another town for a day or two where you can walk around without looking over your shoulder. But after that I...I'm not sure what to do next."

She squeezed his hand, then let go so he could have it free for driving. "That's a first."

"For what?"

She smiled. "The first time you admitted you don't have an answer for everything."

"Am I as bad as all that?"

"Well, sometimes." She hesitated. "I'm not quite sure how to put it."

"You mean I'm a little overbearing."

She nodded. "At times you're like a lion dressed in gentlemen's clothes. You make me feel as if I don't do what you ask when it concerns safety, you'll let out an earth shaking roar."

He looked astonished. "I don't see myself that way at all. Kathy complained that I always had to be in control. Being sure of myself and what I'm doing, it's part of being a man, part of who I am."

"But if someone else will be affected by your decision, don't you think it's fair to let her have a say?"

"But I always take the other person's well being under consideration, especially if that person's in danger."

"I'm sure you do, but—"

"And I'm usually right...except for one time—"

"You actually admit you were wrong once?"

He nodded. Pain showed in his eyes. "I was once, and it cost me—" His voice cracked. He kept his face straight ahead, obviously pretending to be concentrating on city traffic.

"What happened?"

"I don't want to talk about it."

Lee leaned closer. "Talk about me being afraid of life. Now you're the one who's afraid to face something."

"I've faced it—but I can't forget it."

"You can't let something from a long time ago fester inside and poison your life. What happened?"

He frowned and took a deep breath. "An agent from another country, my contact there, had her cover blown. I was supposed to spirit her away. I'd just hailed a taxi when someone shot at us. I thought it was me they wanted and offered to go with them."

He bowed his head, then continued, his voice strained.

"They seemed to agree, but when I started to walk toward them, I left her partially uncovered. She was getting into the cab when someone shot her in the back. I pulled out my gun and got off one shot but they got away."

"Then what happened?"

"I climbed in after her and told the driver to rush to the hospital. He got us there in record time, but it was too late. She died in my arms."

Lee touched his arm. "You must have felt awful. No wonder you're so paranoid about safety."

"I was in a blue funk for days. I almost called headquarters and told them to take that job and shove it, especially after they asked me to fly home and break the news to her family. I knew they'd blame me for her death."

"And did they?"

He shook his head. "They were shocked. They hadn't realized her job was so dangerous. I felt like a damn hypocrite."

"But it might not have been your fault."

"I knew the opposition might find us. I should have taken her to the railroad station earlier under cover of darkness."

"So—did you have a good reason not to leave earlier?"

He shook his head. "There weren't any trains leaving until eight o'clock." His voice sounded strained. "I didn't want to leave her there alone with the station master, and I had a contact I had to meet in the park at seven a.m."

"Couldn't you arrange to meet the contact later?"

Alex shook his head. "I didn't know how to get in touch with him. He had important information. I had to go."

"So did he?"

Alex pulled onto I-35W. "Did he what?"

"Have important information?"

"He didn't show, but going to meet him made me rush with preparations for getting Idelle to the station. I was careless and missed seeing a tail."

"Did that guy contact you again?"

Alex shook his head. "Either he got caught or thought his information wasn't that important."

Lee patted his arm. "Or maybe that was a ruse to catch you."

"I considered that, but discarded the idea. Now that I think about it, you could be right."

"Then what happened wasn't your fault."

"Yes, it was. I've played the scene over and over in my mind, trying to figure out what I could have done to save her. I thought of several things I could have done, but didn't." His chin sunk down toward his chest. "I let Idelle down when I might have saved her."

She took his hand and intertwined her fingers with his. "Under the circumstances, I don't think you could have done anything to change things."

He took a deep breath. "Maybe you're right. But I'll never forget her trusting eyes looking up into my face, expecting me to create a miracle and make her live."

She patted his arm again. "It's useless to agonize over the past if you can't change it, just like I can't change the fact that I may be hunted down and captured."

"Not if I can help it. I want to do what I can to keep you safe."

He rubbed at one eye. "I need to concentrate on the present. I have to figure out some way to convince Kathy not to show Tanya those pictures."

Lee glanced out the car window. "Aren't you going to tell me where we're going?"

"I'm taking you to Waco. As long as we're not followed, we can relax and do some sightseeing."

Lee stretched. "It will be nice not to have to look over my shoulder all the time."

"I almost forgot. Open the glove compartment."

"Why?"

"Must you question everything I ask you to do?"

"Didn't you listen to anything I said about being bossy and overbearing?"

"All right. Would you please open it? There's something in there I want you to get."

She flashed him a smile. "See, that wasn't so hard, was it?"

"No, I guess not."

She pulled down the little door. "Now what?"

"Get out that little box."

She pulled out a small box wrapped in gold paper with a bow that almost covered the top.

He grinned. "That's something I picked up in Middletown for your birthday."

A warm glow spread over her as she grasped the present with trembling fingers. "Thank you."

Tiny tears of happiness welled up in her eyes, tears that kept her from saying anything more. In spite of all they'd been through, he'd remembered her birthday was five days after Libby's. And somehow, although they'd been together practically the whole time, he'd managed to slip off and get her something.

She tore the wrapping off and opened the box to find a tiny gold chamois bag. After loosening the drawstrings, she reached inside and pulled out a pair of jade earrings. Each little green heart hung from a gold bead. "They're beautiful."

"Libby said to get something green to match your eyes, but—" He glanced out at the sky, more gray than blue right now. "In this light your eyes look more brown to me. I guess hazel eyes are changeable. Maybe if I see you in that green dress again, they'll look green.

His gaze met hers. "Kathy's eyes are green. I don't particularly care for her green eyes, but I like everything about the way you look."

She took his hand and squeezed it. "Kathy's a fool not to want you. There's something I'd better tell you. About my eyes—they aren't really brown."

He looked at her face. "They look so natural, but I should have guessed. You're wearing colored contacts, aren't you?"

"My eyes are green, but as long as I'm likely to be hunted down, I'll wear the brown contacts and keep my hair this color."

He glanced at her. "Auburn looks nice on you, but what's your natural color?"

"Strawberry blonde."

He held up her hand. "That's not surprising with your fair skin." He kept hold of her hand until letting go to steer around another car. Finally he pulled off at the Waco exit.

"Are we going to stay here tonight?" she asked.

He nodded as he pulled up in front of a Holiday Inn. "Come inside while I register. I'm not leaving you alone out here."

"You're bossing me around again."

"Sorry, it's hard for an old tiger to learn new tricks."

In the lobby, she sat on a leather couch while he signed in. A few minutes later he held out two keys. "Take one."

"Good. You got two rooms."

He shook his head. "Shhhh. I'm not leaving you alone," he whispered. "But I did get a room with two beds."

She drew a long sigh. Now that the divorce papers had been signed by the judge, would he want to— She looked up to meet his gaze. Grinning seductively, he reached for her hand. "Okay, Mrs. Lance, let's get our stuff."

After they stepped outside, she asked, "Why did you sign us up as a married couple again?"

"I don't want to call attention to us. I told them we were on our honeymoon and not to bother us. I said you might be nervous so I wanted two beds."

She giggled. "You didn't."

He put an arm around her waist and pulled her close. "That's one way to get people to leave us alone." Wearing an engaging grin, he picked up their suitcases. She offered to carry hers. "Wouldn't dream of it. But," he looked at her with invitation in his eyes, "You can give me something to dream about—"

"But Alex—"

"No buts. I'm going to take you out for a great steak dinner at somewhere quiet and romantic and then—"

She drew in a deep breath. "I don't think that's a good idea."

"Just think about, okay?" His smile oozed confidence.

Spending the night in his bed would be wonderful. But would that only intensify the pain she'd feel when they parted?

Wondering how to convince him they had no future together, she walked beside him to their room. His muscles rippled as he carried their bags.

He unlocked the door. "How about wearing that green dress with your new earrings and just for tonight, would you take out those contacts? I want to see the real you."

"You've seen the real me, maybe not my eye color, but you probably know me better than anybody, except my sister."

In the bathroom she put on the earrings and took out the contacts. A moment later she smoothed the green dress over her hips, then slowly opened the door.

Stepping stepped out, she felt like a model on display. He let out a long low whistle. "You look fantastic."

Meeting his adoring gaze, she couldn't help smiling.

He held out his hand. "Come."

"Where are we going?"

"Some place where the lights are bright so every male will be jealous after seeing you with me. Or I can take you some place romantic where the lights are low, and we sit at a corner table."

She smiled in spite of herself. Women might have made great strides, but men still felt having a pretty girl on their arms made them feel successful. But, hey, if he thought her beautiful, who was she to complain?

She smiled up at him. "I prefer a romantic atmosphere, but I want good food, too."

He held out his arm. "Let's go."

Downstairs, he scanned the lobby, then stopped at the desk and asked about places to go. He led her out the door into the warm evening beneath a crescent moon.

Ten minutes later, they sat side by side at a small booth in the corner of an intimate restaurant. Flickering beams from a candle in a glass globe outlined the firm line of his chin and masculine nose.

Soft music played, and smells of grilling beef wafted by. He held her hand as he consulted the menu and the wine list. "What would you like?"

She pointed to the Asti Spumanti. "That and a small sirloin."

Still holding her hand, he waved for the waiter. After placing their orders, he lifted her hand to his lips and kissed her fingertips, one by one.

His gaze met hers. Seeing the look of adoration on his smiling face warmed her all over.

Slowly, he moved closer, crowding her against the wall, moving in like a lion, sure of his mastery.

"But, we can't kiss—not here."

He smiled. "The judge already signed the divorce decree. Give me one good reason why not." His eyes twinkled, as if daring her to pull away. His lips inched closer.

She couldn't move farther away. She really didn't want to. Soon enough, she'd have to leave him. And if he kissed her in a public place—well, it couldn't be too intimate a kiss. What would it hurt to pretend they were really a couple? She closed her eyes.

Chapter 19

Eyes closed, Lee waited in the restaurant booth. She could pretend they were alone — and maybe no one would notice them here in the corner.

His touch was gentle at first. She savored the softness of his mouth against hers. Then his arms came around her, pulled her against his firm chest.

Her breasts tingled. His kiss took on another dimension. His lips roved over her mouth as if he were trying to imprint the feel of her on his heart and soul forever. However, his touch would be forever emblazoned on her heart. Too soon, she'd have to leave him, but she'd cherish these memories forever.

She touched his face, felt the heat of his skin. She let her lips say what was in her heart. Could he taste her hunger? Could he feel how fast her heart was pounding? If he realized she cared for him, maybe, just maybe that would make him feel better about himself, perhaps heal the hurt he felt from Kathy's rejection and the guilt from failing to save the lady spy. "Alex —" she murmured.

"Shhhh." He silenced her with another kiss, more soul shattering than the last.

By the time she came up for air, she felt as if she couldn't get out a coherent sentence, but she had to. "Alex, there's something I need to tell you."

He gazed at her with soulful blue eyes.

How could she say this without sounding asinine? "Alex, what happened — what happened long ago in that country — "

"Bosnia."

"You've done your best to protect me. I'm sure you did the same for her."

"But I couldn't keep her from dying, and — " He sighed. "And I wasn't there either when your apartment blew up."

"You couldn't know Bubba was going to bomb my place. You told me to stay at the trailer, but I didn't. You mustn't keep flogging yourself for things that happened in the past."

She touched his arm. "You're starting a new business. You don't need to worry about small time criminals overrunning your office. That's why after I move to another town, we shouldn't see each other."

He squeezed her hand. "But if something happened to you that I could prevent, I couldn't live with myself."

Azure eyes stared into hers. He might have some feeling for her, but to him she was only a responsibility, one he hadn't asked for. It was better to leave before he got hurt or she suffered any more heartbreak.

She pulled her hand away. "Joe will set me up in another town. I'll meet new people — none as interesting as you but — "

"And maybe no one who kisses quite like I do." He was smiling, but she sensed a need to know he'd touched her. She was afraid to let him know how much.

"Thanks for being my pretend lover."

"Kissing a beautiful woman is never a chore, and I wasn't pretending just now."

His words made her smile, but it was time to pull away. She met his adoring gaze. Her heart skipped a beat. Could he really be falling for her?

The waiter plunked down their salads, as if to remind them why they were here.

Alex said, "thanks," and waved the waiter away. He leaned

forward. "Lee, you can't be serious about leaving right away. I'll miss you like crazy."

Did he mean that or was it just a line? Trying not to meet his eyes, she ate her salad, barely tasting it. The waiter returned, bearing sizzling steaks nestled beside fluffy baked potatoes stuffed with sour cream, bacon bits, and shredded cheese.

Her steak was delicious. As Lee sipped her wine, Alex set his down and took her hand. "There's one thing sweeter than that wine."

"What?"

He leaned close to whisper, "Your kisses."

Basking in the glow of his compliment, she wondered if he really meant it. She met his gaze. His intense look took her breath away. Maybe, just maybe, he felt the same way about her.

After they'd finished, he paid the bill and led her outside. They walked hand in hand along the river, its shoreline gentled by moonlight.

He pulled her into the lacy shadows of a lone mesquite tree. His fingers intertwined in her hair as he backed her up against the tree and cradled her face in his hands.

A hungry, adoring look lit up his eyes. Savoring the anticipation, she took a deep breath. His smile drew her in. His hands slid down her back, pulling her closer against him. His ragged breathing matched her own. Her heart skipped a beat.

She ought to pull away. Never one to live for the moment, she decided this was one time she would give in to her impulses. She raised her lips to meet his.

Gentle at first, enough for her to feel the softness of his lips, his mouth met hers. He planted kisses on her cheeks and her forehead before returning to claim her lips with an intensity that surprised her. He held her tightly as if afraid she'd move away.

She slid her arms around him, felt his rock hard chest

pressing against her breasts, felt his arousal pressing against her and wondered why she should resist him when this might be the last time they'd be together like this.

She kissed him, melting into his firm lips, tangling her fingers in his thick hair, and savoring the warmth of his cheek against hers. In the darkness he cupped her breasts with both hands, squeezing gently. She leaned into his hands. He was driving her wild with wanting.

His gaze met hers. "Spend the night with me, in my bed, please?"

❦

Alex watched and waited. How had he ever thought he could go back to Kathy when Lee made his heart pound like this? He shuddered to think he'd been about to give up all that mattered in the whole world, except for Tanya of course. She was the only reason he'd made that asinine suggestion to his ex-wife.

Thank goodness Kathy turned him down. Somehow he'd persuade Lee to face the future with him — with all its risks. He had to convince her that was better than facing them alone.

Moonlight lit up her eyes, soft green depths he could lose himself in. "Never seen such beautiful eyes." He raised her hand to his lips and pressed a soft kiss on her palm — and waited — and hoped.

❦

Lee gazed at his face, saw his wanting. With all her heart Lee wanted to say, 'yes', wanted to surrender to the desire threatening to overwhelm her. But if she did, could she bear to say 'goodbye' when she had to leave?

A new life loomed ahead. Would it be filled with regret if she passed up this chance to be with him, to bask in his adoration, and lose herself making love with him?

Alex gripped her shoulders and pointed to a shooting star arcing across the heavens. Like the star she wanted to soar for one glorious moment.

Gently, he turned her face toward him, his gaze melting her into warm syrup, making her feel as if she could flow over and around him.

"Lee?" His eyes spoke of longing and tenderness.

"Yes," she whispered and snuggled into his arms, feeling as if she'd come home at last. From now on, home would have to be wherever she made it—if only it could be with him.

Taking her hand, he led her back to the car. Inside he turned on a tape of 'Some Enchanted Evening.' For the short ride, it seemed as if the rhythm of the car matched the music. This would be a night to remember, no matter what the future brought.

Holding his hand, she glided into the hotel and its elevator. Walking to their room, she felt as if she were being wafted aloft by a tropical breeze, warm and magical.

Alex pushed the door shut and fastened the bolt. Seconds later, his warm fingers brushed her back, sending a tingle down her spine as he released the zipper of her dress.

He turned her in his arms and slowly slid the dress from her shoulders. "You looked lovely in this dress, but now you look like a goddess rising from the sea."

She couldn't help smiling as the green fabric rippled to the floor. Eagerness lit up his face as he fumbled with the clasp of her bra, and then filled his hands with her throbbing breasts. He dipped his head and pressed soft kisses on her flesh. Never had she felt so alive or so desired.

Then he stepped back. Puzzled, she looked at his face. His expression seemed unreadable. What now?

His hand caressed her cheek. "You're sure you want—"

"Yes," she said and threw her arms around him.

He grinned. "You'll have to let go of me. I have way too

much clothes on."

Her fingers made short work of the buttons on his shirt. Would he think she slept around? She hadn't, but what if he expected more than she could give? What if she were not as good at this as other women he'd been with?

Suddenly in too much of a hurry to worry about that now, she shoved his shirt off, undid his belt, and slid it away.

She reached for the zipper tab, then saw the awesome bulge straining against the closure. She took a deep breath and pulled the zipper down. His manhood pushed forth, straining the fabric of his navy briefs.

He grinned. "Well, go on."

As she eased his briefs over his hips, he did the same with her half slip, panties and hose, all in one smooth motion.

His eyes seemed to caress her nakedness. She in turn gazed upon him, from his broad shoulders, to his bulging biceps, trim hips, and — well, he was magnificent.

She caught his proud grin before he pulled her into his arms and urged her toward the bed. "I want to touch you all over." He caressed her breasts and kissed the tips of each. "And squeeze." His hands echoed his words. "And kiss you everywhere." His mouth held hers with a lingering hunger. Then he pushed her down onto the bed.

Seconds later, he lay beside her. His hands caressed her breasts. His lips roved over the tip of one and captured it, suckling hungrily. Then he did the other one, sending her into spasms of delight.

Running her fingers through his thick dark hair, she arched toward him, reeling from the sensations flooding her body.

He pulled away. Now what? Surely he hadn't changed his mind.

She heard the crinkle of tearing foil. He'd remembered she didn't want a baby. Silently, she thanked him for that. Anticipation bubbling, she waited for him to return to her side.

After settling beside her, he pulled her close and nuzzled

her neck. He kissed her face, her neck, and her shoulders. He kissed each of her damp nipples, making them tingle even more. Then he slid his fingers over her thighs, moving ever inward.

Roving fingers tantalized her flesh. Something tightened and throbbed inside. She felt like a bull fighter might, waiting for the bull's headlong rush.

His quick push filled her. She gasped at the size of him, then met each thrust with eagerness. Faster and faster she moved. Her breaths came in ragged bursts. Tension built as she gloried in his strong thrusts.

Then, like an orchestra reaching a crescendo, so did she. He followed, quivering in her arms like a cymbal being hit over and over.

His lips met hers in a long tender kiss. "You're everything I dreamed and more.

She smiled, her heart overflowing. "I think I love you."

At first he didn't say anything, but just looked at her with a serious expression.

Then he took her hand and squeezed it. "You make me feel more alive than I've ever felt before. At first, I only wanted to protect you, but now, I want you with me always."

Overwhelmed by his words, she kissed him, and then opened her eyes to meet his gaze. Did that mean he loved her?

"I want you lying beside me every morning, and I want to make love to you every night. We have to get married. I won't let you get away from me, not in a million years."

Thrilled to know how much he wanted her, she felt chained by her situation. They couldn't be together. How was she ever going to tell him?

❧

The gravelly voice grated on his ears. He shifted the phone to his left ear. "But Bart, I can't do that. I'd be arrested for murder. And even if I don't get charged, it could cost me my job."

"That's a chance you'll have to take—unless of course you want me to let the word out—"

The harsh laugh sent chills down his spine. Bart would do it, too. He never made idle threats.

Bart continued. "I got three years rent free, courtesy of Texas Department of Corrections, but you got off scot free."

"Can't thank you enough for not ratting on me. I'd never have gotten on with the bureau with that on my record."

"Thanks won't cut it. You owe me, buddy, for not telling the cops you helped arrange that liquor store hold-up. Would have been a great graduation party if the cops hadn't caught us. Well, now it's payback time."

"But—" He ran a hand through his sweaty hair. "Joe is moving her tonight, but he won't tell me where. Standard procedure. It was only a stroke of luck that I overheard him mention her first name when he talked to her on the phone. No one but the marshal and someone much higher up knows the names of the witnesses he's responsible for."

"Search his desk. He's got to have it written down somewhere."

"Nope. Also standard procedure."

"Damn it. I want that frigging broad silenced. The trial's coming up soon. I don't care how you do it, but you'd better make it look like an accident or your ass is toast."

More ominous than Bart's voice, was the whine of the dial tone, a chilling reminder of the high pitched hum of a heart monitor when someone died. He swallowed. Somehow, he was going to have to get into Icebeg's computer and find Lee's new address.

Chapter 20

Lee squeezed her eyes shut, then opened them and wriggled out of Alex's arms. "I can't marry you. I wish—I wish I could, but I can't marry anyone."

Dismay and disbelief shaped his face. "But I thought—" He pulled her back into his arms and pressed a tender kiss on her lips. He met her gaze, his eyes questioning.

"You thought if you made love to me you could banish all my fears about Sheldon and his henchmen."

Just remembering that day her life was ruined forever made her tremble. "You didn't see the hatred on Bart Sheldon's face when he was arrested. You didn't smell the nasty cigar smoke he blew in my face. You didn't hear him curse and call me a bitch. He laughed and said that he'd track me down like a hungry lion, even if he had to scour the sands of Death Valley to find me."

Alex smoothed back a lock of hair from her face. "Wish I'd been there to protect you."

"You didn't even know me then."

"If I had, we'd probably be married by now."

"But you were married then."

"If I'd known you then, that would have jolted me into realizing my marriage was a sham. Should have agreed to Kathy's terms right away. Material things aren't worth all the bitterness we stirred up." He sighed. "Heaven knows how she'll poison Tanya's mind against me."

"Don't worry about that until it happens. She might realize how upsetting that might be for Tanya."

"And you need to stop dwelling on what might happen and stay with me so I can protect you."

"I want to—but I'm afraid." Runaway tears wet her cheeks. "It doesn't matter what you want or what I want. It can never be. I won't draw you and Tanya into the mess my life has become. At least you'll be able to see her regularly."

"That's another problem I'll have to deal with."

"But the decree gives you visitation rights, and the courts will back you up."

"That may change if Kathy keeps insisting Tanya isn't my daughter."

"What if she's lying?"

"She was very definite on that. Maybe I'm infertile."

"How can you know that?"

"We haven't used birth control since Tanya was a year old. Surely, we'd have several kids by now. Damn woman won't tell me who she thinks the father was."

"Maybe she's just being spiteful."

"Or bitter. Guess it comes with getting divorced."

"Do you think she can prove her claims?"

"Not without a DNA test. But as her husband, under Texas law, I'm presumed to be the father."

"Maybe she wants to collect child support while she looks for a rich husband."

"I don't mind supporting Tanya. After taking care of her for five years, she'll always be my daughter, whether I sired her or not. I only hope Kathy doesn't file proceedings to have someone else declared her father. I couldn't bear to be cut off from seeing her."

Lee caressed his cheek, then pulled his head to rest on her shoulder. "That would be awful. I hope Kathy doesn't stoop to that."

She hugged him tightly, imagining how anxious he must feel

about his daughter. She tried not to think about the heartache she'd feel after leaving him. The coarse skin of his cheek pressing against her face warmed her as nothing else could.

She gripped his broad back. Even more than making love to him, as wonderful as it had been, she'd miss being held in his arms. She sighed.

He pulled back, his blue eyes meeting her gaze. "If you won't let me protect you, you have to let the marshals in the Witness Security Program do it. Joe should be able to keep you safe if he'd only act like a man who cared about your safety instead of an iceberg."

A bitter laugh escaped her lips. "There must be a leak somewhere. You saw how Bubba found me. And Floyd, your so-called burglar was looking for me too."

He scratched his head. "You should be safe when you start your new job."

She sighed. "I hope so, but if you follow me, they'll trail you and find me. For all I know, they have a tracking device on your car right now."

"They couldn't. I check almost every time I get into my car."

"Well, don't take it personally, but I don't want you following me to my new town."

He scowled. "So now, I'm persona non grata, is that it?"

She smoothed the back of her hand down his cheek. "You could never be that. It's bad enough that I have to run from them, but I won't let them hurt you. I have to stay away from you and Tanya until I testify against Sheldon, and—" She swiped at the moisture in her eyes. "Maybe even after that."

She squeezed back tears. "If people who know something don't help convict the criminals, the government can't shut them down. This is something I have to do."

"Why you? Can't the bookkeeper be forced to testify?"

"He may be guilty too, or afraid to talk. Or maybe Sheldon had him killed by now."

"I'll stay away until after the trial, but I won't stop seeing you, not unless you tell me you don't love me, and swear you don't want me around." His earnest gaze met hers.

She took his hand and brought it to her lips. "Maybe after the trial's over, and Sheldon's locked up for a long time, you can visit me—but you've got to stay away until then. I couldn't bear it if anything happened to you." She swallowed a sob. She hated having him see her tears.

"Nothing's going to happen to me. I can watch my back, but I'll worry about you."

She sighed. "I hate living in limbo, but I don't want to you come see me until I call you—maybe by Thanksgiving we can meet somewhere."

He looked crestfallen. "Not until then?"

Intertwining her fingers with his, she met his gaze. "I'll miss your arms around me, miss having you so close you're a part of me."

He pulled her against him and wrapped his arms around her. "Then, we'll just have to make the most of tonight."

Soon he was kissing her in places she'd never been kissed. She quivered with anticipation. Her senses flamed red hot. She planted kisses on his shoulders, massaged his strong back, and kneaded his tight buns. He suckled her breasts until they tingled. Squirming in delight she felt a blaze building inside. It grew and grew until she could hardly stand the pressure.

Exhilaration spurred her on, took her ever higher. With him she scaled the mountainside. They came together in a rush. Exploding on top of the world, she savored the bitter-sweet moment. "I love you," she murmured.

"I love you, too," Alex whispered back.

She clung to him. If only things could be different, if only they could be together for always. She snuggled in his arms, drinking in the feel and the heady smell of him, wanting to keep these memories alive to hold her through the coming months without him and maybe forever. She squeezed her eyes shut. She wasn't going to think about that now.

In the morning she awoke to strong arms holding her tight and Alex sprinkling tiny kisses on her shoulders. After turning her to face him, he grinned broadly, then peppered her face, her neck, and then her breasts with kisses.

One more time, she promised herself—for the memories to cherish in the lonely months ahead. She planted a kiss on his lips, only to be interrupted by the jangling of his cell phone.

*

Alex squinted at his watch. "Who the hell's calling me at this hour?" He snatched it up. "Hello," he growled into the receiver.

"Joe here," came the voice. "Look, I just got Lee's message. What room are you in? I'm coming to take her someplace safe."

"What do you mean safe? She's with me."

"That's the problem. You're too easy to find with that red Jaguar and a business office where you go every day. She can't stay with you any more. It's too dangerous. I've found your car in the hotel parking lot. Just tell me your room number."

"You put a tracer on my car? I checked it before I left. Where did you hide it?."

He laughed. "You're slipping. It's behind the muffler. Tell me your room number."

"206."

"I'll be up in five minutes."

"Damn. We're not even dressed. Go for coffee or something."

"Don't drink the stuff. I'll give you fifteen minutes, but I need to move her right away. And you need to stay away from her until I tell her it's safe to call you. See you shortly."

The whine of the dial tone annoyed Alex, but not half as much as what Joe had said. He had almost convinced Lee to marry him, and now he couldn't see her for he didn't know how long. He groaned.

"What was that about?" asked Lee.

"Iceberg is hot to trot."

"Huh?"

"Joe's coming to get you—in fifteen minutes, he said, to take you some place safe."

"Oh, no." She sat up. "I forgot about calling him. When you said you were going to try to make up with Kathy, I called and asked him to take me to the town where I was planning on moving in the fall. I've got to get dressed."

Alex looked crestfallen. "But I thought we had time to—"

"I don't want him to find me in bed with you."

"Hey, I'm sure he knows the score."

"But that's not the same as finding us actually doing it."

"He'll call before he comes up."

"But I've got to take a shower."

He grinned. "To wash off the sweaty aftermath of mad, passionate loving?"

She nodded and jumped out of bed. At the door she paused. "If Joe could track you here, so can Sheldon's men. That's why I have to—have to leave you." She turned so he couldn't see her tears. They ran down her cheeks as she reached inside the shower to test the temperature of the water. Suddenly, she felt his warm body behind her.

His arms came around her. "I can wash your back and—"

She turned in his arms, leaned against his strength.

"Lee, you're crying." With gentle fingers, he smoothed away a teardrop. "Don't cry."

"I don't want to leave you."

He gripped her arms with strong hands and hugged her, his arousal hard and firm against her. "And I don't want you to."

His gaze locked with hers as his mouth descended on her lips. After sharing a hearty kiss, she couldn't resist his tugs toward the shower.

Inside the stall hot water cascaded over her shoulders. He rubbed soapy hands over her breasts, her abdomen, then slid them to her thighs and between.

In seconds he thrust inside, gripping her shoulders to hold her to him—as if she could find the strength to move away. Right now she'd travel to hell and back with him, if only they could be together.

She met him with strong pushes of her own. She regretted with all her heart they had to part like this with nothing settled.

The climax shook her all the way to her toes and back. Trembling, she savored the delicious tingling and wondered if she'd ever see or touch him again.

"Lee, why do you have to go with him? Can't you trust me to keep you safe?"

"I-I trust you, but he's experienced in protecting witnesses. And he's right about me being too visible in your office. I'd better do what he says."

He pulled away. "You're remembering what happened to Idelle, aren't you?"

She shook her head. "It's not that, but—"

He frowned. "I wish I'd never told you about her."

"Look, you've got to forget that. It wasn't your fault."

He scowled. "I had forgotten it—until now."

"Let me soap your body, and I'll help you forget." She grinned and began to lather him.

Someone pounded on the door.

"Oh, no," Lee groaned.

"Open up," someone shouted. More pounding came.

Alex hugged Lee to him. "Is that Joe?"

"I'm not sure."

"Lee, I know you're in there with him. Let me in." Joe's harsh tones rang with authority and betrayed his impatience. He'd been firm when explaining what she had to do, but never like this. Did he know of a new threat he hadn't told her about?

Her stomach tightened. This might be the last time Alex

held her in his arms. Their eyes met, hers full of 'I love you,' His seemed filled with longing. Life wasn't fair.

He grasped her hands, intertwining his fingers with hers. "I can't let you go."

"You need to rinse off, and we both need to get dry. I'll get dressed and let him in, then come back to kiss you good-bye. He can wait a few minutes, I'm sure."

"Lee, open the door," Joe shouted.

"I'm coming," she said, her tone abrupt. She grabbed a towel and went to the door. Leaving the chain on, she opened it just enough to peek through the crack. "I'm not dressed. Give me a few minutes."

"Throw something on and let me in. I can stuff your things in your bag while you get ready."

"I was taking a shower. Let me get my robe."

He laughed. "You mean all you're wearing is a towel. I'd like to see that."

"You're not supposed to say things like that. It's unprofessional. You're a U.S. Marshal on duty."

"Yeah, but right now you've got my imagination working overtime."

She sighed. "Just let me get some clothes on. Then I'll let you in."

"Four minutes, no more."

Frantically, she tugged on underwear and jeans over damp skin. She could hear him pacing outside the door. Fastening the next to last button on her blouse, she marched to the door and unlocked it.

He stepped inside and slammed the door behind him. "That's more like it. Now, are you packed?"

"How could I be? You didn't give me time."

"You should have been packing instead of—" He glanced at the rumpled sheets.

Heat rose from her breasts to her neck and face. She turned away, grabbed her suitcase, and threw it on the bed.

Joe elbowed her aside and snapped it open. He glared at her. "I told you to keep a bag packed at all times." He strode to the closet, pulled her green dress from the hanger, rolled it up and stuffed it in her open suitcase.

"Hey, it will get wrinkled." She folded her extra pants and shirt and laid them inside.

He frowned. "We're not going to a party. Is this all?"

She shook her head, raced to the closet, grabbed her heels, and shoved them in.

He shut the case and grabbed her hand. "Let's go."

"Wait. I've got to say good-bye to Alex."

"Forget it. Looks like you've been saying goodbye since I called."

Heat blossomed inside. She remembered Alex's arms around her, his body entwined with hers. Her neck and face were grew hot, but being with Alex had been worth more than a few blushes.

Joe grasped her hand, pulling her toward the door. "Come on. Maybe one of Sheldon's men has followed you here."

"But Alex will think—"

He grabbed her arm and pulled her against his side.

She tried to pull away. His grip was unshakable. "What are you doing?"

"I think there's a leak," he whispered. "And it could be coming through Alex."

She pulled away as far as she could. "That's not true." Her stomach twisted in knots. "He loves me. I won't believe it until you can prove it."

"Can't just yet." He shoved her toward the door, pulled it open and scanned the hallway. "Don't say anything now." He hustled her into the elevator. The doors slid shut closing them in. He looked her in the eye. "Show me you're made of sterner stuff. I can't protect you every minute. If you spend all your time mooning over that guy, you won't be alert. Watch for a tail. If you think you have one, call me immediately."

She nodded. Leaving without saying good-bye would make Alex think she didn't care about him. Perhaps it was better that way. She'd send him a message to let him know she was safe and that he should forget about her. What had Joe found to make him believe the worst of Alex?

C

Alex turned off the water and stepped out of the shower. It was strangely quiet. He wrapped a towel around himself and strode out of the bathroom.

Lee was gone.

Chapter 21

Fluffy pink clouds studded the sky above U.S. Marshal Joe Berg's speeding red Corvette. Lee might have enjoyed the beautiful sunrise if her heart wasn't torn in two. Life was so unfair.

She wished Joe had let her say good-bye instead of dragging her off so quickly. If there were a leak, Alex couldn't be responsible. He'd never let anything slip. Someone else had to be behind this.

She missed Alex already, but she couldn't risk his life just because she wanted him near. Turning her head away, she brushed tears from her cheeks. She wouldn't let him see her cry.

He yanked out a handkerchief and thrust it toward her. "This might be hard, but you can make a fresh start in Fort Worth. What kind of job will you get?"

"I don't know. I can't use any of the reference letters I have. They show my real name."

"You can't use that name any more. You're Lee Marshall from now on—unless we have to set you up again." He glared at her. "Maybe you don't realize, how much trouble and expense—"

"I know, and I appreciate all your help."

"I can't believe you were stupid enough to keep those letters. I told you to destroy all prior identification. You don't still have your old driver's license, do you?"

She nodded, then turned to watch the woods along the road, wishing she were going on a picnic instead of moving again.

"Hand it over."

Lee slapped the old license in his hand. It felt as if she were giving up the last tie to her former self.

He ripped it in two. Keeping his eyes on the highway, he stuffed the pieces in his shirt pocket. "I can't keep you safe if you disobey orders. Tear up those reference letters. You'll have to find a job without them."

He didn't speak as the miles rushed by beneath them. She pressed her hands to her roiling stomach. This was all wrong. How was she going to face the days ahead without seeing or talking to Alex.

Half an hour after they passed the Fort Worth city limits sign, he turned off the highway onto a city street. Then he made several more turns. "We're almost there."

"So when can I tell Alex where I am?" Knowing Joe, it might be days before she dared talk with him.

"You'd better not contact him again."

"Not ever?" Her heart sunk. "Do you have any proof that he's leaking information?"

"Every time someone finds you, you're with him. The fewer people who know where you are, the better."

She shuddered. "Alex checked all my things before he found the tracking device on my sister's picture. That's how they found my apartment. Maybe someone at your office.... Who else knows where you're taking me?"

"No one. Not even my boss, though he was the one who pulled up a list of medium sized towns to pick a new place for you. I pulled up the chambers of commerce on the internet and read about each one. Then I decided you'd be less noticeable in a larger city. You won't need to buy a car. The bus runs down Meadowbrook. That's only a few blocks away."

"After the trial is over, and Bart Sheldon and his

accomplices are in the pen, I should be free from them, right?"

"Don't count on it. Sheldon may have contacts who aren't in jail."

She shivered. "You mean I'll never get my life back?"

Joe turned down a side street and pulled up in front of a small yellow duplex with brown trim. "With your help we'll put those guys away, but you'll need to watch your back from now on." He escorted her to a door and unlocked it.

She felt as if the wind had been knocked out of her. It was bad enough that she couldn't contact any of her friends again. This was permanent. She sighed. She didn't want to spend the rest of her life looking over her shoulder.

Joe hefted her bag. With sagging footsteps she followed. He shut the door behind them. "Wait until I check the place out."

Standing in the doorway, she looked the place over. The early American furniture looked comfortable, but no pictures hung on the walls. The windows had blinds instead of draperies. A wide ruffle print of apples and pears hanging above the window over the kitchen sink was the only curtain in the place.

Joe returned and stood beside the front door. "Watch your back. Phone me every week. If you're threatened, call the police immediately, then call me. I can be here in an hour or less. I wish you were closer to Dallas, but then, you'd be easier for Sheldon's men to find." He reached for the doorknob. "Good luck."

"Wait."

"What now?"

"Are you going to put my sister in the witness security plan too? Libby could stay here."

"Bad idea. Then if they find you, they'll find her. I moved her to an apartment on the other side of Dallas. I had her put the house your father left you with a real estate agent. She promised to contact me when it sells so I can bring you the papers to sign." He stepped to the door, then paused, "And don't call that Alex guy from here. I'd like it better if you don't call him at all, but I'm sure you will sooner or later. Use a pay phone in Benbrook or Burleson—and don't talk too long."

He shut the door. Minutes later, the Corvette roared away.

She stared at the walls painted in landlord cream and the drab tan carpet. This place—so empty, so lonely. How am I going to get through all the lonely nights without seeing or talking to Alex?

After sinking onto the brown and yellow plaid couch, she rested her head in her hands. Alex had claimed he loved her enough to chance the dangers she faced. She believed he'd meant it, except it was better he didn't find her. But oh, how she'd miss him.

She wasn't going to wallow in self-pity. Rising, she straightened. She'd find new friends. That wouldn't make up for not seeing Alex or Libby, but she'd get used to it. Now if she could summon up enough enthusiasm to find a job, maybe it would keep her mind occupied so she wouldn't miss Alex so badly.

❦

One month later, on a Friday morning, Lee dished mashed potatoes into a large pan. How ironic, she, who never cooked, now worked in a cafeteria kitchen. As shift supervisor she was glad she didn't have to stand on the hard floor for eight hours straight. The young staff of co-op students and high school dropouts were full of enthusiasm and energy. She enjoyed working with them.

But that wasn't enough to make her forget how much she missed Alex, missed his touch, the way he watched out for her. She'd never forget the anguished look in his eyes when he rode in the ambulance with her, the way he held her hand as if he feared she'd die if he let go.

And most of all she remembered the way he made love to

her. She might never again feel his arms around her, his mouth nibbling on her ear and whispering he loved her. If only she could step out front and see him walking down the line at lunchtime.

But what if he came and gunfire erupted right before her eyes? She'd done the right thing by leaving. She wouldn't have to worry about endangering him and Tanya.

Now Alex could see his daughter regularly without fearing someone might harm her. She wondered how Tanya was doing. Again she wished the three of them could be a family, but it wasn't to be. In her situation she might never be able to have a life with a husband and family. She didn't even know when she'd be able to see Libby again or dare talk to her for more than ten minutes.

She brushed tears from her cheeks. She wished she could just see Alex and feel his arms around her and his lips on hers once more. She even missed his bossing, and heaven help her, she wanted to make love to him again, not just once, but many times. A home and family hadn't seemed important until she met him and Tanya. Her life seemed so empty now.

Sure, she'd made a few friends at church, and one guy had asked her out. Just a quiet teacher who seemed to want to settle down, but he wasn't Alex. Would it be fair to him to start a relationship that couldn't go anywhere?

At the end of her shift she dragged her aching feet back to the little duplex, past the pink and purple petunias blooming beside her doorstep. Afraid she'd have to move again, she'd planted them in a large pot so she could take them with her.

As she unlocked the door, her cell phone rang. Alex's deep voice saying, "Hello, sweetheart," set her heart thumping.

She was so excited, she almost forgot to bolt the door and check to see if anyone had been there. "It's wonderful to hear your voice. How'd you get my number?"

"I couldn't stand not knowing how you are or why you left without saying good-bye. I badgered that rodent marshal of yours day and night until he gave it to me. I had to tell him we were engaged. I wish it were true."

Lee's heart leaped. Did he really mean that? If only....

Alex kept talking. "Of course he made me swear on pain of death only to use my cell phone and not give the number to anyone else — as if I would."

"He practically dragged me out of the hotel that morning," Lee said. "He claims there's a leak in the system. He even had the nerve to suggest you might be involved. It's awful to think anyone who worked there would put an innocent witness in danger. Did you have any rotten apples in the CIA?"

"Unfortunately, yes, but all the known traitors have been eliminated."

"As in killed?"

"We couldn't afford to let them cause another agent's death."

"What if someone thought you were a traitor? You must have had to watch your back every second."

"Sure, but it was exciting as hell. I've always dreamed of running my own business, but all these humdrum details can't compare to being an agent."

"So why don't you go back?"

"I want to be a real father to Tanya. And for that, I need to stay around, not trot all over the globe."

"Maybe you should run a different kind of travel agency."

"What do you mean?"

"Adventure tours, white water rafting, parachute jumping, stuff like that. Once in a while you could even act as a guide for some."

"Hey, that's not a bad idea." He paused as if considering it. "I'll check into it." He paused once more. "When can I see you again? I'd love to spend Thanksgiving with you."

Wishing he were here beside her, Lee sighed. "My sister and I plan to meet in a big city to spend Thanksgiving together. She said she'll tell me all about her new boyfriend, but Joe told her not to bring him. He's someone she met at a charity fund raising gala who might be a prospective buyer for the house our father left us."

"Can I join you?"

"Better not. Joe worries someone will follow you here."

"Maybe he should move you somewhere else."

"I just have to be careful no one else finds me."

"Christmas then?"

A cozy picture of the two of them watching lights blink on a decorated tree sounded inviting, but she had to think of his daughter. "Doesn't Tanya deserve to spend it with her father and mother? Maybe after the first of the year."

"I don't want to wait that long. I miss you."

"I miss you, too, but I'm afraid to take any chances."

"Is it that, or are you involved with someone else?"

He sounded jealous. That shouldn't make her feel good, but it did. "No, I'm not."

"Lee, I can't wait till after Christmas to see you. I'll meet you anywhere you say. How about dinner tomorrow night? We could go somewhere for the weekend."

"What if you're followed?"

"I won't be. If someone tries, I'll shake him," he said in a determined voice. "What's the nearest town?"

She took a deep breath. Dare she risk it? She wanted to see him so badly, she couldn't bring herself to say 'no.' "There's a cafe in Benbrook called 'Mama's Kitchen' just off Main Street. You can't miss it. I can take a cab and meet you there."

"I'll be there around eight. It'll be getting dark then. I'll be harder to follow."

Her heart fairly burst with anticipation. "I can't wait."

His, "Neither can I," set her pulse thrumming.

❧

That voice was getting on his nerves again. It sounded like

the guy had pebbles in his throat. Shifting the receiver to his other ear, he hoped the voice would sound better.

Loud curses reverberated in his ear. "The damn trial's in three weeks, Bart shouted. When am I going to hear about some action?" His voice lowered to a more conversational tone. "Do I need to make an anonymous call to Washington?"

"No, I'll take care of it," he barked. He slammed down the phone so hard it rocked in its cradle. Glancing at piles of papers on his desk, he clutched his roiling stomach. After Iceberg left for lunch would be a good time for another try at getting into his computer. He couldn't fail this time. If he were careful, no one would know. He'd take care of that stubborn bitch and soon.

❦

Next evening, wearing a long black skirt and a clingy green knit top, Lee sat at a corner booth in the rear of Mama's Kitchen, sipping coffee. The jade earrings Alex had given her swung gently whenever she craned her neck to watch the door. Lights were dim. She hoped he could see her from the doorway.

Finally the one she waited for walked in, his tan cheeks flushed with color from the wind, and his kissable lips grinning at her. Smelling of some musky aftershave, he slid into the booth, yanked her close and covered her mouth with his.

She responded eagerly, thrilled to feel his lips hungrily devouring hers. Sinking into his strong arms, she felt as if she'd come home at last. How had she lasted this long without him? Did she really want to face the future alone?

Too soon, he pulled away, and then looked around the room. "We shouldn't attract attention." He smiled broadly, "I like that sweater," he said, smoothing his hand over her shoulder and down the length of her short sleeve. "It's so soft and touchable—like you. Too bad I can't touch you the way I want to here."

Her pulse raced at his words. She gazed into his mesmerizing blue eyes. After so long without him, she could hardly believe he was here at last. She grasped his hand. Big, strong and muscular, his hand held hers tenderly. With a finger he traced a path down her arm from her elbow to her wrist, setting her senses tingling.

Glancing at his hair, tousled by the wind, she wanted to run her fingers through it. And that wasn't all she wanted. She forced herself to sit calmly when the waitress arrived and took their order.

Later, when the waitress set their food on the table, the aroma of fried chicken made Lee's mouth water. Feeling comfortable enough to pick up fried chicken with her fingers, Lee took a succulent bite. Alex did the same.

After they finished, he wiped his hands and grasped hers. "Let's go. I want to spend the rest of the evening with you somewhere we can be close."

Smiling up at him, she wondered if she'd miss him even more after tonight. But she didn't want to think about that, not with her pulse racing in anticipation. She'd worry about that later, and about Joe yelling at her if she took Alex to her house. She swallowed. "You're sure no one followed you or put a tracking device on your car?"

His sultry gaze met hers as he held the door open. Her heart beat faster. "Just to be sure, I had my oil changed and walked under the car while it was on the lift." He slipped his arm around her waist and pulled her close as they walked to his car.

Twenty minutes later, Alex stood facing her in her living room. Glad her landlady was away for the weekend, Lee smoothed down her slacks, suddenly nervous. "How about some coffee? And I baked some cookies." Alex's broad smile tempted her to say, "Never mind," and lead him straight to the bedroom, but that would be too obvious. Besides, she'd already figured him as a guy who liked to make the moves.

He squeezed her hand. "That would be great. I've had a long day, and I don't want to fall asleep on you." However, the look in his eyes said there was no way he would.

Later, trying not to let her hands shake, she carried two mugs into the living room. Their last time together, she'd left him without saying good-bye. He hadn't mentioned that since his phone call. Was he holding that against her?

A television announcer's voice caught her attention. Scenes of a hostage situation flashed on the screen, complete with police shooting at the door of a run-down frame house. Setting the coffee mugs down, she shivered and hoped she'd never have to face that.

Alex's footsteps sounded behind her. His welcoming arms warmed her body and soul. She turned into his embrace as he nuzzled her neck. Maybe they'd forget about coffee.

Hearing a car come to a stop outside, Lee glanced out the window and froze. "There are two men outside. They're getting out of a black car and heading here."

Alex yanked her away from the window. "Stay out of sight till we know who they are."

He flipped off the lights, darkening the room. He pulled her into the shadows. Light from a window illuminated his face. His expression made her heart pound. She'd never seen him scared.

Someone pounded on the door. "Lee, open up, we need to take you to another safe place."

"Carl," Alex called out. "What the hell's going on?"

"Let me in. I need to move Lee away from there immediately."

"Where's Joe?" Lee whispered. "Carl may be his boss, but I'm not going anywhere with Carl. I don't trust him."

"I'll stall," Alex said in low tones. He tossed her his cell phone. "Run out the back. Hide in the woods behind the fence. I'll tell them you're not here. After they leave, I'll call you." Louder, he said, "Lee's gone next door to talk with a neighbor—may not be back a while. You know how women are when they get to talking."

"Bullshit. I know she's in there."

"Hold on a second," Alex said. "I'll unlock the door, and you can see for yourself."

Lee hurried to the back door, hoping Carl would buy the flimsy excuse, probably all Alex could come up with on short notice. In her haste she bumped into the table, knocking some cookies off the plate onto the floor. That jarred her hip, but she held her breath and slipped out the door onto the back porch.

Rubbing her aching hip, Lee heard the front door open, then a shot. She froze momentarily. Her heart pounded. If Carl would shoot Alex, he'd shoot her too. She couldn't help Alex if she were wounded. She ran down the back steps. Raced toward the wooden fence and the woods. She tried the gate to the wooden fence. Stuck shut. Damn. She'd have to climb the fence.

She ran to the fence and grabbed the top. She placed one foot on the lowest horizontal support bar. She hiked up her long skirt. Put one foot on the middle bar.

"Stop, Lee," came Carl's voice. "You can't run away. You've got to come with me, for your own safety." He sounded determined, and angry.

Swallowing her fear, she gripped the fence. Struggled to drag her other foot up.

"Stop," he shouted. "Stop or I'll shoot."

Her heart pounded. He might have killed Alex. Would she be next? She had to get away.

Balancing on the top horizontal support board, she got ready to jump over. Her skirt ripped. One more second and she'd be over. The woods beyond the alley beckoned.

One shoe fell off. She hesitated a second, then jumped over the fence. The blast was deafening. Pain shot up her leg. She slammed onto the ground, hitting her head on the concrete alley. Everything went black.

In the living room Alex struggled to rise. Pain laced his arm. It was bloody, but the bullet had only grazed his arm. He'd played dead until Carl left the room, but if Carl meant to kill him, his aim stank. Another gunshot echoed from outside. Oh lord — Lee — had he shot her? Knots tightened in his gut.

Alex ran to the back door. Gun ready, he edged onto the porch. Braced his body against the wall. Heart pounding, he strained to see. A shoe lay beside the fence. Lee was nowhere in sight. Thank goodness.

Carl stood motionless, his brows furrowed. The gun hung loose in his fingers. The other man emerged from the side of the house. Gun in hand, he pointed toward the fence. "What's going on?" the man asked.

Keeping his gun poised, Alex waited. He had to size up the situation, then act.

Carl frowned. "Don't be an idiot, Harper. Lee has to learn to follow orders to stay in the witness program." Carl glanced at Alex standing on the porch. "She wouldn't stop climbing the fence. Harper was only firing a warning shot, but Lee fell."

Harper stood there, gun in hand, his jaw hanging slack. "But boss, I didn't — "

Carl's brows inched closer together. "Shut up, Harper."

Alex tensed. He couldn't believe it. Carl must have shot at an innocent woman — a witness the government was sworn to protect. Then he'd blamed the other guy. His former classmate had gone wacko or else...or else — or else he was the leak in the U. S. marshal system. That was the only explanation that made sense. An icy trickle of sweat ran down Alex's back.

Gripping his gun, he clenched his other hand into a fist. He wanted to beat Carl senseless. His arm smarted, but he needed to appear calm and non threatening — at least while the other two were armed. "Carl, what's going on here?"

"I told you. Harper fired a warning shot, and she fell over the fence."

Harper scowled. "You're not making me a scapegoat."

"Shut up, Harper," Carl barked.

Alex pointed his gun at his former friend. "Carl, drop the gun before someone gets hurt."

Carl still held the gun, but lowered it to point toward the ground. "Harper, climb the fence and check on our quarry. I heard her fall. She may be hurt."

Harper clambered over the fence. Heart pounding, Alex kept his eyes on Carl.

Harper's head disappeared, then rose up again. "Think she's dead, boss."

Chapter 22

Dead, she couldn't be dead. They might have shared a life together—if only he could have convinced her to marry him and taken her far away. Lord, what will I do now?

He raced to the fence. Looked over it. She lay on the alley's hard concrete, not moving. A breeze dropped leaves on her as if covering her for burial.

A cloud darkened the waning light. Shattered was the promise of a pleasant evening with the woman he loved. She now lay still as death. A crow cawed, seeming to profane the life slipping away. If only he could turn back the clock and keep Carl from shooting her. He squeezed his eyes shut. His dream of sharing a home with her and Tanya vanished. He felt empty inside.

Through a haze he heard the voice of the man Carl had brought with him. "Boss, how you going to explain killing the witness you were supposed to protect?"

"I didn't mean for anyone to kill her, just stop her from running away," Carl insisted.

Alex scowled. "The hell you did." He grabbed the fence, fear almost paralyzing him. A splinter stabbed his finger. Ignoring the pain, he clambered over the fence. Hitting the ground with a jolt, he barely managed to keep his balance.

The concrete felt hard underfoot. How much harder must it have felt to Lee when her head came crashing down?

Her still form jolted him into action. Kneeling, he pressed his fingers against her neck. The breeze died. An eerie stillness ruled the scene. Couldn't feel a pulse. Couldn't see her chest move.

Nothing moved except a tiny rivulet of blood darkening her leg. "Call an ambulance," he shouted, his voice resounding harshly in the hushed silence.

How could this happen?

Then he saw the cell phone he'd tossed her. It lay near her body — he wouldn't think of her as a body, not yet at least. He grabbed the phone, pushed 9-1-1. If it still worked, he could get help.

The cheery answer gave him hope.

"A woman's been shot—" he blurted. "She's behind the fence at a yellow duplex on Pine Street." He hoped this was the only duplex on the block.

"I'll send an ambulance and the police."

He snapped the phone shut and laid his head on her chest. Was it his imagination or did he feel a faint heartbeat? "Lee," he murmured. "Don't leave me. I love you. Please, you've got to live. I need you."

Carl peered over the fence, gun in hand. The gun wasn't aimed at Alex, but if Lee were dead, it wouldn't matter much if Carl killed him too — except he had to take care of Tanya. He studied his former friend's face. Had Carl gone over the edge? "You're not going to shoot again are you?" he asked, trying hard to keep his voice in a matter of fact tone.

Carl shook his head. "Is she dead?"

"I'm not sure." Alex lifted his head, watching for even the slightest breath. Sirens sounded in the distance. Their high-pitched whines as they came closer were welcome sounds. Two difference tones sounded simultaneously, one a high pitched shrill, the other blasting the night with escalating bursts. Good. He hoped that meant both an ambulance and the police were on their way.

Carl stood there, staring over the fence.

Alex kept rubbing her cold hands, trying to bring some warmth into them. Why hadn't that ambulance gotten here yet?

Was Lee in shock? He wished he had medical training. A vision of Idelle dying in his arms flashed before him. He hung his head. He couldn't let Lee die too. "Lee, please don't die. I love you," he whispered. How could he live without her?

The whine of the ambulance got louder, then stopped. Alex stood. A paramedic ran into the back yard. Alex drew a sigh of relief and beckoned. "Over here." He looked around for a gate. There was one about ten feet down. If only Lee had used it, she might not be lying here almost dead.

"Quick, come this way." He motioned to the attendant, who rushed toward the gate. Another man wheeled a gurney across the yard.

He bent down and took her hand. "Lee, darling, it's going to be all right," he whispered. "The ambulance is here. Just hang in there. Please, for my sake, you've got to live."

The first paramedic shoved at the gate. The latch stuck, but finally released. The attendants shoved the wheeled stretcher through the gate. He thought Lee's eyelids fluttered, but couldn't be sure. He kissed her cheek. After chafing her cold hands once more, he backed away to let the paramedics take care of her.

Alex stepped back beside the fence and glared at Carl. "If she dies, her death will be on your hands, and I hope you fry." He rubbed his eyes. Had Carl followed him to Lee's place? If so, Alex was as much to blame for her getting shot as Carl. Why hadn't he seen this ruthless side of Carl before? He'd have to live with that failure for the rest of his life.

He wanted to shake the daylights out of Carl. But if Lee died, that would be small comfort. His heart would be wrenched from him. He'd be left without the woman who'd made him want to enjoy life again.

"It was an unfortunate accident," Carl insisted.

"Tell that to the judge," Alex spat out.

The paramedics lifted a blanket-covered Lee onto the gurney and wheeled it through the open gate. Alex held his breath and followed them. She had to survive. He didn't know how he could make it if she didn't.

Two uniformed policemen ran into the yard. One with an authoritative voice barked, "Police, drop your weapons."

Alex heard two soft plops. Thank goodness his former friend and Harper were cooperating.

"What happened here?" said the authoritative voice which belonged to the taller cop. The shorter one snatched up the guns.

Carl pulled out his wallet and flipped it open. "We're U.S. Marshals. Our government witness was trying to get away."

"Did you shoot her?" asked the taller cop.

"I'm with the Dallas division of Wit-Sec, the Witness Security Program. We came to move her to a safe place. When she ran from us, my man fired a warning shot. She was hit in the leg by accident," Carl lied.

Harper spoke. "We never shoot to kill anyone except in self-defense."

The taller of the two policemen stepped closer to the gurney. "Looks like she's out cold. How could this be an accident?"

"She tried to climb the fence and fell," Carl said.

Alex stood as if rooted to the ground. The paramedics held something over Lee's nose. Her face moved as if she were trying to avoid whatever it was. He let out his breath. She looked so pale, but at least she was responding.

The paramedics pushed the gurney away from the gate and started through the yard. A knot gnawed at his gut. Lee lay there motionless, dampening his hope. Alex was torn between wanting to follow Lee and wanting Carl to be charged with shooting her.

Carl leaned against the fence, one hand gripping the top. "I-we—didn't mean to hurt her, just scare her into stopping. She was trying to climb over the fence—must have hit her head on the pavement when she fell."

"And you weren't aiming to hit her?" asked the shorter cop.

"No. Harper didn't mean to shoot her. I told him to just fire a warning shot," Carl insisted.

Alex pointed at Carl. "He shot her, not Harper." Couldn't they tell Carl was trying to cover his ass?

The shorter cop beckoned to Carl and Harper. "Both of you need to come with us—for questioning."

Harper and Carl walked with the two policemen toward the front of the house.

Alex shoved his hands into his pockets. "Will she be all right?" Not sure he wanted to hear the answer, he waited, his stomach churning.

"Can't tell yet," the attendant said.

Lee lay so still. Damn the paramedics. Why couldn't they give him an answer? What if she were dead, and they weren't telling him? His stomach knotted. That couldn't be. It just couldn't.

Alex grabbed Carl's arm and spun him around. He couldn't help lashing out. "It's all your fault. You meant to shoot her. Why the hell would you do that?"

"Get your hands off me." Carl wrenched himself free, his face radiating hatred. "You always got everything I wanted, even Kathy, the woman I wanted."

"So why did you let her marry me?"

"That was her choice, not mine," Carl said. "And Tanya's my daughter, not yours. Haven't you noticed she has red hair just like me?"

He was lying, trying to rub salt in Alex's wounds. "Why would Kathy say she was expecting my baby if it wasn't mine? And why not marry you if the baby was yours?"

Carl scowled. "She claimed you had better prospects so she

let you think Tanya was yours. She swore if I said anything to you, she'd deny it."

"When we were getting a divorce, she conveniently forgot to mention that." Even as he said that, Alex figured there might be some truth to Carl's statements. His gut twisted. "Why would she claim that now?" he asked. Would Kathy hide the truth from him and Tanya to get child support? He thought a moment. Yeah, she probably would.

Alex glanced at the gurney the paramedics were wheeling toward the ambulance. His heart was breaking, but Carl didn't even seem to care that Lee might be dead or dying.

"I don't know why she waited until now to tell me Tanya's my kid. Could be because she wanted to divorce you and marry me, now that I'm successful."

Alex clenched his fists so tightly his nails bit into his palms. A knot of anger burgeoned inside. He shoved his fists into his pocket. It was all he could manage not to cold cock Carl just to remove the smug look from his face.

Was he, like Carl, turning into some kind of crazed animal? Kathy, with her scheming, had made a mess of things. Tanya and he were the ones who'd suffer.

Carl shot Alex a determined look. "Now that I know the truth, I'm suing for custody. A DNA test will prove it once and for all. Then you'll have to let me have my daughter. She's all I'll have if Kathy doesn't marry me."

"No judge will give her to a man in jail for attempted murder."

"I'll beat any trumped up charge you file, damn you. Then I'll see your sorry ass in court."

Alex shook his fist at Carl. "The hell you will. I'll see you in jail first. You and your marshal will face attempted murder charges."

"It was an accident, I tell you. And I'll get my daughter if I have to hire Racehorse Haynes. He got that axe-wielding Candy Montgomery off from murder charges, and her case was tougher than mine will be." His 'I'm going to win' smile mocked Alex.

A good right cross would clobber his jaw and wipe off that insufferable smirk, but it wouldn't solve anything. Alex took a deep breath. "I've taken care of Tanya since she was born. She's my daughter whether or not she's got my genes."

Carl scowled. "If you and your damn girlfriend haven't screwed things up royally, Kathy and I might still get together and be a family with Tanya."

As the cops led Carl and Harper to their police cruisers, Alex hoped Kathy would be her usual perverse self and refuse Carl's offer. If not, Carl was welcome to her spendthrift ways and all her complaining when she didn't get her way.

The paramedics carefully lifted the gurney into the ambulance. One paramedic slid behind the wheel. The other climbed up into the back and reached for the door.

"Wait," Alex shouted. "I'm coming with you." There was nothing he could do for Lee now except hold her hand and pray, but he wanted to be near her.

Alex climbed into the ambulance. He took her cold hand in his, trying to warm it. Alex ran his fingers through his hair. Deja Vu lodged a bitter taste in his mouth. He might be responsible for another innocent person's death—again. Carl might have pulled the trigger, but it was partly Alex's fault Lee was shot—just like when Idelle was killed. This was ten times worse than losing Idelle, and it wouldn't have happened if he hadn't gotten involved with Lee and taken her to Carl's picnic.

Idelle had been a dear friend, but he loved Lee and he might not even get a chance to tell her that again. That chilled him to the bone.

"Move please," said the paramedic. "I need to start an IV." He pointed toward the rear of the ambulance. "Sit back there out of the way."

Feeling useless, Alex let go of her hand and watched the

medical technician taking care of Lee. Thank goodness, the man seemed to know exactly what to do.

He couldn't help wondering if he hadn't been here, if Lee might have been peacefully transferred to another place. Except Lee didn't trust Carl. Alex couldn't be sure what Carl might have done if she were there alone.

❧

Alex sat on a hard couch in the hospital waiting room. As far as he could tell, the air conditioning was working, but the air seemed muggy, and the vinyl fabric stuck to him.

He picked up a magazine with Julia Roberts on the cover, then threw it down. He didn't want to read about her latest movie. All he wanted to know was if Lee would survive.

He thought of her pale face the last time he'd seen her. It had been alive and glowing when they made love. He loved seeing her sweet smile shining only for him. He hadn't appreciated how lucky he'd been to have her love—he could only hope she felt the way he did. He didn't know how he'd manage to face each day if Lee died and Tanya were taken from him. Surely, if that happened, a judge would allow him visitation.

He'd thought seeing Tanya only once a month was bad, but sharing her with Carl would be worse. He'd spoil her rotten and probably wouldn't discipline her. His little darling would be a confused wishbone being pulled three ways.

Hours later, Alex checked his watch. He couldn't stop worrying about Lee. Why didn't someone tell him something?

A male nurse in green scrubs approached. "The operation's over. A doctor will be here to talk with you shortly." Before Alex could ask if the operation had been a success, the man left.

Would the doctor come to tell him Lee hadn't survived?

With his fingers drumming the coffee table, he waited, hardly daring to hope.

Chapter 23

Restless, Alex rose from the hard vinyl couch in the hospital waiting room and paced the floor. It had been hours since they'd brought Lee here. Why didn't the doctor come? It shouldn't take that long for him to clean up.

His cell phone rang. Who the hell was calling now? "Hello," he growled into the phone.

"Alex," said Carl. "How's Lee?"

Alex frowned. "I'm still waiting to hear—as if you cared. You'll probably be free of a murder charge, for now that is."

"And you're free to carry on with another woman after dumping Kathy. You always got everything I wanted, even her." Bitterness laced his tones.

Alex wasn't about to tell him that Kathy was the one who dumped him. "So why did you stand by like a coward instead of fighting for her?"

"I'm no coward, you S.O.B. She made her choice. But things are different this time," Carl said. "I'll be the one with better prospects. She'll want to marry me now. We'll have a great life, me, Kathy, and little Tanya."

"You shot Lee. You're not getting Tanya."

"That was an accident."

"The hell it was. You're lying about that. You're not fit to be Tanya's father."

"Bullshit. She's my daughter whether you like it or not.

That red hair says so. I've already talked with a lawyer. He'll keep me out of jail, and he's preparing a petition for custody to file." Carl's voice rang with determination.

Carl's words slammed Alex's heart. He couldn't let Carl have his daughter. "We'll see about that. I'll get my own lawyer."

Slumped on the couch, Alex cradled his head in his hands. His stomach twisted at the thought of losing the two people most precious to him. Lee couldn't die, she just couldn't. He didn't think a judge would give Carl custody, but if the DNA tests were positive — it could happen.

A white-coated doctor strode into the waiting room. Surely, he wouldn't stride unless Lee was going to be all right. Alex jumped to his feet. He couldn't tell from the man's serious expression if the operation had been a success or not.

The doctor's voice was calm, but revealed nothing. "Are you a friend of Lee Marshall?"

His heart in his throat, Alex nodded. "How is she?"

"We removed the bullet. She'll have some pain for a while, but she should regain the full use of her leg. Aside from a slight concussion, she seems okay."

"Thank you, doctor." Filled with relief, Alex breathed a silent prayer of thanks. "Can I see her?"

"She's not conscious yet, but they'll soon be moving her from recovery to room 308."

Half an hour later, inside room 308, Alex watched a nurse bustling around. She adjusted the blinds and smoothed the covers over Lee's still form. "Don't try to wake her. Just let her come to naturally. Here's the call button." She pointed to a buzzer on the bedside table. "If you need assistance, push it."

With a swish of nylon skirts she left the room. A faint odor of bleach hung in the air. Outside a mockingbird sang several tunes, reminding Alex life went on regardless of any drama or heartache inside these walls. But his life would be meaningless without Lee.

She looked so pale, so still. He took her hand. At least it felt warm. He slid his thumb up to her wrist and rejoiced to feel a steady pulse. A lock of auburn hair dangled over her forehead. He smoothed it away, wondering when he'd be able to see her hair spread over his pillow and her soft brown, no green, eyes looking up at him. Hell, he just wanted to know she was all right.

He brushed a kiss on her delicate forehead. Slowly, her eyelids rose. Her green eyes had never looked so beautiful.

Alex squeezed her hand.

She looked up at him with wondering eyes. "My leg feels numb. All I remember is a sharp pain in my leg…and falling. What happened?"

"You were shot in the leg. The doctor took the bullet out. He said it might hurt for a while, but you should be okay." He patted her shoulder, blinking his eyes to hold back tears. "I was so scared—" His voice broke. He took a deep calming breath. "I was so scared I'd lose you."

"I can't believe Carl shot me…just because I rejected his advances."

Alex brought her hand to his lips and pressed a soft kiss on it. "Don't blame yourself. He may have been trying to get back at me."

"For what?"

"He told me he wanted to marry Kathy, but she turned him down and picked me."

"That wasn't your fault." Lee took a deep breath. "Maybe he was afraid I'd report him."

"Why?"

"Remember all his new furniture?"

"So?"

"It looked like some I saw loaded into trucks when I worked for Sheldon."

"You're sure his new furniture is stolen goods?"

Lee nodded.

Alex scratched his head. "Maybe Carl's working in cahoots with Sheldon."

"He's Joe's supervisor. He could be behind the leaks in the Witness Security Program."

Alex frowned. "Carl's bad news." He wouldn't tell Lee now about Carl claiming to be Tanya's father. If a blood test proved it, and Carl sued for custody, Alex would fight him, but that wasn't Lee's problem. He'd deal with it himself — later.

Aloud he said, "It all fits. In high school I felt sorry for him when his dad died, but then he took up with a bad crowd. He must have been crazy to take a shot at you."

He kissed her tenderly on her lips. He wanted much more, but she seemed weak. He shouldn't press her. She responded, her mouth warm and welcoming, then raised her hand to his face. For a moment he enjoyed her soft touch, then pulled away. "You need to rest. I'll be here to protect you, so don't worry."

Her eyes closed, and she drifted off to sleep. Alex settled down in the easy chair. It was going to be a long night, but he wouldn't leave her.

❧

The next morning Lee struggled to wake up. Finally focusing on Alex, she mumbled, "Coffee. I need coffee."

He rose. "I'll get you some." Her eyes drifted shut again.

She awoke to an empty hospital room and a ringing phone. "Hello?"

The voice wasn't one she wanted to hear. She gripped the phone tightly. She wanted to slam it down, but didn't dare. "Bubba, how'd you get this number?"

"Name's Frank, you know. We have our ways, Sheldon and I." His harsh laugh sent chills down her spine. "Better think twice 'bout spilling your guts in the witness chair."

"You can't take a gun in there. They have metal detectors."

"Yeah, but what about afterwards? You can send Sheldon

to the slammer for a while, but I'm still out on bond, and so is Floyd, you know."

"You may not be after I testify." She gulped. Shouldn't have said that.

"Gotta find me first, you know. Sheldon's got others who owe him. He can call in a favor anytime. And then you'll be history."

His harsh tones made her skin crawl. She swallowed. "I'm telling the police everything you say."

"You do and your boyfriend and his little girl may suffer. We can always find out where he lives." With that the line went dead. She caught her breath. She had to testify, but she didn't want to put Alex and Tanya in danger.

Would she and Alex and Tanya would ever be free of threats? Would Bubba come here and attack her while she was weak? Her pulse raced. What was taking Alex so long?

With trembling hands she groped for the call button. Realizing the nurse couldn't do anything about the phone call, she stopped reaching for the call button just as Alex walked in carrying two cups of coffee.

He handed her one. Her hand trembled so badly, she had to set the cup down after one sip. "I'm glad you're back. Bubba just called and threatened me."

"Damn," he said, "I was only gone a few minutes. I'm not leaving you alone again. I'm calling Joe. You need a guard round the clock."

"Wait. That's not the worst of it. Bubba threatened to hurt you and Tanya."

She clamped her lips together. She shouldn't have gotten involved with Alex. She'd brought danger to them. She might as well swear off all men. She was too dangerous. But she had to testify, didn't she? She was damned if she did and damned if she didn't.

She watched and listened as Alex called Joe, the local police, and then spoke to Joe again.

"Okay, I'll call you from there." Alex closed his cell phone.

"What now" Lee asked.

"As soon as you're released, I'll take you to a hotel in another town. Joe will find you another place to stay."

"To stay", he'd said. Was that all she would ever do — stay somewhere until her U.S. Marshal decided she needed to move? Even her petunias wouldn't have a chance to set down permanent roots.

Well, if that was going to be her life from now on, she'd make best of it. She'd testify and move on with her life — even if it were only half a life. She'd get some kind of job and volunteer as a tutor in her spare time. She didn't need credentials for that, and she could help some children make it through school.

❦

Two days later Alex paced the bedroom of the duplex on Pine Street while Lee threw things into a suitcase. Knowing Joe waited outside to take her away, Alex glanced at Lee with a troubled heart. All the while he was in the CIA, he was never afraid. He could take care of himself. Lee must have been in constant fear ever since Sheldon got arrested.

He gripped the door frame. "When Carl came after you, he yanked the floor out from under me. All I could think of was how I'd feel if I lost you or Tanya. For a few seconds reason flew out the window. If I'd been more alert, I could have stopped Carl and kept him from shooting you. But then he shot me." Alex sighed. "If he'd killed you, I wouldn't have much to live for — except Tanya."

Lee took a deep breath and slammed her bag shut. "I lived through being shot, and I'll be okay. I won't be ruled by terror anymore. That's not living; that's cowering behind a wall of fear." She stepped closer and took his hand. "I've too much to live for.

He pulled her into his arms. "Does that mean you'll marry me?"

The look of longing on his face pulled at her heartstrings. Being wrapped in his strong arms felt wonderful. With all her heart she wanted to say 'yes.' Did she dare hope for that? She couldn't—not just yet. Too much was at stake.

"It's not that simple. I can't commit to anything until after the trial." How she wished she could. Gently, she eased herself from the haven of his arms, feeling bereft immediately. "My life is too risky right now. I won't take a chance on someone else getting hurt because of me."

"You're the bravest woman I know. Look at all you've been through. You shot Bubba in the arm when he broke into your apartment, you survived the bomb he planted, and you lived through being shot in the leg."

He squeezed her hand. "And you can talk about it without even a quiver now. I think you've come through it all miraculously. If you can just learn not to worry about things unless something bad's occurring, you'll be fine. After all that's happened, I'd like to see the U.S. Marshals give you more protection, but even if they don't, I want to be able to protect you as your husband."

Lee met his gaze. He was right. She had survived a lot. And she didn't need to worry herself sick about things that might not happen.

If things went right at the trial, she'd be happy to share a home with him and Tanya for the rest of her life. And maybe, Alex might be content with only one child. She didn't want to chance dying in childbirth like her mother had.

He was watching, waiting for her to say something.

"The U.S. Marshals can't be everywhere, but I'll be all right. However, I don't think they will okay protection for you and Tanya, too. If the bad guys aren't all sent away for a long time, I'd put you and Tanya in danger just by being with you. And what if Tanya comes to love and depend on me, and then I'm shot or killed, and she has to suffer through that?"

His face took on a determined look. "I won't let that happen."

She shook her head. "I can't let you take that chance. You and Tanya have got to stay away from me until after the trial. Tanya needs her father as well as her mother."

"I want Tanya to be safe, but I'll be thinking about you, wishing you were with us, counting the days until we can be together again."

A warm glow spread throughout at his words. It was wonderful to be wanted, but she had to think of his safety. "No, you shouldn't even come near me until I'm sure all of Sheldon's men are locked up for good."

He swallowed, his Adam's apple bobbing. He took her in his arms. "I won't like it, but you're right. I need to protect my daughter."

"I'm so sorry I put you both in danger. I never meant to get you involved, but you were a Godsend when I needed someone."

He kissed her long and hard, then feathered kisses on her cheeks and forehead, his lips lingering on her skin as if he couldn't bear to move away.

How had she managed to deserve such a loving, honorable man? If things went right at the trial, maybe she and Alex could live happily ever after with his little girl filling their house with laughter and questions. And maybe he might not miss having another child.

But a baby in her arms, cuddly and trusting, like his nephew, Danny, might be worth the risk. She'd been afraid to see a doctor before now, but if she did, he could tell her if she were likely to have trouble bearing a child. Just because her mother died from childbirth didn't necessarily mean she would. That was a fear she'd have to get over.

Joe pulled out a key and unlocked the door to a white clapboard house. "I checked out this place out. The front and back doors have security bolts and peepholes. There's a security system, too. You should be safe here."

Wistfully, Lee watched the city bus pass through the quiet north Dallas suburb where he'd found her a new place to live. She followed him inside and up the stairs to the room he'd rented for her. "I hate having to depend on public transportation," she told him.

"Sorry, but the budget doesn't cover cars for our witnesses. The bus or the DART train will take you to Galleria or Valley View Mall. Better go on sale days when the stores are crowded, but be back well before dark."

"What makes you think I want to go shopping with a bum leg?"

"I thought all women liked to shop. I bet you will when you feel better." He set her bag down in front of a door and took out another key.

"Have you heard anything about Carl?"

"He's been suspended without pay pending an investigation."

"Tell them to check out all the improvements to his lake home. His furniture looks like some I saw being loaded from Sheldon's warehouse. I think it was stolen."

"After Carl shot you, I figured there must be a link between him and Sheldon. That may be the proof we need." He set her suitcase down just inside a room with a maple rocking chair and a matching early American bed. Braided rugs and a patchwork quilt made the room seem warm and homey.

He straightened and brushed a lock of straw-colored hair from his forehead. "Take care, and call me at least every other day. If no one bothers you during the first month, you can cut back to once a week."

His red Corvette soon disappeared from view. Lee sighed. She had to unpack and find a job, but what she wanted most was to be with Alex. Would they ever be able to have a life together?

Three weeks later, Lee's cell phone rang. "Hello," she said, hoping it was Alex.

"Lee, it's so good to hear your voice." His voice, deep and reassuring, made her heart beat a little faster. "Every day, I wonder and worry, hoping you're all right. Do you have any plans for Labor Day weekend?"

"Are you kidding That's three weeks off. Besides I hardly know anyone here, and I can't visit Libby or any of my friends."

"Pack a bag with camping clothes and plan to meet me somewhere at four-thirty on the Friday before Labor Day."

"There you go again, being bossy. I told you to stay away until after the trial."

He chuckled. "I just thought you might like to go white water rafting with me."

"That sounds exciting...and dangerous."

"We'd wear life jackets and go with a guide. I'm thinking of offering that in conjunction with trips I sell, and I need to check this guy out. Can you get permission from Iceberg, I mean Joe?"

"I think so. I'll ask him if it's okay, but isn't that your week to have Tanya?"

"I'd like to take her with us, but Kathy will probably veto it. What better testimonial than to say a five-year-old made the trip safely?"

"Maybe, but do you want to risk your daughter's safety?"

"No, I guess not. I'll ask to have her for a different weekend."

Lee swallowed. Time to practice being brave. This shouldn't be that risky. After all, her leg should be healed by then, and she could swim. "Okay, you're on." She told him where to meet her — a well-frequented bookstore she could walk to.

On the Friday before Labor Day, she stepped inside the

bookstore, set her back pack down and waited. Her life was going to be risky. She hoped she could learn to live with it. She had to think of this as an adventure. And she wouldn't let Alex see any fear.

"Hello, darling," said a deep voice behind her. She turned into his arms and hugged him, feeling safe and welcome.

Alex led her outside and settled her in his car. Though it was warm, he'd left the top on, but the windows were open. He took her in his arms. "In here I can kiss you the way I want to, well maybe not quite, in my bed would be better." He grinned, then lowered his mouth to hers. The smell of freshly mowed grass from outside mingled with his aftershave. She sank into the softness of his mouth. Everything else faded. It felt like eons since she'd tasted such sweetness.

Later, after flying from Dallas Love Field to Colorado and spending the night wrapped in his arms in a wooden bunk bed, Lee dressed quickly in the chilly morning air.

Following breakfast she climbed into a tour bus and rode with a group of twenty chattering tourists. Her heart pounded. Did anyone ever drown on these trips?

When the bus stopped, Lee swallowed. Eagles battled in her stomach. Why had she agreed to this? What if she got tossed out into a raging current and were dashed against the rocks?

Alex grabbed her hand. "Come on, this will be fun."

Ashamed to admit her fear, she let him help her down from the bus. With every step, her legs threatened to turn into jelly.

Above them a lone bird soared and dipped, then let out a piercing cry that rang in the cool clear air. Trying not to think about what lay ahead, she looked across the river and studied a towering cliff with its different hued layers.

Here in the shadow of the cliff, olive drab waters raced on, more turbulent than she'd imagined. Sounds of the rushing river engulfed her, making it hard to concentrate on the guide's words. Wet earth near the water's edge smelled like damp dirt after a rain.

The two rafts weren't as big as she'd expected, especially for this large group. Lee imagined being knocked overboard, swallowing the dark water, and banging her head against the rocks. She shuddered. "What if I fall out or the boat tips over?"

"That's what these are for," said the muscular guide, a man in his late twenties, handing out puffy orange vests. "But no one's fallen out in the last five years."

Numbly, she accepted one. She hoped she wouldn't be the one to break their record. With fumbling fingers she struggled to fasten it. "Wait a minute. How can you say that? This life preserver's damp."

The guide looked sheepish. "I dropped it in the water after the last trip."

"If it's damp, will it still keep me up?"

"Of course," the guide said. "But no one will fall out. I'll see to that."

Alex touched her shoulder. "Slowpoke. I've got mine fastened. Want some help?" The weak sun hadn't warmed the air yet. She nodded. His warm hands on her shoulder helped alleviate the chill from the damp preserver. As he fastened it, she looked at the fast-moving river and swallowed. Beneath her feet, the solid soil felt comforting. Was she ready to forsake that for the flimsy rubber bottom of a raft?

When Alex pried his hand loose from hers, she realized how tightly she had been holding his. Why on earth had she agreed to this?

She didn't have long to think about it. The tour guide told them to climb into the rafts tied to posts on the shore. As she stepped down, the flimsy bottom of the boat wobbled under her feet, making her grab Alex's arm. The craft tipped alarmingly.

The guide glared at her. "Sit down. You're making the boat rock." As she settled down next to Alex, she tried to remember the safety tips she'd heard, but couldn't think of any except not to lean over the edge. She certainly wouldn't do that.

She snuggled against Alex, glad for his arm about her shoulder.

He grinned, then squeezed her shoulder and looked deep into her eyes. "Relax Lee. This will be fun."

He knew she was shaking in her seat—despite her attempts to hide her fear. Relieved she wouldn't have to pretend any more, she leaned against him, trying not to shake.

When the guide untied the ropes, the raft jerked forward. The ride was bumpy. Was that a rock that hit the raft beneath her bottom? Boulders loomed ahead. Spray flew into the air even before the raft reached them. There didn't seem to be room enough between the rocks to pass. They were heading right for a huge rock.

Lee shuddered, afraid to close her eyes for fear she might be tossed out and have to dodge those behemoths in the surging water. She gripped Alex's hand, too tightly, she was sure, but she was too scared to let go.

The craft bobbed and bucked. Miraculously, they sped through the narrow opening. Maybe the driver, steering at the rear, knew what he was doing after all. Another rock jabbed at her bottom. When would this ride be over? She'd had enough excitement to last a lifetime.

The boat headed for a large boulder, the passage even narrower than the last. She held her breath, hoping they'd squeak through as they had before. At the last minute the raft dipped way low on her side.

The next thing she knew, icy water was closing over her head. Sputtering, she grabbed for a large rock. It slipped through her fingers. The current slammed her against another

The raging waters drowned out her cry.

Chapter 24

Lee struggled to keep her head above the icy water. Water filled her nose. She spat out muddy water. The roar of the river's rushing waters made it hard to hear. She could barely make out Alex's shout. "Woman overboard."

The boat was sliding downriver. Away from her.

Shouting behind her made her look back. Another craft, full of people hurtled right for her. At that speed, no telling what would happen if the heavily loaded raft slammed into her. How ironic it would be if an accident instead of Bubba kept her from testifying. Well, she wouldn't let that happen. She'd be there if at all possible.

She grabbed a protruding rock. Its green, slippery growth made the rock hard to hold. Her fingers were cramping. She tried to swing her legs closer to the rock. The strong current kept pushing them out to the middle. What if the heavy craft knocked her against the rock and made her lose consciousness? She'd drown.

Her heart raced. She didn't want to die. Not here. Not now.

The boat slowed, how the driver managed she wasn't sure. A dark-haired man leaned toward her, holding out a hand. "Grab on," he yelled.

It was all she could manage to reach out her cold numb arm. The man clutched her wrist and yanked so hard she felt as if her arm would come loose. She let go of the rock, and he grabbed her other arm and pulled.

The man rolled her over the side of the raft. The boat rocked and dipped alarmingly. What if she caused the whole craft to dump its passengers and they all had to flounder in the rapids? That would be disastrous.

Heart pounding, she lay there as the craft righted, too spent to do anything but shiver.

The man wrapped a blanket around her shoulders and patted her face dry with a corner. "You're safe now," he said.

A woman whispered, "Spose she'll catch pneumonia now?"

Lee barely heard another man's "Hush, she'll hear you."

"You all right now?" her rescuer asked.

Lee took a deep breath. "I think so. Thanks a million for pulling me out."

He smiled. "You're welcome. He pulled her to a sitting position. "You might as well enjoy the rest of the ride then."

Her teeth chattered. "Yeah, right," she mumbled under her breath, not wanting to sound ungrateful. She pulled the blanket tighter around her. At least the waters were calmer now, and the sun warmed her face.

A little girl patted Lee's hair. "You're all wet. You went swimming, didn't you."

Lee bent down. "I sure did."

The girl turned to the man beside her. "Daddy, why didn't you let me jump in the water, too? That looked like fun."

Lee shook her head. "It wasn't fun. I kept getting shoved against sharp rocks. I was afraid I'd get hit by the boat and drown."

"Oh," the little girl said. Her face grew serious as if pondering what Lee had said.

The boat picked up speed, and another narrow passage loomed ahead. Lee grabbed hold of a metal ring on the side and held her breath. When the raft sailed through without a hitch, she relaxed.

A flock of birds flew overhead, wings flapping lazily except for the one at the head of the vee-shaped formation. Then another took over the lead, taking the brunt of the wind, and the former leader fell back, slipping into the relaxed rhythm of the rest of the flock. They all worked together, helping each other. Like them, she could rely on others to help her, others who cared about people instead of money or power like Sheldon and Bubba. She'd make new friends wherever she went.

The waters rolled along more calmly now. She'd seen the worst already. There wasn't anything more to be afraid of, for now at least. She might be wet, but she was getting warmer and dryer by the minute.

Another bump rubbed her rear. She was getting used to the bouncing and jerks. The boat slowed again. The guide pointed to the multi-layered face of the cliff. "Each different colored layer represents a separate time period, perhaps thousands of years before humans ever saw this river."

Pulled from her reverie by the thump of the boat against the shore, she let the blanket drop. A cool breeze chilled her momentarily.

Alex helped her step out onto the bank, then hugged her. His gaze bored into hers, his face solemn. "It scared me plenty to see you flounder in those rapids. You okay?"

Afraid her voice would come out squeaky, she nodded.

He put his arm around her waist. "Come on. Let's get you into the bus and out of the wind. I don't want you catching pneumonia. I might have to marry you in a hospital room. Maybe Tanya can be a flower girl."

"I'm not getting married in a hospital. Besides I don't 'think they'd allow a young flower girl to enter the building."

His eyes twinkled. "We can talk about that later. Now let's get in that bus and go get some lunch." He helped her into the bus. After settling into a seat, she nestled against him, loving the feel of his rough, warm cheek against her forehead. Her hands and ears came to life again, tingling briefly, then warming.

She took a deep breath. Being tossed in the water hadn't been so bad. She wasn't ready for another white water ride any time soon, but she wouldn't be as terrified of it now. Maybe she was ready to face other risks, too, if she could face life with Alex beside her. She'd make an appointment with a doctor about her risks in having a baby. But she couldn't plan a future until after the trial.

Alex shifted his arm and turned to face her. "Know what?"

She shook her head.

"I really enjoyed that ride. Think I'll concentrate on adventure tours and take some myself occasionally, just to break the monotony. It may not be as exciting as what I did in the CIA but I can live with it—as long as I can take you with me or have you to come home to."

Lee squeezed his hand. "I can't promise anything until the trial's over and the bad guys are in jail."

"Then I hope it happens soon" His eyes bore a shining promise, enough to hold her through her upcoming ordeal.

❧

The day of the trial dawned, cool and rainy, filling Lee with a sense of impending doom. Her stomach roiled. Everything depended on her testimony. She had to get it right so the jury would put Sheldon away for a long time.

She arranged the strawberry blonde wig the way she used to wear her hair and removed her contacts. Blinking in the glare of the bathroom light, she studied her reflection in the mirror and wondered how Alex would react to her changed appearance when he saw her. For his own safety, she'd begged him to stay away from the courtroom today.

After hearing a knock, she hurried to the door. Joe must be here to drive her to the Dallas court. She still didn't feel ready to face Sheldon and his lawyer. The shark would probably cross-examine her and try to get her to change her story. Well, she might sweat, but she wouldn't let him win.

She peered through the peephole and saw Alex's welcoming smile. Heart pounding, she yanked the door open, letting in the scent of honeysuckle and the sounds of dripping rain.

He looked at her intently. "I like your green eyes and your strawberry blond hair."

She couldn't help smiling. "It's a wig. However, flattery won't get you anywhere you wouldn't get otherwise."

"You can call it that, but I really mean it." He took her hand and squeezed it. "I'm here to support you. Don't be afraid. They have metal detectors in the court building. All you have to do is tell the truth. If you feel shaky, just look at me, and I'll nod in reassurance."

Lee pulled her hand away. "You're not going near that court. Iceberg, I mean Joe, will drive me to the courthouse and walk me to the courtroom."

"Now who's being bossy? Don't you want me there? I want to share your tough times as well as the good."

Lee shook her head "I adore you for wanting to be there for me, but I don't want anyone knowing you're connected to me. It's not safe for you."

She put her hand on his arm. "I'm willing to take the chance that one of Sheldon's henchmen might put a bullet in me someday. I won't let that stop me from living a full life. But, I won't risk your life too. They could kidnap you as a means of getting to me, or Sheldon could kill or torture you and Tanya to make me suffer."

Alex took her hand and held it next to his heart. "Bubba and Floyd already know what I look like. They could come after me anyway, whether I show up at the trial or not. I want to be there to reassure you so you'll be calm and remember all the facts. You've got to explain them well enough to put those guys away for life. Now come on, so we won't be late."

After following him out the door, she locked it, then hesitated. "I don't want you putting your life in danger. I'll just wait for Joe."

He stopped, and stood there, unmovable as a defensive line football player. "I'll take my chances." He stepped to his Jaguar and opened the door. "Now, are you going to get in or not?"

She got in. "You're so stubborn. I guess I can't stop you from watching the trial, but for heaven's sake, sit in back of the courtroom and pretend you don't know me."

She called Joe to let him know Alex was taking her to court. "Can you ask the DA to provide an escort afterwards? I want someone to drive me around to be sure we don't have a tail, then take me somewhere I can meet Alex, say the Anatole Hotel."

"I'll try to arrange that. I'll see you in court."

Alex started the car. "That takes care of today, but Carl and probably Sheldon, too, may find out where you live and probably where you work. Don't you think it's time to move on?" He turned onto a road leading toward downtown Dallas.

She nodded. "I explained my situation to my boss when I asked for time off to testify. He said he hated to lose me, but he didn't want to endanger his customers by having me there. He mentioned a manager in another town that needed a worker immediately and would be willing to take me on his recommendation."

"Are you going to do it?"

Lee nodded. "He wants me to start next month."

"But what about you and me?"

"I can't ask you to move somewhere else. You'll lose all the good will and the customer base you've built up for your travel business."

"With my computer, I can do business anywhere. You said you didn't want to have a baby, but would you consider a guy and a five-year-old daughter?"

Lee smiled. "If that daughter were Tanya, I would in a minute. Was that a proposal?"

"Well...I had thought of doing something more romantic, a nice restaurant, wine, violins playing, that sort of thing."

She placed a finger over his lips. "Wait until after the trial. If Sheldon's isn't convicted, I don't know if I can make any plans with that threat hanging over my head."

"Listen, damn it. I'm willing to take you and all the risks. For all I know you may have a terrible temper. Just don't hit me with a rolling pin or pour cold water over me to wake me up."

"I don't have a temper, and I'm not that handy in the kitchen. I might splash a few drops on cold water on your face, but I'd be careful not to pour it in a strategic place. On the other hand, think how much fun it would be to warm you up afterwards."

He grinned and grasped her hand. "I can't wait."

She pulled away. "We need to get to court. How much farther is it?"

Alex glanced at her. With that strawberry blonde wig, she looked different but still adorable. He needed more time, time to take her in his arms, kiss her silly until she gave in. This was one stubborn woman. He loved every inch of her, even her chin that stuck out so resolutely. Hell, he could stop here beside the road for a few moments. The trial wouldn't start until she got there, would it?

Traffic was light on this farm-to-market road, perfect for what he had in mind.

He pulled the car over onto the shoulder and turned off the engine. "I'm willing to take my chances with you. Our version of for better or worse may be more exciting than most. If you get threatened, I can take you on a vacation in Barbados or some other exotic place until the police nab the culprits."

"Alex, why are you stopping? Is something wrong with the car?"

He shook his head.

"You going to leave me here beside the road so I can't testify?"

He laughed. "Course not. Here, hold the keys if you don't believe me." He let the keys dangle from his hand. "Put them in your pocket."

"Now you're bossing me again."

He sighed. "Old habits are hard to break. Please, just do it."

She did, then met his gaze. "What if I don't give them back?"

"I want to show you something. Unbuckle your seat belt."

"There you go, bossing me around again." He blew out an exasperated breath. "Please, just do it." He got out and came around to open her door.

She hesitated, and then stepped out. She turned toward him, a breeze lifting her hair.

He led her across soft grass to a large oak tree and backed her up against it. He took her in his arms. "If you don't return my keys, guess I'll have to buy another car, but what's mine can be yours, my heart too if you'll have it."

Lee felt the soft touch of his lips on hers. Then he kissed her nose, her cheeks, her forehead. The ever changing song of a mockingbird hung on the air. The smell of grass wafted about her. From somewhere came the smell of honeysuckle. It mingled with his woodsy aftershave.

His caressing hands on her shoulders spoke of tenderness and want. His slumberous eyes focused on her face, drawing her into a magical spell. She felt as if they were connected by invisible threads binding her to him. He held her face close, only a breath away.

She shut her eyes, wanting, waiting for another kiss from the one man she couldn't say 'no' to, even if that meant she'd risk losing him to the same dangers she faced.

She moved to close the wisp of distance between them, but he pulled back. Surprised, she opened her eyes, peered into his.

His gaze caught hers and held it. She could barely hear his low whisper. "Promise you won't leave me?"

Shaken, she murmured. "I'd never want to. I don't know if I could bear to lose you—if one of Sheldon's hit men found you…." She choked up at the thought.

"You lost your mother and managed to live without her, didn't you."

"Yes, but that was different. She couldn't help dying."

Alex swallowed. "My sister couldn't either. I miss her, but I learned to live with her death. Accidents can happen to anyone, anywhere. You can be careful, and still live life to the fullest. You're the one I want to share my life with. You and Tanya."

He handed her a small gray box. She rubbed the dove-soft covering, knowing what must be inside. It was so tempting. She wanted to say, 'yes,' and be held in his strong arms, to become lost in his kiss. She wanted to go on tasting his lips, snuggling in his arms and sharing the glorious passion that erupted whenever they made love. Dare she chance a future with him? No, she couldn't. Living without him couldn't be worse than seeing him killed.

She handed the box back without opening it. "I can't promise anything until after the trial, much as I'd like to." She hoped he understood.

Chapter 25

The oak tree pressed against Lee's back as a yellow butterfly fitted by and landed on a nearby honeysuckle bush. Its fragrance teased her nose as Alex's warm brown eyes met her gaze. "If you won't wear my ring at the trial, will you at least keep the box in your pocket? I want you to have it close to remind you that I love you, that I'll keep on loving you no matter what happens?"

She wanted to — more than anything, but she couldn't in all honesty take it. "I love you, too, but I'm not sure that's enough with Sheldon's curses and threats hanging over my head."

"I've lived dangerously before. This will add spice to my life. Since you don't cook, I don't think I'll get any on my dinner plate."

"Are you trying to give me a hard time?"

Smiling, he squeezed her hand. "I'll take a great lover over gourmet food anytime." He caressed her breasts, set them tingling with desire. She leaned closer, pressing her breasts into his hands. He was driving her wild. She wanted to rip the buttons, tear off his shirt and make love to him on the soft grass, but she couldn't. Not now — maybe not ever again. If this trial didn't go the way she hoped, she'd have to let him go. She couldn't bear to see him hurt or killed because of her. She blinked back tears. Why did she have to be the witness Sheldon wanted dead?

He kissed her long and hard. She threw her arms around him. Pressed all her pent up love into that kiss, knowing it might be her last. She ran her fingers through his hair and smoothed them over his firm cheeks. She wanted to touch him all over. If only she could store up everything about him, his kisses, his adoring glances, his welcoming smile, all those endearing things to remember when she was alone in a new strange place. Without him.

He pulled away, leaving her chilled and wanting. "We need to get going, but first I want you to promise you'll marry me, no matter what happens at the trial." He placed the velvet box in her hand, closed her fingers around it, and pressed a kiss on top of them.

She sighed. "I can't give you an answer. Not unless Sheldon gets put away for a long time. We have to think of Tanya's safety if not our own."

"With your testimony, he's bound to be found guilty. And even if Carl can prove Tanya is his child instead of mine, I don't think a judge will grant custody to a man who attempted to kill you."

"What? You mean Carl is claiming Tanya is his child?"

"I'm afraid so. He says that's what Kathy told him. I may face a custody battle."

"But he'd make a horrible father."

"I know. That's what I'm hoping a judge will decide. But I'll worry about that later. Just start thinking about where you want to get married." He kissed her gently on the lips. "Aren't you going to look at the ring? I think you'll like it."

Unfolding her trembling fingers, she stared at the box. "I'm sure I'll love it because you gave it to me." Suddenly, she couldn't wait to see it.

She snapped the box open. Inside, a golden rose with delicate petals adorned a ring. The large diamond center caught the sunlight, its edges sparkling with glints of red, green, and amber. "Ohhhhh," she murmured., catching her breath. "It's beautiful. Everyone who sees it will be green with envy. And any woman who has known your kisses will be sorry she let you go."

He smiled. "I'm the lucky one." He cradled her face in his hands and lowered his mouth to hers for a long sweet kiss. "Now, put it in your pocket. We really have to get going."

Lee walked into the federal court building beside Alex. Outside the courtroom she stopped short and gripped his arm. "There's Carl." Her mouth dry, she forced her hands not to tremble.

Alex patted her hand. "This is a federal court building. Not likely he'll try anything. Wait here. I need to talk to him."

Gritting his teeth, he strode across the hall. He wanted to beat the man to a pulp, but keeping Tanya depended on him maintaining his cool.

"Hello, Carl."

Carl glared at him, but said nothing.

"Do you really think a judge will grant you custody of my daughter — of Tanya?"

Carl stepped closer. "She's mine. A DNA test will prove it."

"But how can you be a real father to her — with criminal charges hanging over your head?"

Carl shook his fist in the air. "It's all your fault. You turned Kathy's head with your promises of a great future. You married her so fast I didn't have a chance to change her mind. Even now I can't be sure she'll marry me."

"Tanya needs me," Alex insisted. "I'm the only father she knows."

"You won't be if I can help it." Stepping away from the courtroom door, Carl threw a right punch. Alex barely dodged it. Then Carl's fist slammed into his stomach. "That's for stealing Kathy from me."

Alex grimaced and tensed for a fight. Fists ready, he blocked the next punch, then slammed his fist into Carl's face.

Running footsteps sounded behind him. Two guards grabbed hold of Alex's and Carl's arms, restraining them.

Alex said, "I'm charging you with assault and battery. Just see how that will affect any move you make to get custody. And I intend to insist on a psychiatric exam. No lunatic is going to raise my daughter." He turned to Lee. "Write down the guards' names. I'll need them as witnesses."

Pulling out a note pad, she glanced at their name tags and wrote their names.

Carl assumed a more sober stance and turned to the guard holding his arm. "I won't cause any more trouble. Just let me go sit in the courtroom. I need to hear what happens."

The taller guard shook his head. "We can't have anyone likely to cause a disturbance in the building. You'll have to leave."

Carl's face turned red. "If I have to leave, then he should go too."

"He can stay," said the shorter guard. "I saw you throw the first punch."

The two guards escorted Carl away from the courtroom. His muttered curse echoed in the quiet hall.

Hoping Carl wouldn't cause any more trouble, Lee stepped into the courtroom and glanced around. Her gaze roved over the spectators seated in the benches arranged like pews in a church. Were any of them Sheldon's henchmen who might show up later with a gun poking into her back? At least she didn't see any she recognized.

The U.S. attorney and Sheldon's defense attorney presented their opening arguments. The U.S. attorney charged Sheldon with transporting stolen goods to other countries, money laundering and not reporting all income received. When the attorney called Lee, she walked toward the witness chair, hoping no one could see how she was shaking inside. She sat, forcing her hands to be still. Crossing her legs at the ankles, she vowed to keep them that way and not fidget. She was nervous as a squirrel in the street eyeing an approaching car.

As she swore to tell the truth, she studied Sheldon. He seemed more subdued than she'd ever seen him. She figured his lawyer had coached him to act that way. His brown plaid suit and flashy tie seemed incongruous beside the gray and navy pinstripe suits of the attorneys. He drummed his fingers repeatedly on the table, probably wishing for one of his awful-smelling cigars.

The hate in his eyes seemed to follow her every movement. Her confidence was slowly oozing away. That wouldn't do. She straightened her spine against the hard oak witness chair. She had to convince the jury that Sheldon was guilty so he'd be put away for a long time.

Drawing a deep breath, she waited for the first question from the U.S. attorney, a restless lean man in a navy pinstripe suit.

He asked her to explain how Sheldon operated his business.

She sat up straight and held her head high. In a firm voice, she said, "He ran an import-export business. At first I didn't realize he was also selling stolen goods, running a money laundering operation, and taking bets on the horse races."

Sheldon sprang to his feet. "The bitch is lying. I didn't do all those other things she said."

The judge frowned and rapped his gavel on his desk. "Counselor, control your client." His lawyer pulled him down and spoke in low tones. Sheldon clamped his mouth shut.

The U.S. Attorney stepped closer. "When did you realize Mr. Sheldon was keeping two sets of books?"

"When the man from the IRS came to do an audit and asked to see the books, I gave him the maroon covered account books I'd seen the bookkeeper working on last. I thought Sheldon had bought new ones because the others I'd seen were black, but then Sheldon rushed into the office. His face was red and sweaty. He shouted at me that those were the wrong books. He dropped a stack of black books on the table in front of the investigator, then grabbed the maroon ones. He claimed they were books his bookkeeper used to do the accounting for another small company and had nothing to do with his business."

The U.S. attorney walked over to the jury seated nearby, then turned to her. "Did you believe him?"

"Mr. Sheldon sounded so emphatic. I knew I'd better not contradict him or say anything else. As mad as he looked, I didn't know what he'd do to me if I said anything then."

"And did you see what accounts were in the maroon covered books?"

"I peeked at them later. It looked like they held records of stolen property Sheldon sold to overseas companies."

The government attorney rubbed his chin. "What made you think the books referred to stolen property?"

"I never saw any invoices, or typed any letters to accompany any payments for anything mentioned in those account books."

The U.S. attorney asked, "Was there anything else that made you suspect he was selling stolen goods."

"When we got deliveries during the day, Sheldon always paid the driver in cash. Sometimes as much a thousand dollars. I heard him count it out once." She glanced at her former boss, his ears protruding from his blow-dried, well shaped hair. He sat glowering at her from the table next to his attorney.

"And did he receive receipts for this cash?"

"I never saw any."

Sheldon jumped up and pounded the table. "That's a Goddamn lie. I paid for all those goods."

The judge scowled and rapped his gavel on his desk. "Counselor, as I directed earlier, you need to control your client or I will hold you in contempt of court."

Sheldon's lawyer frowned and spoke to him in low tones.

The look of malevolence on Sheldon's face sent shivers down Lee's spine.

"Can you tell us the names of the men he paid cash to?"

She glanced at Alex. His expression seemed to say, "Hang in there, Sweetheart."

She took a deep breath, wishing this were over. She hoped they'd provide a guard to protect her when she left the courthouse.

Ignoring Sheldon's scowling face, she listed all the names she could remember. Some she knew only by a nickname.

"When did you ask to be put in the Witness Security Program?" the U.S. attorney asked.

"The day the IRS came. I told Sheldon I was going out for lunch. Before I left I saw him getting arrested. Then I went straight to the U.S. attorney's office."

Then she answered more questions about the day she'd finally figured out what was going on—the day that changed her life forever. She hadn't realized then all that could happen. Meeting Alex was the one bright spot.

The U.S. attorney held up the two sets of books taken from Sheldon's office as exhibits. He asked Lee to identify them, which she did. He also offered into evidence subpoenaed bank statements from several banks and asked if she'd seen them. She claimed as secretary, she'd looked at them when she opened Sheldon's mail.

The questions went on and on. Sheldon's attorney kept interrupting and objecting.

Then it was time for Sheldon's attorney to cross examine her. Sheldon glared at her as if daring her to say anything against him.

However, his attorney's demeanor as he approached her was calm and professional. She sat back and relaxed. This might not be so bad.

His gaze raked her over, then focused on her chest. His arm extended, he pointed a finger at her. "Isn't it true that you and

Sheldon were intimate, and after he threw you over for another woman, you decided what you thought you knew could send him to prison?"

She gulped. Where had that come from? She felt the eyes of the crowd assessing her. Did they see her as a kept woman?

She twisted a lock of hair around her finger, then dropped it and caressed the soft gray box in her pocket to bolster her courage. Sitting up straighter, she clenched her fist and leaned forward. "That's not true. I never—"

The U.S. attorney held up his hand to stop her. "Objection," he said. "That's immaterial, irrelevant, and asks the witness to make a legal conclusion."

Sheldon's lawyer started to say something, but the judge rapped his gavel and barked. "Objection sustained."

After a few more questions, she was excused. As she stepped down, Sheldon's eyes flashed a wish to kill her so palpable she could almost feel his hands around her neck, choking the life out of her. She watched the stony faces of the jury, hoping her testimony had convinced them of Sheldon's guilt. If he didn't get convicted, she'd be looking over her shoulder for the rest of her life. She swallowed. That wouldn't be much of a life.

When it came time for Bubba and Floyd to testify, they took the fifth amendment and refused to say anything more.

In his closing argument, Sheldon's attorney belittled and denied all the charges against Sheldon, painting her ex-boss as a maligned upstanding businessman who brought in much needed business. She wished she could take the stand again and tell them how he treated his employees, how he cheated bettors out of half their winnings and sent enforcers to beat up those who couldn't pay loans he'd made to them. Except she'd been told not to say anything except to answer the questions.

Sheldon's lawyer told the jury they'd be deciding against logic if they didn't acquit his client. Of course, the U.S. attorney argued they should convict Sheldon, but his remarks didn't seem near as persuasive as Sheldon's attorney's.

By the time the two attorneys finished their closing arguments, and court was adjourned, her insides were a mass of quivering Jell-O.

However, she wouldn't let anyone see that. Summoning up all the confidence and poise she could muster and a consummate amount of acting, she strode from the courtroom with her head high.

Outside the courtroom she sank into a wooden bench along the wall beside the courtroom door. She let out the breath she'd been holding and tried to stop shaking. Alex eased down beside her. "You did great. I don't see how the jury could rule any other way except to convict that scum."

"I wonder if Sheldon paid Carl to kill me."

"He probably did, but that could be hard to prove." Alex squeezed her hand and whispered, "I love you, and I want to marry you. I'm even willing to take the chance we'll have to move at a moment's notice." He pulled her into his arms and kissed her. "Whatever happens, I want to keep you safe from those bastards. If you're willing to marry me, I promise I'll protect you."

Lee savored his kiss, then raised her face for another. "With kisses like yours, I don't know how any woman could say no to you."

He grinned. "So stop resisting and say 'yes.'"

She whispered, "I can't until I know what happens in there. The U.S. attorney told me Sheldon would get twenty-five years for each count if they convict him."

The next day Lee sat with Alex on a bench outside the court. Finally, the courtroom door opened, and someone said, "The jury's back."

Lee walked into the courtroom on shaky legs with Alex beside her. She sat next to him in the back of the courtroom.

The judge addressed the foreman of the jury. "Have you reached a verdict?"

The courtroom became silent. Lee twisted the material of her skirt and shoved her hands into her pockets.

She hoped things would go right, that her troubles would be over soon. She held her breath and waited.

The ticking of the clock on the wall was the only sound.

The jury foreman rose. The paper he held crinkled in his hand.

In a steady voice, he stated, "On the charge of money laundering, we find the defendant guilty as charged. On the charge of transporting stolen goods, we find the defendant guilty as charged. On the charge of not reporting income to the IRS, we find the defendant guilty as charged."

He handed the judge the paper he held. "I signed this statement certifying that the jury voted unanimously on all three charges."

A buzz of conversation erupted. The judge rapped his gavel. "Order, I call for order in the court."

The room quieted. "Will the defendant please stand and face the bench?"

Sheldon and his attorney rose.

"As you have been found guilty on all three counts, you are hereby remanded to the custody of the Federal Correctional Institution for three twenty-five year terms to run consecutively." He rapped his gavel. "Court is adjourned."

The bailiff led Sheldon toward the exit. Sheldon pivoted and faced Lee. In a voice laced with hate, he said, "I'll sue your skinny ass for defamation of character."

Lee gasped. "I can't believe he had the nerve to say that. He can't do that can he?"

"Be quiet," the bailiff said to Sheldon. "You had your day in court, and it's over." He hustled Sheldon out the side door.

Alex took her elbow. "I wouldn't worry about that. First he has to find a lawyer who'll take his case. And I doubt he can."

As Lee walked out the courtroom door, a woman in front of her brushed back a lock of gray hair. "I don't see how the jury could have ruled anything else," she told her companion.

The person beside her, a plump older woman in a flowing dress said, "He got what he deserved. I heard that the men who worked for him, that fat guy and the one called Floyd couldn't make bail. I heard on the news that their trial starts next month. I bet they nail them, too."

Alex clapped his hands on Lee's shoulders. "You hear that? Now will you marry me?"

"Yes," she whispered. "I can't believe you're choosing to share all the risks I face. We can't be sure Bubba and Floyd will be put away too."

He led her outside the building. "We won't dwell on the risks. Sure, we'll be careful, but we'll live life to the fullest as much as we can. Where's that ring? I want you to wear it when I take you out to dinner to celebrate."

She pulled the soft gray box from the pocket of her blazer.

He snapped it open and slid the ring on her finger. It shimmered in the sunlight as a gentle breeze brushed her skin.

His lips met hers in a tender kiss. Then he grinned. "Let's go. I'm taking you to Dakotas, that fancy underground restaurant with a courtyard open to the sky to celebrate."

"That place is so expensive they don't even have prices on the menu."

"We can go there or somewhere else, wherever you want to go. See. I'm trying to remember not to be so bossy. And afterwards—" His smile was captivating. "I can't wait to share your bed tonight," he whispered.

She gazed at his handsome face, remembering his soft caresses and fevered kisses. Filled with warmth and happiness, she smiled at him. She now had a lifetime of that to look forward to.

Epilogue

Lee parked her car and snapped her cell phone shut after talking to Joe Berg, her U.S. marshal guardian angel. Joe assured her Sheldon, Bubba, and Floyd had been sentenced to long prison terms. Joe said Carl had been indicted by a grand jury on charges of endangering a government witness.

Lee could hardly believe she was free at last. After getting out of her car, she ran to the door of the lake cottage she shared with Alex as his wife.

Breathless, she pulled the door open. Alex sat in an easy chair, reading a magazine. She grabbed the magazine, tossed it aside, and pulled him to his feet. "You know what?"

He kissed her, and then looked at her quizzically. "I can't guess."

"Joe asked a friend at the CIA to check the records. His friend found a report which exonerates you from any blame for Idelle's death. Joe also told me that Sheldon, Bubba, and Floyd will be locked up for a long time.

Lee hugged Alex. "Joe also apologized for thinking you were behind the leaks before figuring out it was Carl. Carl has been ousted from the U.S. Marshal Service. When he goes to trial, he faces a long prison term for conspiracy and for endangering a witness."

"Thank God. I doubt he'll try to sue me for custody of Tanya now."

"Can he do that?"

"My lawyer told me if DNA tests proved it, he could ask for visitation privileges, but it's unlikely a judge would allow that as long as he's in jail."

"Do you ever plan to have the tests done?"

Alex shook his head. "As far as I'm concerned, she's my daughter."

Lee smiled. "Now, you want to hear the rest of my good news?"

"What?"

She ruffled his hair. "I went to the doctor, and he said I'd have no problem delivering a healthy baby."

He winked at her. "There's no time like to present to make our family grow."

She met his gaze. How could he help but see the excitement bubbling inside her.

"And I have even better news."

"What could be better than what you already told me?"

"I'm pregnant! I just found out today."

He grabbed her in a bear hug and swung her around. Then he kissed her.

The kiss went on and on until Tanya ran up to her and tugged on her skirt.

"What's pregnant mean? Is it something you catch like the measles that I got a shot for?"

Lee ruffled her red curls. "It means you're going to get a baby sister or brother."

"Can I play with the baby?"

Alex bent to hug her shoulder.

"Not at first, but you can help me and Lee bathe and feed the baby."

Alex squeezed Lee's hand. "Let's call your sister, Libby, and tell her our family's about to become merrier. Then, after we put Tanya to bed, we can celebrate."

"What's celebrate mean?" asked Tanya.

Lee smiled. "Go get in bed. I'll tell you when you're older."

Later, after Tanya was asleep, Alex took Lee by the hand and led her to their bedroom door. His lips caressed hers. His arms surrounded her with warmth, filling her with promises of love, joy and contentment for years to come.

Dear Reader: If you enjoyed *Hiding from Love*, a review at your favorite retailer would be appreciated, and you'll want to read the next books in the Witness Protection Series.

PROTECTED BY LOVE
Witness Protection Series, Book Two

Fashion designer, Elizabeth Leventhal, Lee's sister, wants to escape her abusive ex-husband, who works for The Elites, a Texas crime ring. When he beats down her door, she calls U.S. Marshal Joe Berg to put her in the Witness Security Program. Handsome and muscular, he swears to protect her, but insists her evidence is thin. He asks her to learn more by attending an Elite's party at a huge honky tonk. That fills her with dread.

Joe Berg's sympathies and his heart are drawn to the plucky Elizabeth. He struggles with his obstinate boss, his forbidden attraction to Elizabeth, and the Elite's attempts to turn her over to her ex-husband.

Available Now in print and digital formats

––––––––––

TEMPTED BY LOVE
Witness Protection Series, Book Three

U.S. Marshal Sheila Talbot, picks up a rebel ex-cop as her first witness. She tries not to be impressed with his good looks or his more than a touch of arrogance, which she finds hard to ignore. He runs her ragged trying to keep him safe. Despite rules against involvement with witnesses, he tempts her at every turn. When he bolts, fearing for his safety, she follows him to Hawaii, where they barely escape danger.

Brent Broussard didn't want to be set up with another U.S. Marshal. She and he were good together, and yes, he knew that was breaking the rules, but why did she have to trade him for the scum bag he was supposed to testify against? He can hardly wait until that damn trial, but will she still want to be with him then?

Available Now in print and digital formats

––––––––––

Also by Carolyn Rae

ROMANCING THE GOLD
MuseItUp Publishing 2014

Adventurous Megan McKinley finds searching for gold more exciting after hunky, bearded photographer, Joseph Logan, a man with a hidden past and a secret agenda, arrives at the dig.

When Megan's archaeology professor boasts he found the terra cotta bowl she dug up, she suspects he's not the benevolent mentor she'd thought him. Then she discovers the photographer is actually Josh Seward, the clean-cut high school teacher she had a crush on years ago.

Available Now in print and digital formats

––––––––––

Check my website at Carolynrae.com and Carolyn Rae Author / Facebook for excerpts from *Romancing the Gold.*

About the Author

As a teenager, Carolyn Rae told stories to kids she babysat. On a long road trip, she entertained her younger sister with stories she made up.

Later she taught home economics, family living, and English in Michigan, Illinois, and Texas, where she earned a master's degree. She worked as a researcher for a mincemeat company and met her neighbors by bringing samples of mincemeat pies. She taught ironwork, painting, and carpentry residents at the Fort Worth Federal Correctional Institution in Texas. While there, she also wrote and directed videos on nutrition and fair fighting for married couples

Carolyn Rae wrote the text and many recipes for *There IS Life After Lettuce* (Eakin Press, Fort Worth, Texas), a cookbook for heart patients and diabetics. Her profile and travel articles have appeared in the *Romance Writer's Report*, *Fort Worth Star Telegram*, *The Dallas Morning News*, *Positive Parenting*, and *AAA World, Hawaii and Alaska*. She has worked as a paralegal and follows her passion, writing romantic suspense where bullets are flying, people are dying, and lovers are resisting attraction until they can escape the danger following them.